SNAG

Snag (Conduit 2)
Copyright © 2025 Meghan Ciana Doidge
Published by Old Man in the CrossWalk Productions 2025
Vancouver, BC, Canada
www.oldmaninthecrosswalk.com

Library and Archives Canada
Doidge, Meghan Ciana, 1973 —
Snag/Meghan Ciana Doidge — PAPERBACK

Cover design by Jay Aheer (Simply Defined Art)
Zaya and Rought Illustration by Barbara D Soares (drsoaresrex.com)
Maps and other graphic design by Eternal Geekery

ISBN 978-1-989571-79-8

CONDUIT TWO

SNAG

MEGHAN CIANA DOIDGE

AUTHOR'S NOTE: CONTENT

The Conduit series is set in a secondary world that shares many common traits with our own. The divergences in language, governing bodies and countries, technology, and geography are all intentional choices by the author.

Content of Note: Adult 18+, violence (on the page), explicit language, attempted suicide (recounted), discussions of child abuse, sex and sexual situations (on the page), attempted incest (not children, one unwitting partner), partially shifted sex, eventual why choose (MFMM; half-brothers and no MM).

Specific content of note and a list of tropes can be found on MCD's website: www.madebymeghan.ca/snag

AUTHOR'S NOTE: READING ORDER

Snag is the second book in the Conduit series, which is set in the same universe as the Mirth duology. While it is not necessary to read all the series, <u>in order to avoid spoilers</u> the ideal reading order of the greater Conduit World is as follows:

- *Awry* (Conduit 1)
- *Grand Romantic Delusions and the Madness of Mirth, Part 1*
- *Grand Romantic Delusions and the Madness of Mirth, Part 2*
- *Snag* (Conduit 2)

(Chronologically, *Snag* comes before *Mirth Part 1* in the series timeline, as does part of book 3.)

FOR MICHAEL

My hand clasped in yours, beyond death and back again.

INTRODUCTION

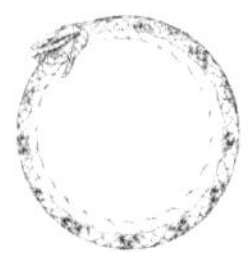

I've awakened to find bits of my missing past — memories and bonds that I didn't know had been torn from me — captured within photographs arrayed across the walls of the caretaker suite. Displayed for me to find them, to discover everything my aunt has actively hidden from me for over thirteen years. Secrets she's taken with her into the After, leaving me all the power but none of the foundation I need to be the Conduit.

Then I discover that my aunt's secrets go beyond her betrayal, creating a systemic rot, an unraveling, that began before I was even born. The resulting ramifications weave together to unsettle, to overwrite, any attempt I could make to fortify the connection between me and my universe-promised mates.

Without them, I'm unmoored. And unmoored, I cannot possibly wield all the power the world needs me to wield. That the universe needs me to wield.

Jealousy, envy, grief ... love?

Only choice matters above all else.

Just not for me.
I move as the universe wills.
Or I suffer the consequences.

ONE

"No threads connect us," I repeat numbly, listing toward Rought. He's still gently holding both my hands, and I'm not fighting him over it.

All the fight has drained from me.

I trace my eyes over him, anchoring myself in all the little details because everything else, each revelation tumbling down over the next one, is too much. Dark-blond hair, curling at his temples against naturally tan skin. Even barefoot, he's easily eight inches taller than me. He hides an intricate web of tattoos under his black T-shirt, including a memorial tattoo of a floral anatomical heart for his lost childhood love.

Marrow.

Me.

"No threads connect us ..." I whisper again, my gaze on the feathers peeking out from the collar of his shirt, kissing his neck. More tattoos decorate his forearms and the backs of his hands.

Feathers because his inner beast is a gryphon. Half-eagle, half-lion. A guardian of the divine. Which is ridiculously appropriate because I'm ... I'm ...

I'm the aspect of a goddess myself.

That power is still unsettled within me, though. As if it hasn't infused itself on a molecular level yet, hasn't completely permeated my soul. I press my hand over the necklace tucked under my sweater — a massive pink-diamond amulet caged in threads of gold that teem with power separate from my own. That artifact, heavy with metaphorical weight rather than actual physical mass, appeared around my neck at the moment of my aunt's death. It's supposed to help me navigate ... well, all of what it means to be the Conduit.

Rought tightens his hold on my left hand and draws it against his chest, so I can feel his heart beating. Steady and sure. His body heat radiates through his shirt, warming my chilly fingers.

And I know now ... I know the other reason I haven't felt wholly realized in a very long time. One of three reasons, at least.

Including the male staring at me with concern, in wonder, with the burnished gold of his gryphon ringing his blue-green eyes.

Rought.

My soul-bound mate.

Mine.

I've been ... rudderless, aimless, reckless. I thought that was just my nature. Because I was destined to be the next Conduit, pulled back from death numerous times because I had a duty to the fucking universe. Not truly a person, just a vessel-in-waiting.

And also ... banished, I now realize, from the property, from the intersection point my aunt held — one of only seven active secondary anchors for all essence. Though once there were nine intersection points in total. Energy, or life force depending on various belief systems, is first anchored in the Conduit, then woven around the globe through the intersection points in a protective boundary.

I've been banished from the family that could have been mine.

"Thirteen years ago ..." I murmur, starting to piece it together. Thread by thread. Maybe I can weave it all back into place? First in my mind, and then ... gathering the missing pieces of my soul?

Rought swallows harshly, drawing my gaze back to the tanned skin of his neck. "Yes. Almost thirteen years now ..." The Southern drawl to his accent is tinged with old grief. "We had part of that summer together."

His gaze flicks to the black-and-white photograph on the wall behind me. One of the numerous photos I've just discovered in the second bedroom of the caretaker's suite in the workshop-barn. Taken by Mack, the former occupant of these rooms and my aunt's recently deceased chosen. The space is just white-painted walls, worn wood floors, and at least twenty identically framed eighteen-inch photographs.

All taken without our knowledge, according to Rought — and to my still-hazy memories of the time I spent at the Gage estate, from childhood through my teenage years.

I don't have to turn to recall the photo that's captured Rought's attention over my shoulder. The moment immortalized within it, of which I have no actual memory, is already burned into my brain.

The three half-brothers and me by a campfire on the beach in monochrome. Rought, Rath, and Reck. Starlight overhead. And anatomical hearts tattooed across all our chests.

"I died … that summer," I say.

"Yes."

"I don't remember that either."

"I do." Rought's thumb brushes against the back of my hand still pressed against his chest. His caress is tender, comforting.

It was my instinct only a day ago now to reach for him, to lay my hand across his chest, to touch him exactly like this at our first meeting. Or what I thought to be our first meeting. I stopped myself for a multitude of reasons. Because I don't touch easily. Because anyone remotely aware of what the energy roiling around me portends, or what the vibrant violet of my eyes indicates, is wary of my touch, of my mere attention.

I am a power in this world. And not by choice.

But even without the threads that should connect us, I felt that urge, that need to touch him. To connect us. I felt it, questioned it, and tried to ignore it.

I tear my gaze from his neck, from the wretched sadness in his gaze, and look at his hand. His right hand holding my left. I twist that hand, maintaining contact with his chest — and uncertain as to whether I can actually pull away right now. I brush my thumb across the scar on the pad of his thumb.

My teeth marks.

He shudders under my touch.

A sliver of warmth cracks through the grief that has numbed me from within. I've lost so much … and the framed photographs lining the walls of this otherwise empty room are a visual map of all that loss … yet …

Rought is standing here now, with me.

"You … loved me."

"I love you," he says, utterly intent.

The word, the steady assertion, fucking tears through me, taking the rest of my breath with it. And I welcome the sensation. I can't remember a single person other than my mother who ever said those words to me. And truly meant them.

Then grief-fueled pain streaks through my head, through my eyes, and more tears take my sight.

No one loves me. No one truly can love me.

Because I'm not a person. Not really.

"I'm the Conduit now," I say dully. "I'm not the girl in the pictures. The girl you loved."

"Tell me about the threads," he rasps, speaking through whatever emotion clogs his throat.

Confused by the topic change, I blink up at him. I'm still holding his hand. I should let him go. I know I should.

I don't.

I don't let him go.

It's possible that I'm suddenly and irrevocably unable to let him go, not ever again.

"Do you mean threads that should bind us?" he asks, clarifying because I can't find focus, can't find my voice. "Actual essence that you can normally see? Tell me about those. And how we create new ones if those have been taken from us."

My chin trembles as I struggle to not be overwhelmed by the magnitude of the loss he's describing. "It's not that … that's not … it shouldn't be possible to take those sorts of bindings. Even death … even the death of our physical vessel cannot … shouldn't be able to snip those threads, those soul-deep connections … we should … if we're … soul-bound mates are …"

He brings his free hand to my cheek, brushing away a tear while still barely touching me. "I will never, ever be dragged away from you again, Zaya. Half dead myself or banned from the property, I will never —"

"What do you mean?" A chill slithers down my spine, my tears drying in an instant. "Banned from the property?"

Rought snaps his mouth shut, grimacing.

"All this time," I say, feeling as if I'm clawing through a thick fog that I can't actually shift, can't actually find clarity within. But still piecing it all together bit by bit. "You thought I was dead."

"Yes." He shakes his head. "No. I knew ... my beast knew you weren't."

"You didn't say anything." My voice cracks. "Why?! Why wouldn't you ... and Rath ... he ... he must have recognized me?"

He exhales shakily. "You didn't know me, Zaya. And I didn't know why. I didn't want to force anything that might cause further damage. I thought if I could show you, spend time with you, that maybe you'd remember me ..." He swallows again, then shakes his head. "And Rath. That's not for me to say or even to know."

"Did you ... were you involved in my death that summer?"

He blinks at me, slightly taken aback.

"Aunt Disa banned you from the property," I say, clarifying.

"I tried to protect you," he whispers. "I failed. I was ... some of it is still hazy for me. I think I blacked out a few times. I didn't have my beast then."

"You saw me die."

"Heard it ... felt it ..." His chest heaves under my hand.

"Wished I'd gone with you when I woke up in the hospital a week later."

I take a shuddering breath, still not processing things at the same pace they're being revealed. Rought takes a deep breath as well, his chest expanding under my hand.

"I was banished too, I think," I say. "But I didn't know it."

He nods his head reluctantly, thoughtfully. "Maybe this is too much right now … trying to figure that part out right now."

"The part where I died?" Anger flushes through me, making me even more shaky and a little lightheaded. "Then my aunt, my mentor, my protector, did … what? Did she just decide I would never cross paths with my soul-bound mates again? Why? Why would she …"

I shake my head. My chest hurts from all the emotion I'm trying to navigate, to contain, to process.

"Yeah," Rought says, offering me a completely inappropriate grin. As if he finds my anger delightful. Though maybe anger is better than the numbness I've likely been radiating. "Maybe we figure that part out later."

I laugh involuntarily. It's a harsh, ragged sound full of disbelief. But it is a laugh. "You want to just be here in the *now*?"

He tilts his head in that shifter way, lots of eagle in the mannerism, grin widening. "With you, yes."

"I'm good in the now," I say agreeably, mostly to myself. "I exist in the now. The Conduit always exists in the *now*."

"All right." Rought gently runs his free hand down my arm, capturing my fingers lightly with his. A gentle, almost meditative energy stirs between us everywhere we touch.

"Then I'll exist here in the now with you. And when you're ready for tomorrow, we'll figure that out as well."

I blink at him again. It can't … it can't be that easy. There are ramifications extending from what has been done to us. Plus, everything is different now that I'm the Conduit. The Conduit doesn't get to have —

Rought places my hand on his waist. I instantly fist the fabric of his T-shirt, gazing up at him. I settle my left hand flat across his heart again. He pins it in place with his right. Not that I'm going anywhere.

"These threads you want to see … need to see … between us." His voice is low and intimate. "Tell me how we … spin them."

He hesitates over the analogy, just a little.

It's enough to make me smile, just a little.

"Can we start over?" he asks.

I think about that for a moment. Just think about that one thing instead of trying to understand and then solve everything else all at once. How would that work? He has years of memories of me, and I have none.

"The pictures."

Rought smiles. "Yeah. Seems like you were meant to find them, hey?"

"You think Mack left them here for me to find?"

"Did he know you were coming home?"

I slowly scan the room around Rought's wide shoulders, once more taking in the photos lining the walls. All black and white, all the same size, all framed in the same black metal with a thick-edged mat.

"There was a letter for me …" I whisper. "From my aunt. And an ice-cream maker."

Rought nods. "So they knew you were coming."

"Maybe. I thought it might have been a part of a

knowing, from Disa to me, but …" I continue to scan the photographs. "All these dates. There aren't any photos from before I came to live here."

"Or after you left."

Sliding my hand down to capture Rought's, my left in his right, I drift toward the first photo of him and me. It's partway down the wall, adjacent to the upper hall of the caretaker's suite.

Perpetually hovering on the edge of my consciousness, I can still feel the energy, the life force, of everyone else on the property. Presh, DeVille, Doc Z, and Cayley in the main house, either still asleep or just rising. Muta in the kitchen, likely still basking on the oven where I last saw him. Rath is still in the vicinity of the beach house, still completely ignoring that he doesn't have my permission to be anywhere on the estate. Annoyingly, two Authority agents have the entrance to the estate staked out.

"Start at the beginning," I murmur, keeping my attention on the *now*. Then I look at Rought and point to the photo of him and me.

In the image, according to the date, I'm nine. Rought and I are perched on a weather-bleached driftwood log, facing the beach and the open ocean beyond with our backs to the camera. Even captured in black and white, the sun glints off Rought's unruly hair. My skin is pale next to his deep tan. Two other blurred figures are in the background, farther out on the beach.

"You think Mack knew about what I'm … missing. That I lost all of this …" I struggle as renewed grief, hot and sharp, slices through me. "And he … wanted to help me find my way back?"

"I think … I never even knew Mack was a photographer." Rought's gaze is fixed on the photo, though I know he saw all the framed pictures only a day ago. Saw them and tried to show me. "I've never seen any of his photos framed and hung anywhere on the estate. Of course, I haven't been here for ..."

"Thirteen years."

"Right."

I inhale deeply, holding his hand a little tighter. "Do you remember this day?"

"I remember every day with you, Zaya." His gaze is now riveted on my face, meaning it, believing it. He clears his throat and seems to force himself to look away, to look at the photo again. "You can't see it from this angle," he says. "But my leg is in a cast. You got your arm cast removed that morning." He taps the greenery edging the back of the driftwood log. "Muta was never more than a couple of feet away from you in those days."

I lean closer, but it still takes a moment for me to discern Muta hidden among the mint that grows wild in various places on the property. Reputed to be a Gage-bloodline ancestor, Muta — an aspect of a death god trapped in the body of a bushmaster snake — was left to me by my mother moments before her death ... and only days before this photo would have been taken ...

A flicker of a memory surfaces, even as I'm speaking it out loud. "Ingrid. Disa's potions mage —"

"The healer."

That little bit of info neatly slots itself into place in my mind, my memory. "Yes," I breathe, trying to hold onto the recollection and not the reality of the preserved body of my aunt's chosen just downstairs, awaiting transportation to the crematorium. Ingrid, who I didn't remember when I found her dead in the beach house. Ingrid, who died at the same moment the Conduit powers transferred to me, the same moment my aunt died. "She healed me after ..."

"After your mother died."

Old pain, old grief stirs in my belly, but I keep my attention on the now, on the photo. "Ingrid said that mint shouldn't really grow on the edge of the beach like that. Not so abundantly. Next to the open ocean, at least."

"It's you," Rought says with pure conviction. "Your essence smells ... tastes ... like that wild mint. The mint grows like that in all your favorite places on the property."

I knew that. I knew that.

I remember that. But not who first told me.

And ... 'tastes' not just 'smells like mint,' Rought said. He knows what I taste like because ... he ...

We were lovers, not just friends.

I sway a little on my feet. Rought shifts his hold on my hand so he can crowd up against me, his chest to my back. I don't lean into him, but he's there if I need him to hold me up.

He reaches past me to touch the photo. To touch the shoulder of the young girl, the young me, within it. "You want the story."

"If that's our beginning, yes."

"We met that day. In this lifetime, at least. Though I'd seen you a couple of days before from a distance."

"Tell me, please."

He brushes his cheek lightly against my temple, inhaling deeply. "I was beaten badly at my ... father's compound. You know he's the Cataclysm? Founder and president of the motorcycle club of the same name, right?"

I nod.

"I was beaten regularly by his men under the guise of training, but that time —"

"You're not even ten here!" I say, instantly incensed.

He chuckles quietly. "Yeah, you were pissed about it back then as well. Even with your own arm in a cast. I'm only two months older than you. So we're both nine here."

Jaw clenched, I shake my head, my anger not at all assuaged by his amusement.

"Do you want to hear the story or not?" he teases.

I huff. "Yes."

"My sperm donor wasn't around," he says. "If that makes you feel better. Oddly, the Cataclysm never actually laid hands on us ... then." He takes a fortifying breath.

And I know ... I know there is something deep and dark hidden in that breath, that pause and hesitation. "That's not the beginning," I say, not certain if I'm protecting him or my own fragile psyche.

"Right." Rought sets his chin lightly on top of my head. It is not a remotely dignified position, but I have absolutely no desire to push him away. "My mother intervened. Her and Reck, though he was still a kid himself and almost as badly hurt as me. Rath had gone for help. I'd mouthed off to some of my father's enforcers, though I can't tell you what was said. The Cataclysm was, is, all about survival of the fittest. His club followed that edict, even with his bastards." He trails off thoughtfully.

"Your mother?" I prompt.

"Took a fucking crowbar to the two idiots. And they were scared of fucking too much with the Cataclysm's current fuck. My mother held his attention longer than anyone before or after her. Anyway, she took off with all three of us. Me, Rath, and Reck. Stole a truck. Dead of night. Drove us all the way out of the Federation, somehow passing through the heavily fortified Navajo Nation to meet up with the Outcast, our uncle, just over the California border. Though none of us had met him yet, or even knew about him. She asked the Outcast for shelter. For us. Just us. She went back to the Cataclysm.”

My chest is aching, for him, for his mother. “They’re married now,” I say softly, not certain if I’m trying to comfort him or myself. “Your mother and the Outcast?”

“They are. For about twelve years. DeVille is my half-brother through my mother, but not my uncle’s kid. And my half-sisters, my mother and the Outcast’s twins, are technically also my cousins.” He flashes a grin at me. “But that’s a different story.”

I grin back at him, because I apparently can’t maintain any sort of emotional equilibrium right now. “Right.”

Rought settles his attention on the photo, his expression turning grim. “I think my mother thought the Cataclysm wouldn’t drag us back right away if she stayed with him. But no matter how many bastards he has ... we have half-siblings we don’t even know about. Reck is his oldest. And Rath and I are ...” He doesn’t complete the thought, just stares at the picture for a moment. “There are still things I don’t know all the details about. It was Grinder who brought us to Ingrid, not my uncle. The Outcast drove us to the estate, here, straight from California, but then left us at the gate. I think the Club traded a favor with Ingrid for the healing. All three of us needed it. None of us had our beasts then.”

“Most shifters don’t fully transform until their late teens,” I murmur quietly, to let him know I’m listening. Intently.

He nods. “Grinder brought us to the main house first to speak with Ingrid, but we didn’t go inside. Then three days later ...” He touches the photo, then looks down at me.

"You came out to the cottage in the woods, demanding to meet me, meet us."

I laugh. And I realize that I'm here. I'm here in the *now*. With him. Just like I was for that moment on the front patio of the main house yesterday. The moment I first saw him, even if he'd first met me when we were both only nine years old.

I want to be in the now with him. I want to ignore the terrible revelations erupting all around me, and all the conclusions sure to come. I want to ignore everything I thought was the truth, that I've now learned was some sort of a lie, and skip forward.

I feel as if Rought would be more than willing to jump into the now with me.

"Your arm was in a cast. You asked me ..." He clears his throat. "You looked at my leg, at the bruising on my face. Ingrid had to heal me in stages."

"Me too," I say quietly, not wanting to interrupt him.

"You asked me if my mom was dead too."

My heart suddenly feels as if it's lodged in my throat. "And what did you say?"

He chuckles darkly. "I said no, but that I wished my father was. Three days here, by the ocean, surrounded by people who actually fucking cared about me, and not worried what my next so-called lesson was going to be ... and I already knew I never wanted to go back. Then I met you. And you just cemented all of that."

"But you did go back."

"I did. The Cataclysm didn't let us get away that easily. But he let us come every summer, to train with our uncle, the Outcast, because he thought it would get him a foothold in Cascadia."

"Why here? The Federation seems more his ... style."

Rought snorts, then shrugs. "Power. It's always about the accumulation of power, isn't it? That's why he ..." He shakes his head.

"Why he ... ?"

"Let's put that on our list of things to figure out later," he says, angling his head so he can look me in the eye. "Not that I enjoy looking back at anything other than you, Zaya."

I flush, actual warmth threading through my chest.

"You want to know something?" he asks, all low and rumbly.

"Anything," I whisper, like an utterly breathless, utterly beguiled idiot.

"You've taken my vengeance for that day. For all the beatings before and after."

I blink, confused. "How so?"

"The Cataclysm enforcers who liked to beat the shit out of Reck, Rath, and me under the loose guise of training us? Of making sure we were the biggest, baddest shifters around? The best assets for our father? You've killed them both." He laughs harshly.

He means Chains and Breaker. Breaker fell by my hand on the beach, albeit with Muta's venom slowing him down first. And I snipped the threads of Chains's future, his life force, to stop Presh from manifesting her powers too early. Too quickly.

"What a blow to their fucking egos," Rought says with a smile. "To be put in their fucking place by a girl."

"I am the Conduit," I say wryly. But I rub my forearms, where I can still feel Chains's threads of fate scoring my skin. It's usually not for me to question my past, my path. But for a moment, I wonder if I would still be standing here, right now, with Rought, if I hadn't rescued Presh from the two Cataclysm lieutenants. If I hadn't died on that beach. If I hadn't snipped Chains's threads before his time.

I was already heading for the estate, to claim it and to try to figure out what had happened to my aunt. But would there have been any reason for my path to cross Rought's? Any reason to pop into the Outcast clubhouse, then — completely out of character — dance with a near stranger?

I don't think so.

I shiver, rubbing my arms. Again.

Rought's gaze drops to follow my movement, his brow thoughtfully pinched. But he doesn't ask if I'm hurt or cold. "Others don't understand power like what you hold, Zaya."

"And you do?"

He pauses for a moment, actually thinking about it. Somehow, that makes me like him even more.

'Like him.' What an utterly trite way of encompassing everything I'm feeling.

"I'll learn the new you," Rought finally says. "Though I think I understood the you of before, so that's not a bad start, right? For our threads?"

He reaches for my hand and ever so gently brushes his thumb across the smooth pad of my left thumb.

"If ... if you were mine ..." I whisper. The idea is overwhelming, mind-boggling. I never thought, never even hoped —

"If I was yours," Rought says, "we would walk on the beach together, like this, hand in hand."

"Yes."

"Snuggle on the couch together ..." His gold-rimmed eyes ensnare me. I can't look away, as if he's weaving some sort of spell between us. A binding. "Sharing our favorite films and snacks. Do you still like licorice All Sorts?"

I haven't had any in years, but —

He adds, "Not the jellies, though. Your favorites are the triple-layered ones, leaving me the coconut rings and the solid black licorice."

I close my mouth. He's right, of course.

He tilts his head, assessing me. Maybe seeing if I'm still with him.

I am. Completely.

"And we would go for drives up the coast, blasting music and stopping anywhere that serves milkshakes and fries. If I was yours."

"Yes." I exhale shakily. I'm not ... that life ... that's not supposed to be mine, but ... he knows me.

Maybe he only knows little bits of me, but I want to know all about his favorite things as well. I want to know how to make him smile, make him laugh, make him tighten his arms around me. "I want that."

He crowds up against me, lowering his voice again. "And dancing, like at the clubhouse?"

I nod, head fallen back to look up at him, cheeks flushed and utterly fixated. On Rought. I've never wanted anyone as much as I wanted him while dancing last night. And with Rath watching us together ...

"And at night?" Rought teases knowingly. "When the darkness encroaches on the day. I'm in your bed, yes? For more ... cuddling?"

I laugh, again involuntarily. "Cuddling? Is that how you earn your keep?" Just about everything I knew about my past has been blown wide open. I've been dealt what should have been a mortal wound, even a death sentence, for most — the loss of three soul-bound mates — and I'm fucking flirting with him.

"Well," he says feigning seriousness. "I'm pretty good at fixing things. Cars, appliances ..."

"I see," I say, pretending to consider his proposition.

"And I'm a great tech."

"I have Coda for that."

He blinks at that, absorbing it. "You have ... Coda ... ?"

"Not like that!"

He barks a laugh. "No ... I didn't think ..."

"We rescued each other years ago," I say, feeling oddly earnest. I haven't been without sexual partners, as sporadic as the impulse to connect with another human has been, but I don't want any misunderstandings between Rought and me. "From awry hunters. But there has never been anything other than a mutually beneficial ... partnership between Coda and me."

Still grinning at me as if I'm utterly adorable, he says, "I know who Coda is."

"I know you do."

"Which ... that means ..." His face crumples, shoulders suddenly sagging. "That I ... I ... could have fucking asked! I could have asked Coda about you. I fucking searched and searched on my own —"

"I'm impossible to find that way, Rought."

Head bowed, he scrubs a hand over his face. His heavy despair, his old grief, actually rips through me. Viscerally. And that should frighten me, should concern me, because I'm not empathic. But somehow, it only anchors me further.

I'm not alone.

I'm not alone in this world. In my grief.

I grab his shoulders, suddenly desperate to patch this newest wound. "You couldn't have found me like —"

Rought pulls me into his arms, lifting me up — chest

pressed to chest. I twine my legs and arms around him, as if it is pure instinct to do so. Maybe even muscle memory? I bury my face in his neck. Skin to skin.

He holds me tightly. Though I'm so much smaller, I'm not fragile to him. Though I'm so much, much more powerful, I'm not dangerous either.

He takes multiple deep breaths, of my hair, of my neck, filling his lungs with me over and over again. Essence — mine, his, and the power underlying the intersection point — twines all around us, cocooning us.

I *know*. I know what he needs in this moment. And I know how to give it to him. I want to give it to him.

Because he is mine. He feels like mine. Oh, fuck. He felt like mine the first time I saw him. And right now, I don't care that there are no actual threads between us. That I can't see or sense our soul bond.

"Have you got me?" I ask, whispering into the skin of his neck. Because this is what he needs. He needs to know I'm here. That he's found me.

"Yes," Rought says gruffly. "Always."

I pull back just enough to look him in the eye. He shifts me slightly up in his arms so that my legs twine around his torso rather than his hips, leveling out our faces. I thread my fingers through his hair, greedily snatching thick handholds of it, gazing deeply into his eyes.

He groans, dropping his head back. Gold-rimmed eyes narrow contentedly ... like a cat's.

"You want to know how we create more threads?" I ask. "More anchored connections between us?"

Those golden eyes glint knowingly. "Cuddling?"

I laugh. "Well, I was trying to seduce you, but ..."

"Zaya. I'm already seduced."

"There are probably a lot more things we should talk about."

Rought hums in disagreement. "After the kissing."

"You want me to kiss you?" I tease, my gaze flicking down to his full lips.

"I want to press you against this wall," he growls, not the least bit playful. "Between these fucking pictures of our past. Sit you on my fucking shoulders, and bury my face in your perfect cunt, Zaya. I want you to come so hard, you fucking trigger me. I want you begging, then flushed and satisfied. And then I want to do that over and over again until you're so undone, so content, that you fall asleep in my arms and you dream of nothing. No worries, no fears. Just all the sleep you need."

"Oh … I …"

I'm warm all over now. Hot, achingly wet, between my legs. I want the pleasure he's promising, yes. But it's the sleep … I can't imagine it even being possible to be that settled, that content.

"So, yeah …." Rought says. "I want you to kiss me."

I tilt my head thoughtfully, as if I don't suddenly, rather desperately want to be pressed against the wall with his tongue on my clit. And I don't normally like that. It's too intimate. I feel oddly disengaged whenever a lover tries to —

Maybe my body knows?

Maybe my body has always remembered …

Him.

"Zaya …" he growls playfully.

Smiling just a little, I hover my lips over Rought's. This is another sort of dance, isn't it? Because he could have just kissed me. He could have kissed me on the front patio yesterday when I was so enthralled with him at first sight.

"I wanted to climb you like this when we were dancing," I whisper, only a breath away from his lips. "I wanted to work your jeans off and fuck you right there in the middle of the clubhouse."

Rought groans quietly.

"And ..." Despite the playfulness we're both using to keep us in the *now*, I feel the need to add, "I don't ... like fucking all that much."

His gaze practically spears into mine. I open my mouth to ask him if I did like fucking. Did I like fucking him? Have we fucked? He has a bite mark on his hand, the impressions of my teeth scarred across his skin. We definitely fucked as teenagers. I can't imagine exchanging bites in the shifter way of claiming a mate without knowing, truly knowing, each other first.

Rought doesn't make me articulate any of that. He slides me slightly down his body so he's looming over me again, and threads his free hand through my hair. I cinch my legs around him tighter, his head still caged within my arms. Completely wrapped around each other like this blocks everything else from my sight, focuses me solely on him, on the desire threading through me. Until I feel nothing else.

"I've never felt so whole as I do when I'm buried deeply in you," he says. "So realized. So who I'm supposed to be. As I do when you're clenched and coming around my cock. So we can tease and cuddle all you want, but when you want to fuck, I'm ready for that too."

"But ..." I say, still a little shaky. "Without ... without the threads that should bind us, how do you know ... ?"

Rought kisses me then, silencing my doubts. At least for the moment. His lips are firm and steady against mine. I press back into him, gripping him as hard as I can. Holding him to me. But I already know he's not going anywhere.

I know that. Don't I?

Connection. That's what he's offering. And that is what I want. With him.

Something shifts deeply within me, possibly soul deep. I don't try to analyze it. I just part my lips under Rought's and slide my tongue against the seam of his mouth. He opens his mouth with a groan that reverberates through me, echoing from his chest to mine.

"Fuck, Zaya ..." His grip tightens on my ass and in my hair.

That groaned 'fuck' burns through me like an essence-laced shot of whiskey, all the way down to pool between the apex of my thighs. I press my tongue against his, and —

The intersection point taps me.

Taps me.

On the shoulder.

Then I get a flickering sense, an impression, of a powerful woman with wildly curly light-blond hair touching the fence that separates the property from the main road. A large vehicle idles at the entrance to the estate, unable to cross through the boundary wards without permission despite the gate being fully open.

Gigi. And Coda.

"Fuck," I groan.

"Unexpected company?" Rought asks against my lips, as if he too felt the tap.

"Expected." I sigh. "And ... needed."

Smiling, he brushes his lips against mine once more, then slides me down his body until I find my feet. I force myself to step back, though it physically hurts to do so. My gaze falls on the photo behind him on the wall. On all the photos. I hesitate.

"You want me to grab these?" Rought asks, anticipating me. "You get your guests settled. I'll put these in your bedroom?"

"That would be ... that would be ..." I blink away renewed tears. I'm still utterly overwhelmed — and now also ridiculously turned on.

He touches my shoulder lightly, turning away to grab the first photo.

I grab his hand. "Maybe come with me to meet Coda and Gigi, then we'll grab these together. They ... it's okay if they see them. It doesn't make any sense to keep this kind of info from Coda, from either of them. But Coda might want to set up in this room."

Rought's grin is warm and inviting. Pleased. As if I've done something spectacular. For him. He threads his fingers through mine and allows me to tug him out of the room.

I don't look back at the photos. Hand cradled in Rought's warm grasp, I latch onto the *now*. I hold onto it tightly.

As we descend the inside stairs, then head out of the suite, I focus on the energy of the intersection point, willing it to accept Gigi and Coda, to allow them entry.

That is actionable.

That I can do without second-guessing myself, my past, or my future.

A BIG-RIG BLACK TRUCK TOWING WHAT APPEARS to be a shiny black cargo container speeds along the driveway toward us as if the driver is being chased by dire werewolves. Or is in desperate need of a hot shower and a comfy bed.

I lift my face to the misty rain, closing my eyes against the cloudy day because it's still bright enough to hurt them. The chilly late-winter morning actually helps settle me. Though thankfully, it doesn't dampen the kernel of gentle energy I can now feel free-floating in my chest. I press my hand against it, as if I can protect it from the elements. From myself and all my vast — possibly self-destructive — ability to push away anything that tries to touch me more than skin deep.

Rought squeezes my other hand lightly, and I open my eyes to confirm that he's staring at me, eyes bright with his gryphon and a soft smile on his face.

And I *know* ... I know I'll never have to stand alone again, except by choice.

How did I not realize how desperately alone I was?

"It goes both ways," he murmurs, as if he can read my mind. As if he can read me.

No one looks at me that closely. No one is allowed, either by myself or the greater universe, to look at me that closely.

I squeeze Rought's hand back, though being gentle, intimate, doesn't come at all naturally to me.

The photographs lining the walls of Mack's second bedroom flit through my mind. Maybe it was once natural for me to ... love? Then someone, something — the universe? — took that away from me. From Rought and me and —

"Breathe," Rought whispers, raising his free hand to direct whoever is driving the truck.

I inhale steadily.

The truck is close enough now that I can see Gigi driving — her wild mane of light-blond curls and ever-perfect slash of red lipstick is a dead giveaway. Coda isn't in the passenger seat, meaning the awry tech is no doubt hooked up to all their equipment in the trailer.

"Behind the barn, Zaya?" Rought asks. "I'll have them back it in."

I have no idea. Other than crossing around it to get to the estate cemetery, I'm not certain what's actually behind the back of the barn with its workshop and garage. "Coda might just want to work out of the trailer section. Can we … hook it up to power … there?"

Rought nods. "The wind sweeps up through here, between the buildings. Coda no doubt has satellite dishes. The barn will act like a windbreak. There's a secondary … or maybe it's the primary … entrance to Mack's old suites beyond the kitchen."

Right. Not having to cross through the garage and workshop would give Coda and Gigi a bit more privacy to come and go from the suite.

Gigi slows, then slides the truck to a stop alongside us, rolling down the driver's-side window just enough to scowl down at us. Well, down at me. Rought is tall enough to be closer to eye level. For someone who was all but thirsting over a mere picture that Coda unearthed when looking into the Outcast Motorcycle Club, Gigi barely gives Rought more than an offish glance now. Though perhaps the thirsting was more about the idealized dick that might accompany the guy in the picture, not the guy himself.

The combat mage's normally pale skin is sun kissed. Black mascara and red lipstick are her only makeup.

"This rain is outrageous, Zaya," Gigi grouses in that French accent that I'm still not certain is natural or adopted. "It's been like this for the entire drive up the coast!"

Rought stiffens defensively beside me. It's subtle enough that if I weren't still holding his hand or suddenly so in tune with him, I might not have noticed. He doesn't like the combat mage's tone. It's a protective, possessive reaction that should piss me off.

Not, as it does, send a warm thrill through me.

"Gigi, my friend," I say for Rought's benefit — and just a little pointedly. "Let's get you settled. There are scalloped potatoes and a warm fire awaiting you in the main house."

"Fine!" she huffs playfully.

"Can you back it in?" Rought asks, gesturing toward the back side of the barn beyond the garage.

The combat mage gives him a withering glare, slams the truck into reverse, expertly spins the wheel, and somehow manages to back the trailer up without taking off the side of the barn. She even manages to avoid the low eaves — low compared to the height of the trailer, at least — plus all the gutters, downspouts, and overfull rain barrels.

I'm fairly certain that the barrels are supposed to be feeding into a watering system for the garden and green-houses, not all backed up. But I don't have it within me to do more than just note the issue.

A combination of energies shift behind me, and a more specific brush prickles up my neck and the side of my face. I glance back toward the main house to find Rath exiting through the front door. His gaze is on me as he casually pops the last quarter of a purloined muffin in his mouth.

Apparently, he wandered up from the beach house while I was otherwise distracted, just in time to steal my food before attempting to intimidate my guests. My invited guests.

Presh, swathed in double-layered blankets and also holding a muffin, hovers in the doorway behind him, blinking as if she's just woken up. Realizing I've seen her, she gives me a tentative, questioning wave.

As if she's the one worried about her welcome, rather than the other way around.

She should hate me. For not saving her friend Kris from being manipulated and then killed by a dire mage.

Shouldn't she?

With all but the front of the truck tucked away behind the far side of the barn, Gigi jumps from the driver's side as if leaping for freedom. "Thank the fuck!" she cries, slamming the door behind her and striding toward me. "You know you have some asshole Authority staked out at the top of the drive, right?"

I twist my lips in acknowledgment. "You left them alive, didn't you?"

She laughs, sharp and bright. "Yeah, alive and even unmaimed. Unfortunately, they'd already seen me. You know how dialed in those fuckers are with their stupid automated reporting system. But I didn't want to bring any shit down on your head."

Energy flickers across my shoulders — the only warning of Muta's sudden appearance as the snake twines possessively around my neck. With his broad head and eyes fixed in Gigi's direction, the bushmaster flicks his tongue to scent the air.

Gigi's step hitches, her fingers twitching as she instinctively readies a defensive spell. Then, recognizing the snake decorating my neck, she covers by pressing that same hand to her chest. "Muta! You sneaky fucker!"

"A little late, aren't you?" I say teasingly to the massive gold-and-brown bushmaster — my sometimes guardian, but mostly just a pain in my ass. "Was the fireside just too compelling?"

Muta cinches tighter around my neck, clearly sulking. He's not a fan of rain, not even the current light mist. He could easily avoid it by transforming into his solid gold-and-bronze topaz-bracelet aspect — usually worn around my forearm disguised as a piece of jewelry — but he enjoys the freedom his snake form offers. No need to hide or be circumspect on the vast estate, though there are usually fewer people around that he's allowed to terrify.

Gigi takes the last few steps to close the space between us, stopping just short of touching me — eye to eye, mostly due to her short-heeled boots. Her printed silk top flutters loose around her hips, instantly soaking up the misty rain. Her designer blue jeans are so bleached they're practically white, artfully ripped and worn at the knees.

Muta slithers down my arm until he's twined around both my and Rought's wrists, because we're still holding hands.

I raise my free arm to Gigi, offering an embrace. She steps into me. Her blond curls twist wildly in the breeze as she just barely brushes her right cheek against my right, then her left cheek across my left. She releases me as quickly as possible, stepping back and not quite looking at me.

My energy is usually seriously off-putting, or at least quite intense. Not that I'm generally so demonstrative. Or offering to be demonstrative.

"Thank you for coming," I say.

"Anytime," Gigi says, meaning it.

"Coda?"

She jerks her chin back toward the trailer. "Plugged in as usual. Last I bothered to check. I need a break ... where's the nearest fucking spa?"

"We'll get you sorted," Rought says.

Gigi finally acknowledges the shifter, glancing down at our entangled hands and Muta all but binding our wrists and arms together. "I wouldn't expect anything less from you, AD." 'AD' meaning 'Adonis dick.' That was Coda's nickname for Rought. Because he looks like an idealized Greek god, not because the awry hacker successfully hunted down actual dick pics.

Rought frowns deeply. I'm so accustomed to him smiling that I'm a little shocked, and admittedly just a little turned on, by the pure, focused intent threaded through his abrupt displeasure.

"Gigi, Rought," I say. "Rought, Gigi."

Gigi tilts her head coyly. Her shoulder dips just enough for the silk blouse to slip low enough to expose a sexy flash of her lacy, bright-red demi bra. "My pleasure ... Rought," she purrs.

Rought deliberately looks away from her, utterly dismissive and practically seething with indignation. "I'll get the trailer hooked up." He squeezes my hand, then loosens his hold.

Muta releases Rought, settling fully — and way too heavily — on my wrist. Ignoring that I feel instantly untethered without Rought's steady touch, I cradle all of Muta against my chest. Even though he hates being cuddled like a pet. "What have you been eating?" I mutter to the weighty death god.

Muta hasn't yet taken his full focus off Gigi, but he spares my comment a pissy flick of his tongue.

Rought crosses toward the truck and trailer without acknowledging the combat mage again. My long-lost soul-bound mate ...

I'm not certain I've completely managed to wrap my mind around it all yet. So I just snuggle Muta against my chest, against that warm ball of energy that might be the beginning of a new bond —

"Singularly focused," Gigi murmurs, though likely still loud enough for Rought to hear. "Good." She knows he's a shifter — the tenor of his essence factored in with his physical size would be unmistakable to a mage of her caliber — though she doesn't know about the extra powers that come from his gryphon. Yet.

I sigh, shaking my head at the combat mage, even though I'm still watching Rought walking away. Watching him as if I can't bear to tear my eyes from the breadth of his shoulders, or the taper of his waist, or the remembrance of his mouth on mine, his grip on my —

"Goes both ways, I see," Gigi says, eyeing me now and slightly amused. "That's good too."

Rought disappears from my sight around the truck and the side of the barn. I can still feel him, though. His presence is potent even within the energy of the intersection point. Almost as if the gryphon shifter feeds into that energy, and it into him. That's another of the revelations to be explored when my mind, my soul, doesn't feel quite so ... threadbare.

Muta writhes around my wrist and forearm, tucking under my sleeve as he transforms into the gold-scaled, dark-brown topaz bracelet. Too many people, maybe. Or maybe the misting rain is finally too much for him.

"Introduce me to the rest?" Gigi asks almost gently. Her

gaze levels on the front patio of the main house over my shoulder. "We should warm up and eat, yes?"

I follow her gaze, taking in Presh, still swathed in blankets and nibbling on her muffin, and Rath, huge and forbidding, standing watch like he's some ancient guardian. A guardian in dark-gray sweatpants and a ridiculously tight black T-shirt.

And fuck.

The celestial dragon sharing a body — and a soul — with the imposing shifter actually is an ancient guardian.

So that's two.

Two of my supposed soul-bound mates transform into mythical guardian beasts. The third is a creature even more terrifying. If the mythology is built on truth, Reck's beast, the cu-sith, is a type of grim reaper — the personification of death, aka a demigod. And based on what I saw of it last night, the cu-sith is nowhere near as well contained as the death god currently twined around my forearm.

"Is this one a problem?" Gigi asks, eyeing Rath with narrowed eyes.

The dragon shifter glowers right back at the combat mage, crossing his arms and widening his stance.

"No," I say with a sigh, starting for the house. "He's mine as well."

Rath's amber-bright gaze shoots to me. Surprise or some similar emotion eases the tension threaded through his shoulders.

"I just didn't know it," I add.

"Okay, then," Gigi murmurs, just a little doubtfully. "And the little one is Precious?"

I smile at that, locking eyes with the young awry intently watching me approach. The purple in her eyes marking her as awry is more obvious today, even against the gray light. She manifested a lot of unanchored power last night, so I'm not surprised that it's all settled close to the surface. "Yes. She is Precious."

"I see that." Gigi picks up her pace, jogging up the stairs to the patio ahead of me and grinning down at Presh. "Hello, darling. I'm Gigi."

"Hi," Presh says shyly, glancing over at me.

"Gigi and Coda are old friends," I say, mounting the stairs.

"Yes," Gigi says. "Friends."

Though I'm not certain of my welcome, I open my arms to Presh. The young awry rushes the last few steps to me, grabbing me as hard as she can through the layer of blankets she's swathed herself in, and pressing her face to my chest. Her pastel-rainbow hair is damp from a shower, the colors muted when wet.

Presh sobs, just once, then attempts to burrow into me further.

Holding back the emotion suddenly clogging my own throat, I meet Gigi's worried gaze over the young awry's head. "The kitchen is down the end of the hall," I say, pleased that I sound sure and steady. "Just beyond the bathroom on the right. Will you put another log on the fire?"

"Already done," Rath says, though not unkindly.

Gigi steps into the house without further invitation, giving us a moment.

I hold Presh tightly, angling my head enough to gaze up at Rath.

He stiffens as if expecting a chastisement. And I should give him one, for being on the property uninvited. But the revelations among Mack's photographs press into my mind, as if the memories contained within them, printed in black and white, are slowly overwriting everything else that has occurred between adult Zaya and adult Rath. For the moment.

He's larger and way harder hewn than the teen in the photos, though, presumably going through his last growth spurt when his celestial dragon manifested.

I have so many questions. Those at the top of the list are nebulous, and the rest … overwhelming.

Why didn't Rath tell me he knew me?

Would I have believed him if he did?

"Have you seen Mack's photographs?" I ask him quietly.

He tilts his head, glower deepening.

That's obviously a no.

"Of us."

His expression softens, just slightly. "Us?"

"Yes. All four of us. They're in the second bedroom of the caretaker's suite off the workshop." I inhale unsteadily, tightening my hold on Presh. The young awry squeezes me back just as fiercely, angling her head to peek at her brother from within my embrace.

"All four of us …" Rath echoes a little hollowly.

"I'd like to bring them into the house so Coda and Gigi can feel free to claim the space."

Rath nods stiffly. "I'll get them for you." He steps close enough to touch me, opening his palm to reveal a pair of my sunglasses.

Keeping my hold on Presh, I take the offered glasses. "Thank you."

Rath palms the back of Presh's head, towering over the both of us for a moment and holding my gaze.

I don't put on the glasses, though the daylight is still too bright for me, even under the layer of cloud and the roof of the front patio.

Tilting his head thoughtfully, tension shifts through Rath's jaw as if he wants to speak. But he simply shakes his head, then steps past us, shoulder lightly brushing against mine.

A gentle energy shifts between us under that point of contact. I don't shove it away.

All is not okay between us, but now isn't the time to go over any of that. I understand Rought's reaction to my return a little better, but not Rath's. Not at all.

Presh and I watch the dragon shifter cross through the misty rain toward the barn.

"We can argue after breakfast," Presh says resolutely.

"You and me?"

She scoffs, pulling away just enough to thread one of her blanket-wrapped arms through mine and pull me toward the house. "No! Them. My three asshole brothers!"

I let her tug me into the house, welcoming the warmth as it closes around us. I narrow my eyes. "When have they been assholes to you? Recently?"

"To you, Zaya!" Presh declares with another huff. "I'm not stupid! They all know you, right? That's what you mean by photographs 'of us.'"

I blink at her for a moment. "You're right. They are all assholes!"

She cackles, delighted by my vehement agreement. "But first, breakfast?"

"Yes. First, breakfast."

Just beyond the front entranceway, where I pause to remove my boots and jacket, DeVille is sprawled across the lower stairs leading up to the second floor, as if he slipped on the dark wood and broke his neck on the way down. Otherwise naked and barefoot, the medium-brown-skinned, unmanifested shifter is wearing light-gray sweatpants that bunch above the splint still encasing his lower left leg. He has a light-blue T-shirt clutched in one hand, as if he expended all his energy just to get down the stairs, then decided to take an impromptu nap before pulling the shirt on.

Presh huffs, hands instantly falling to her blanket-swathed hips as she widens her stance to glower down at DeVille. "Doc Z told you to stay in bed!"

DeVille jolts awake — confirming that he's just sleeping, not moments away from slipping into the After — then instantly glowers at the young awry. His dark-gray hair falls around his face, longer than it was even a day before and shadowing his green eyes. It's that same shade even at the roots, making it likely that it isn't dyed.

The hair growth is presumably due to whatever healing potions Doc Z has been pumping into his system. Either that or he's only weeks away — maybe even days away — from taking the form of his beast for the first time. He's the perfect age for it, late teens.

DeVille tilts his head back, eyeing Presh as he runs a hand down his bare torso, then pats his stomach. "I'm hungry."

"I could have brought you up something."

"Would you have?"

Presh just snorts at him, then dismissively saunters up the main hall toward the kitchen at the back of the house without replying.

DeVille's face instantly falls, gaze now cast around my feet. "I think maybe Precious blames me. For Kris."

"You did everything you could," I say, my tone harsher than my sentiment. Because when the cu-sith showed up, I was the one who defied the universe urging me to protect Precious, DeVille, and Kris. I don't usually question a push by the universe, because doing so always comes with consequences. But I placed the lives of the dozens of shifters fighting in the streets first.

I made a choice. And Kris is dead.

She had likely been hovering on the moment of her death hours before, but none of us knew it.

DeVille hunkers forward, elbows on his bent knees now, head bowed. "You said the beach. You said straight to the beach ..." His voice cracks. "I let ... I knew something was wrong. Kris's scent shifted. Then she darted away from me ..."

"Kris wasn't Kris anymore." Movement draws my gaze down the hall. Both Precious and a jeans-clad Doc Z — Zephyr, the medic for the Outcast MC — hover in the doorway to the kitchen area, listening to our conversation. Precious might have been in love with Kris. Doc Z was her sister. The golden-red-haired pegasus shifter brought Kris to me in the midst of the battle last night, trusting her to my protection.

"Exactly." DeVille shakes his head. "I knew ... I knew. I should have grabbed Precious and run. But she really never would have forgiven me."

He looks up at me, eyes glassy with unspent tears.

I step forward to touch his shoulder. He shudders under that touch, under the press of all the power I hold. Uneasily. And I *know* ... I know he's looking for absolution.

Unfortunately, no matter the sects that worship the Conduit as such, I'm not that sort of divine being.

I can, however, offer him retribution.

"I will track down the dire mage," I say, resolute and firm. Unwavering. "I will get you definitive answers. But I'm already certain there was nothing you could have done in the moment. Kris was compromised the instant the dire mage decided to take her. Presumably hours before. Possession spells are ... complicated. They aren't set or triggered in the spur of the moment. And never without thoughtful — and malicious — foresight."

I look down the hall to meet Doc Z's gaze, ready for her questions and condemnation. She blinks back tears, shakes her head, and drops her eyes.

Beside Doc, Precious rasps, "At the salon. The dire mage took Kris to get to me. Get me away from the pack house protections."

Still seated at the base of the stairs, DeVille pivots to look over his shoulder down the hall. His spine stiffens, shoulders squaring.

Next to Presh, Doc Z's face crumples. "At the salon? But ... when Cay and I were there? But who ... we would have scented dire essence ... we should have ..." She presses a shaking hand over her mouth, to contain a sob, maybe? To try to weather the realization that she could have intervened if —

"Maybe if you weren't so worried about getting in my brother's pants," Precious spews viciously. "And gossiping about shit you shouldn't be talking about in public, you would have!"

Doc Z actually stumbles back from the young awry, hitting her shoulder against the kitchen doorframe.

All of Precious's sudden anger drains from her. She

buries her face in her hands and sobs — the force of her grief racking her small, blanket-swathed form.

DeVille heaves to his feet, hobbling, then using the open edges of the stairwell risers and the walls to get to Presh.

Doc Z reaches the sobbing teen first, pulling Precious against her chest and holding onto her tightly. Tears silently roll down her own cheeks.

"I'm sorry, I'm sorry," Precious whispers, voice muffled against her hands still covering her face.

Reaching the two of them, DeVille wraps himself around Presh from the other side. The trio hold each other for a moment, just navigating their combined grief.

When Precious finally drops her hands from her face, resting her head on Doc Z's shoulder to look down the hall toward me, I meet her gaze steadily.

Unvoiced promises pass between her and me, threading through and along the tie that instantly bound us together in the bathroom of the Choices Cafe only three days ago. I had never felt a connection snap into place like that to anyone before.

And now I know the *why*, don't I? I've seen the foundations of our soul-deep connection in black and white, in the photographs lining the walls of the suite's second bedroom.

Precious is a blood sibling to the three people who were my soul-bound mates. Who *are* my soul-bound mates?

"Breakfast?" I ask, shoving away all the confusing thoughts and the ramifications of those revelations unfolding all around me. Food and more sleep will make navigating all of that, all of this, easier.

Presh nods, just once. "Breakfast."

Doc Z releases the young awry, running her hands over her own face to brush away the streaks of tears. "I squeezed us some orange juice." She heads back into the kitchen without another word, her back stiff, fingers curled.

"You're suffocating me, Andy," Presh grouses, complaining.

DeVille — who Presh insists on calling Andy just to piss him off — huffs and releases her as well.

But he doesn't move more than a step away, still holding onto the wall, then the countertops, to support himself as I join them, and we cross into the kitchen together.

@drsoaresrex

TWO

I SLIP AWAY FROM THE EATING AREA OFF THE kitchen, leaving Gigi to not-so-subtly interrogate the others in attendance — aka gathering ammunition — as Cayley and Rath cook up another round of breakfast for everyone. Or maybe it's now an early lunch?

The kitsune shifter took off after Coda and Gigi arrived, only to reappear with enough groceries to feed a small army. Which isn't an inaccurate assessment of the power gathered around the overly full breakfast table. The eggs, milk, and butter I found in the fridge earlier — presumably also thanks to Cayley — were apparently only enough to make muffins, scalloped potatoes, and feed the bottomless pit DeVille calls a stomach.

Gigi took one look at Cay — the patch-decorated leather jacket, the skintight black jeans, and the perfectly manicured maroon nails — and decided they were destined to be friends. Gigi doesn't have friends. She has responsibilities, of which I assume I'm one, but I'm honestly not sure the combat mage even likes Coda. But Cay's answering smiles are just as sharp edged, so I have no doubt the two will find a level just below outright mayhem and maiming.

Neither Rought nor Coda have yet made an appearance in the main house.

As I cross into the mudroom for boots and the back door, Rath's gaze is heavy on me. I have no doubt he wants to discuss Mack's photographs. But between that expectation and the smell of frying bacon, I need to focus elsewhere, on something actionable.

The dire mage.

Also, what the fuck happened to my Aunt Disa? And why the fuck whatever she *knew* was coming — with enough time to order an ice-cream maker and for Mack to curate his photographs — wasn't worth a phone call to me, her supposed successor?

And to solve both of those nagging issues, I need Coda.

The rain has increased enough to leave small pools of water on the weathered back steps. Ignoring my continued confusion over the general neglectful upkeep of the property, I hike up my silk skirt so I don't trip over it for the dash through the rain from the back of the house toward the barn.

The rig that Gigi parked behind the barn is now in the driveway, leaving Coda's sleek trailer all but hidden from view between the barn and the orchard. Though the still-winter-bare apple and pear trees don't offer much protection.

I assume the truck is a rental and needs to be returned. Which means Coda and Gigi are planning on staying. For a while, at least. And oddly, that pleases me. Comforts me?

I usually don't like people in my space.

But how much of that individualistic behavior might have been tied to what's been stolen from me?

I skirt the shiny black-metal cargo container, looking for the entrance. A single satellite dish is affixed to the top, and two more have been set up on the peak of the barn. I have no doubt there are more, or will soon be more, that I can't see from this low angle.

Coda has put Rought to work rather efficiently.

I find a door about a third of the way along. But it's high enough off the ground, the container still set on the wheeled trailer, that I have to strain to reach the handle. The door swings open outwardly easily enough when unlatched, but with nothing to step on, my skirt is going to be —

Rought appears in the doorway. Reaching down for me, he effortlessly swings me up into his arms. His energy instantly wraps around me, and I shamelessly cling to that, to his warmth, even though I haven't been outside long enough to get truly chilled.

I also haven't been away from him long enough to miss his presence quite as much as I obviously am.

"Close the door," Coda snaps from somewhere deeper inside.

When we first met in Belize — or rather, when we rescued each other from the mercenaries hunting the awry tech — Coda's accent hinted at Latin American origins. But after all these years, it's a more neutral North American now. Even as the political landscape on this continent tends to keep Coda elsewhere as much as possible. With the essence they wield over tech and the digital realm, Coda can work from anywhere and still reach every part of the world they wish to reach.

Between the Authority and the Federation, North America isn't that friendly to awry. It isn't that friendly to other unaffiliated essence-wielders in general, though there are pockets where the awry and those with essence are protected and nurtured. At least as much as that's possible when those without the ability to wield essence, aka the nulls, vastly outnumber us, and power-hungry individuals or organizations hunt us.

The Phrontistery Academies are one such pocket. Fortified by generations of protection — both financially and literally — the academies' primary objective is to nurture talent.

Which is exactly why that's where I should send Precious. With DeVille.

Rought, still holding me tucked firmly against him, reaches out with his free arm and yanks the door closed behind me, shutting out most of the light.

For a moment, before my eyes adjust to the low ambient light emanating from all the tech lining the walls and the low lighting around Coda's workstation situated at the far end of the container, we're sheltered within that sudden darkness.

I shove back my unsettling thoughts about sending Presh away. I will if that's what's best for her. But it's ... too soon. Too soon to make any other significant changes. For either of us.

Rought runs his hand down my back, fingertips lightly caressing my spine through my hand-knit sweater. I burrow closer to him, then press a kiss just under his jaw as if it's a tiny secret I'm sharing with him.

He palms the back of my head, angling to press his own kiss to my lips. I breathe him in, reminding myself — a little shakily — that it's okay, even if just for a moment, to be this dependent on another person. It's okay that his presence steadies me. After all, that is his purpose according to the universe. Or it was before those threads of fate were stripped from us.

Who am I to argue with or deny what the universe wove for our souls?

"Fuck off," Coda grouses, startling me even though the awry tech's essence permeates the darkened space.

A quick glance in their direction confirms they aren't talking to me or about us.

"Fuck the fuck right off!" Coda snarls, fingers tapping harshly on their keyboards.

Only three of the dozen screens surrounding Coda's main workspace appear to be working properly. The others glitch occasionally as Coda's fingers continue to fly over the three keyboards set on a narrow desk — if 'keyboard' is still the correct terminology for the custom-built tech the awry hacker has rigged to their extensive systems. One of the boards appears to be cobbled together from old mechanical keyboards — the central one, which glows a soft lilac and clacks with each touch of Coda's fingers. But the other two are sleek, with nary a letter or symbol on any of their buttons. Keys? Pads? Trackpads?

I really have no idea what I'm looking at.

"Might need to get a dish on top of the main house," Rought says helpfully. His voice rumbles through his chest, warming me in places that really have no reason to be warm. Certainly not while in the heart of Coda's command center.

"Is it the intersection point?" I ask.

Coda flinches, then spins around in their chair to glare at me as if they didn't sense my presence when I entered. Possibly owing to the set of black headphones they wear, though one cup is skewed behind the tech's ear. With their purple eyes darkened by black-rimmed, blue-tinted glasses, the tech appears paler than usual. Tall but slim, verging on skinny, and with chestnut-brown hair long enough to brush their jawline. And badly in need of a shampoo. "What the fuck, Zaya!?"

"Hey!" Rought reprimands the tech.

I lay my palm on the center of the gryphon shifter's chest, and he settles into a glower. Rather than beating Coda into submission.

I once again ignore the inappropriate thrill that runs down my spine at Rought's display of dominant possession. Over me, about me.

No one protects me. Not outright like that. Not even my aunt did so.

The awry tech completely disregards the pissy shifter. "Stop blocking me."

"I'm not doing it," I say calmly, understanding that being at all cut off from their tech — or at least restricted in reach — is going to upset Coda on a visceral level. "You said it was a blank spot, remember? When I first called you from here? Even with one of your phones."

"Tech works here," Rought says, just a little unhelpfully.

"Maybe well enough for your insignificant reach," Coda snaps back at the gryphon shifter, spinning in the chair to turn their back on us.

Rought opens his mouth to retort, but I shake my head at him. He huffs, then nods with a grimace.

I close the space between Coda and me, ignoring that I'm suddenly chilled in all the places that were previously pressed against Rought. Because while I might be willing to entertain the idea of a soul bond, that reaction is just irrational.

Stacked against the walls with wires running overhead, tech hums around us at different frequencies. I have no idea what any of it is or does. Batteries? Hard drives? Servers?

"Don't touch anything," Coda mutters, fingers clacking across the keyboard directly in front of them.

The first few times I met or visited Coda in person, I inadvertently dispelled months of the tech's work with a brush of my arm or hip. Even before I was the Conduit, my essence instantly canceled out the power of the other awry. Despite the fact that little trick is usually reserved for spells and such with malicious intent.

I always suspected it was the same reason that made me near impossible to track via tech. The same reason Rought was unable to find me, no matter the years he spent searching across his own screens and keyboards.

"I know," I murmur soothingly. To Coda. I'm still not managing to keep my own whirling mind from perpetually hovering at the edge of what feels like unhinged chaos.

Back turned and still ignoring me in favor of the monitors, Coda huffs belligerently.

"Thank you for coming." Following a whisper of a knowing, or maybe it's just my subconscious stepping in to defuse the tension, I gently lay my hands on Coda's shoulders. "Thank you for being here for me when I needed you, but didn't know how to ask you for something so ... personal."

Coda shudders under the touch of my energy, and the tech awry's fingers fall still on the keyboard. It's rare that I touch anyone without invitation, and Coda might honestly be touch-phobic. But they don't flinch away from me, so I maintain the contact.

Their head drops forward, hair falling all around their sharp-edged jaw. "I should have come sooner. I'm sorry. I ... I knew something was wrong, and I didn't even ... ask. I felt it, under my fingers, in my mind ... not a disturbance but a shift in the fundamental energy that ..." Coda trails off, but out of reluctance to continue rather than confusion or a lack of understanding.

"I wasn't ready then." I level my gaze on the glitching screens arrayed on the three walls surrounding us.

"Tell me what you need of me," Coda says hoarsely, almost pleading.

And for a moment, it sounds like more than a simple request.

It sounds like ... prayer.

I push that sense away. I want to be Zaya with Coda. Not the Conduit. Not some goddess to be worshiped. "Find me the dire mage. Chains called her Bellamy."

Energy shifts under my hands, spreading across Coda's shoulders.

The tech awry shudders again, fingers twitching.

The screens before us blink awake. Or at least that's how it appears.

Coda lurches forward, excited and instantly focused.

My hands fall to my sides.

The energy of the intersection point settles into a quiet hum under my feet. It's difficult to distinguish between that endless reservoir of power and my own essence while I'm on the property — or perhaps those two energies are now so enmeshed that I can't feel the difference without reaching for it. Either way, I didn't realize it was so agitated before.

Perhaps Coda, being awry, needed a more formal invitation onto the estate.

"Give me a starting point," Coda mutters, already pulling various feeds up on their screens. A wall of text is scrolling over another. Some sort of coding, maybe. "I got rough highlights from Rought about your last twenty-four hours, and I've got the tracking off your phone." Coda casts a narrow-eyed look at me over their shoulder. "You know, keeping the fucking phone on you would be way more helpful."

"For stalking purposes?" Rought mutters from behind us.

"For cleaning up your fucking messes," Coda snaps, focusing back on the multitude of screens.

"A beauty salon in town. In Newport, I think," I say, ignoring the minor pissing contest taking place between the two techs. "Yesterday afternoon at best guess. Cayley's family owns the chain. The … um …"

"The Nail Bar," Rought says. "On First Street."

Before the shifter even finishes speaking, Coda's screens are already flashing through what appear to be vid feeds along with multiple social media profiles.

"Kitsune," Coda mutters, flicking their eyes behind their blue-tinted glasses over various screens as if they've pulled Cay's background up somewhere, though I don't see it. It's also possible the tech is simply recalling the info. "Cayley Harvey, sister of Kiki. Both interconnected with your timeline, Zaya. About eighteen months ago, when you rescued Kiki and the other teens from the shifter-trafficking ring in Tokyo."

Rought's arm jerks, as if he's just stopped himself from grabbing for me. "That was you? You're that fixer?"

Coda cackles. "The universe has a sense of humor when Zaya is involved."

"I'm not laughing," Rought snaps.

Coda shrugs one shoulder, eyes still glued to the monitors. "That's a choice."

Rought's gaze is heavy on me. "I tried to pick up the kids and Cay from the airport, but fucking Reck got there before me, flashed his badge, carted them off. Were you ... were you on that plane?"

The real question he's hesitant to ask is: Was his older brother hiding the fact that I was alive from him?

"No," I say. "I was ... otherwise occupied."

"Dead, she means," Coda interjects unhelpfully. "Fell right off the fucking grid. Took me three days to find her. And only then because Muta got a little feisty at the morgue." The tech cackles.

At the mention of the enraged death god trapped in the body of a snake, the gold-and-brown-topaz bracelet on my right arm gets slightly heavier.

"Muta's still pissed about being curtailed," I mutter. "In defense of me, of course." That last bit is sarcastic and aimed at the sulky bushmaster. Because though the care and feeding of Muta has been passed down through my family for generations, he neither likes nor dislikes his minders. Still, my waking in the middle of my own autopsy did seem to be what set him off that particular time.

Thankfully, when Coda and I are working together, the tech always has a line on mage-brewed antivenom, so no one died at the morgue. Not that it always works. Muta is rather powerful, and I was too incapacitated to get him under my control quickly.

"Perfectly understandable." Rought's voice rumbles through his chest. He's crossed his arms, presumably because he wants to be doing something else with his hands. I can literally see all the questions flitting through his mind in his sharp gaze. Then he inhales deeply and lets those questions and concerns all drop away.

Because we're living in the *now*, he and I. If only for today.

I, rather sappily, just grin at him.

An answering self-deprecating grin eases the remainder of the tension threaded around Rought, around us. "Why do you think the dire mage was at the nail salon, Zaya?"

"Something Kris said to Precious. Doc Z's sister," I add for Coda, just in case. "Last night after I picked the three of them up at the warehouse rave but before I brought them to the Outcast clubhouse."

"Rave ..." Coda murmurs, adding in the keyboard on the left and amazingly adept on it with only one hand. "I need access to your security, AD. Unless you just want me to crack it."

In a blink, I can suddenly see cobweb-thin threads of essence twisting around both the tech's hands, flowing through their fingers into the keyboard and its built-in trackpads.

Rought steps forward, leaning over the right-hand section of Coda's main keyboard to pull up some sort of scrolling script on the monitor directly in front of him.

Coda grunts, pissed but keeping otherwise quiet about the intrusion.

"The clubhouse feeds are fried from last night, but here's access to all the backups," Rought says.

The threads twined around Coda's hands feather outward to the keys Rought is touching. The gryphon shifter steps back, flicking his fingers as if he feels the touch of that essence.

I blink again, clearing my sight.

Rought steps to my side, brushing his hand against mine. I want to lean against his shoulder, to sink into him, to use him to anchor me.

I don't.

I focus instead on the puzzle — and on the threat right

before me. Working through that will hopefully give my system, my mind, the time I need to adjust to my *now*.

I'm not just the Conduit at least a hundred years before my time. I'm not just the holder and protector of one of only seven intersection points. I've been stripped of bonds I never knew existed for me. Soul-bound mates, who were supposed to —

I shove that unhelpful thought away. 'Supposed to' is as useless to me as 'should' and 'should have.'

"Kris said she got a reading yesterday at the nail salon from a purple-eyed seer," I say, clearing my throat and forcing my focus. "That reading prompted Kris to get Presh to the rave. Away from the protections I assume surround the main pack house."

"You assume correctly," Rought mutters under his breath.

Coda snorts derisively. "An awry seer? Hanging out at a nail salon on the edge of the wilds of Cascadia?"

"It's pack territory," Rought says, just a little irritated.

"Exactly." Coda sniffs snobbishly.

"I also did the security on the salon ..." Rought steps closer to Coda. "I can —"

Coda holds up their hand. "I've got it. You just gave me access to everything you've ever constructed, shifter." The tech snickers derisively. "Should have thought twice before touching my tech."

Rought shrugs. "Whatever Zaya needs."

I expect another pissy rebuttal from Coda, but none is forthcoming.

Multiple feeds appear across the top center screens. An exterior shot of the Nail Bar, which appears to be closed. Plus two interior angles showing the salon and a small office. Both are also empty.

The windows and glass door of the salon have been boarded up.

"Break-in?" Coda asks. "This is the live feed."

"Rath," Rought says, sliding his gaze to me questioningly.

Rath? He means the celestial dragon. And he's not certain how much I want Coda to know. "That was him? All the glass blowing out?"

All that glass shattered all over the streets as we fled the clubhouse with Chains and two berserkers on our heels. From all the windows facing those couple of blocks of Newport. Shattered by a single roar from a pissed-off celestial dragon. Likely essence-enhanced, though I don't remember feeling a specific push or tenor of essence at the time.

Not a single shard of that glass hit us as we ran. That might have been a universe-directed intervention — aka my own inadvertent essence-wielding, uncontrollable and capricious as that is. But ...

"The rain as well?" I ask quietly, my mind momentarily stuttering over the sheer power contained within a single shifter. Celestial dragons, gryphons, and cu-sith are all supposed to be mythological. "The fog?"

Rought nods stiffly, gaze flicking to Coda. The tech appears to be ignoring us, though I know they're memorizing, quite possibly even documenting, everything we say.

Rath — or more specifically, his dragon — can control the elements. Water and air, at least. Which explains how he can fly without wings.

Powerful mages, usually wielding in concert, can use spells to harness the elements. And I've heard of awry who can wield one or two elements — earth, fire, air, or water. But —

"Grinder and Pinky are in charge of the crew going around town today," Rought says, not-so-subtly redirecting the conversation. "Temporarily boarding up the windows and cleaning the streets. The replacement glass is already on order."

"I don't keep secrets from Coda," I say, answering Rought's previously unvoiced question.

Coda snorts belligerently. "Yeah, right."

"I don't keep relevant information from Coda," I say stiffly.

"Sure you don't." Coda makes a production of pointing at a currently blank monitor to their upper right. Then, with two more clicks on the keyboard, a different interior shot of the salon appears on-screen. It includes the entrance, the cash register, and Kris seated near the perfectly intact front windows. Coda's already sifted through hours of vid.

Rought whistles under his breath, quietly impressed.

Kris's dirty-blond hair is up in a few curlers, and she's wearing a sage-colored printed T-shirt over blue jeans. The print on the shirt is a faded sunset, trees, with a rock formation jutting out of a beach. Maybe it's a vintage tourist design?

Not what she was wearing when waiting tables at the Tasty Tart diner where we met, and not what she was wearing to the rave later that same day.

The person talking to Kris is partially cut off on the edge of the vid screen. They're seated across from each other on either side of a narrow table. The type usually used to do manicures. The angle of the vid isn't quite wide enough to fully cover that corner of the salon. Or the camera has been subtly nudged out of alignment ...

There are other people moving around in the background of the salon, but I focus on the stranger across from Kris.

Is this the dire mage? Bellamy? She's very ... average looking. But I can't see her eyes — or sense the corrupted essence I already know she wields.

"Recognize her?" Coda asks, grabbing a series of still shots of the stranger in profile, shifting them over to a neighboring monitor, then triggering some sort of facial-tracking algorithm.

I mean, I'm guessing that's what they're doing, but it seems like a logical conclusion.

"No," Rought says, settling a hand on Coda's desk and leaning forward to peer at the screen with a frown. "Is there something wrong with the vid or the feed?"

"Essence interference," Coda says. "I can work around it."

Apparently, I'm not seeing the same images or vid they're seeing, presumably because of my inherent resistance to essence-laced ... well, anything to do with essence, really. No matter that my hold on it all is still shaky, it's difficult to fool the senses of the Conduit, through whom all the essence that fuels the world flows. Supposedly.

"Like ... a cloaking spell?" I say. "Or a glamour?"

Coda shakes their head. "Not certain. Yet."

"Cay and Doc Z are right there in the room with them," Rought says grimly. "Kris hadn't manifested her beast yet, but there's no fucking way that a mage powerful enough to obscure their identity could be sitting only feet away without two shifters noticing. Not only do dire mages stink, but shifters with the ... talents of those two would pick up more than just scent. Cloaked or otherwise."

Kitsune and pegasus, he means. Both beasts likely lend their human counterparts extra abilities, even while not transformed. Rought's being circumspect about the nature of Cay's and Doc Z's beasts, but Coda already knows.

The problem with being powerful? I often don't notice things such as glamours or other essence spells, not even when they're directed toward me. Not even before I was the Conduit. Though if this is the dire mage who compromised and killed Kris, they're powerful enough to have armed Chains with spells so malignant that they took down a club full of shifters. And those spells, I felt.

As well, even when wielding essence through Kris, the dire mage erected a shield barrier that momentarily stymied my senses last night. That level of essence-wielding isn't as simple as a nasty spell that can be precast and contained in an essence-twisted object.

Not that there was anything simple about the casting that forced an entire motorcycle club to wither in pain, transform to save themselves, then seemingly get stuck in their beast forms. And my eyes would have adjusted to the dire mage's barrier spell that Rought's gryphon easily tore through. Eventually.

Speaking of rare shifter abilities — the gryphon not only sensed the barrier, but dispelled it without any blowback.

"I just see a dark-haired, tanned-skinned woman," I say. "Heart-shaped face, big eyes, thinner upper lip. She's got a set of oracle cards, or a custom tarot deck maybe, laid out on the table before her. Her nails are extra long, painted dark red."

Both Coda and Rought turn to me, mouths slightly agape.

"Why?" I ask, just a little pissy. "What do you see?"

They both look back at the monitor.

Rought grunts.

Coda mutters, "What the fuck?" Then they capture a new set of screenshots.

"What?"

"That's what, or who, we see," Rought says quietly. "Now that you've pointed it out."

"That a new party trick, Conduit?" Coda asks, like a total asshole.

I sigh. "I need to know if the dire mage is still in Cascadia."

"And if she's not?" Rought asks.

I think about that for a moment. I shouldn't leave the intersection point when everything still feels so unsettled. "She's near."

"You know?" Rought voices that deceptively simple follow-up as if he knows on a different level what it means for me to *know* something.

I pause, giving that question the consideration it deserves. Also, just in case the universe wants to chime in with a contrary opinion. It doesn't. "Yes, I *know*."

"Fine, good," Coda grouses. "Give me some space and a few fucking minutes of peace and I'll find her for you."

Rought's fingers twitch as if he wants to offer to help. But then he slides his hand across my lower back and waits for me to move toward the door.

I shudder under his delicious touch — but thankfully only internally. Perhaps even on an essence-only level.

"You were tracking Devlin for me," I say to Coda, trying to keep on track. Then I add, for Rought's benefit, "Disa's combat mage wasn't on the property."

"I know," Rought says quietly. "I've been looking for him as well. I've never been able to track Disa directly."

That isn't at all surprising. The universe wouldn't allow

its Conduit to be vulnerable to any sort of tracking, friendly or otherwise.

"I've got something for you. Took my algos way too long to find it, but ..." Coda sounds uncharacteristically cautious. "You want to hear it in front of AD?"

Rought stiffens, though I'm not certain if it's the condescending nickname or the inference that I might not trust him that bothers him. But he looks at me instead of responding directly to Coda.

"Do you need to keep secrets from me right now?" he asks, surprisingly gentle.

"Did we keep secrets from each other ... before?" I ask, not at all certain why that's a question I suddenly need answered.

His eyes narrow thoughtfully. "I don't think so. Not you and me."

"Yeah," Coda interjects. "I'm still piecing together all this past shit you've all got going on, but secrets are a little too cutesy to encompass what might have happened here right before ... you know."

"Before I became the Conduit," I whisper. My gaze is already riveted to the images Coda is pulling up on the screen. It's mostly pictures of various people, including a recent shot of Disa that the tech got off my phone, and a few snippets of vid of locations and vehicles. Unfamiliar at first glance. To me, at least.

Rought jerks forward as if to get a closer look. Though with his beast rimming his eyes, there's no way he'd miss any of the details of what Coda has uncovered.

"Authority agents like to run around with these little devices that knock out tech in a localized area." Coda pulls even more images up on the screens, moving too quickly for me to follow the threads the tech is pulling forth.

"Black boxes," Rought rasps.

"My algos didn't key in on Devlin until I decided to look at the issue … let's say through a different lens."

Rought grunts, impressed. "You're tracking the use of the black boxes."

Coda shrugs offishly. "Let's call it a hobby. I fuck with the Authority in my spare time."

"You've got to be up the chain of command to have a black box," Rought says. "Legally. Which helps narrow your focus … to anything the Authority might be trying to hide, specifically from people like you."

"There aren't any other people like me." Coda's tone is flat. Usually the awry tech is ecstatic while on the cusp of a major reveal. "A black box might be an impediment to any other hacker, though its focus is narrow. But me … I can grab the feed from the bank across the street, find what I'm tracking … in this case Devlin … and sharpen it enough to see inside the cafe."

Coda punches a couple of keys, expanding a vid on the top middle monitor so it fills the screen. The footage clearly shows a light-blond-haired, tanned-skin male in his midthirties sitting at a corner booth by the windows, facing the entrance of a small but bustling cafe.

Seeing him after almost forgetting he even existed is disconcerting. Because of course I recognize my aunt's chosen.

Devlin.

Devlin, whose eyes crinkled around the edges when he laughed. Devlin, who loved surprising my aunt with small treats, roses and seashells and hand-painted greeting cards from whatever city my aunt had chosen for our training sessions. Devlin, whose explosive essence, similar to Gigi's but with many more years of experience and the connection to my aunt to fortify it, parted crowded markets or side-walks without any effort.

Devlin, who was much older than he appears in the vid. Just like my aunt's other two chosen, Mack and Ingrid. Because the tie to my aunt came with almost enough advantages to outweigh its one gigantic complication.

My aunt dying — being murdered? — also killed all her chosen. Though I haven't yet found Devlin's body, an easy extrapolation puts the combat mage at Disa's side when she died.

"When was this? And where?" I ask Coda.

The tech doesn't answer, tapping a key to slow the vid to half-speed as two dark-suited Authority agents slide into the booth across from Devlin. My aunt's chosen greets them with a stiff nod and a sip of his coffee. Though Coda is extremely talented, the vid isn't sharp enough for me to read the expression on the combat mage's face, but his body language seems tense.

"What the fuck?" Rought snarls. "That's Reck's current crew."

The Authority agents, he means. The red-haired, ruddy-skinned shifter, Brett Shaw, and the tall, slim, dead-gazed mage, Clara Wilson.

My heart twists in my chest. An odd reaction, so I try to ignore it.

Coda pulls up another feed from a camera I had no idea existed. Maybe it's new. It's a live feed that displays the mouth of the estate driveway. My driveway. It's angled toward the two Authority agents sitting in their armored SUV.

Shaw, the shifter, has half-healed red slashes across his lower face and neck, running below the collar of his white dress shirt. Wilson, the mage, appears unharmed from the shoulders up. As far as I can tell. She's rolling, or maybe dipping, her dark-wood wand in an ornate silver-plated box situated on the dashboard. I can't see the interior of the box, but even through the vid, I can see a glimmer of essence threaded around it. Most mages who work with wands or other essence-enhanced objects refuel them with salt-and-herb-based spells.

That said, with the easily-discernible-even-on-vid deadened look in Wilson's eyes, I wouldn't be surprised if her fuel of choice was more like … nightshade and arsenic.

"Fuck," Rought snarls. "Gigi said something about the Authority when she pulled up, but I got distracted."

Coda snorts knowingly, presumably because they share the same distraction addiction — anything tech related.

Grimacing, Rought pulls out his phone, seriously pissed and already texting. "Were they here all night?"

"No," I murmur. "Early this morning, I think." Though I'm able to sense the Authority agents on the edge of the property, for me in the now, the Authority as a whole is just another pending confrontation that I'm not interested in triggering yet. So I'm ignoring them.

Rought huffs and turns away, still texting.

"Coda. I need to know when they met. And where." I haven't shifted my attention from the vid of Devlin and the agents in the diner, but I'm still not quite certain what I'm witnessing. An arranged meeting between my aunt's chosen and agents of the Authority? Or just an opportunity to harass Devlin while he was off the estate, where the Authority has no jurisdiction?

Usually piecing together the *why* of it all isn't my purview.

Or, let's be honest, even a specific talent of mine.

I fix things.

But I can't fix the past. So I generally avoid it.

What I now know of my own past has settled in a low-grade ache around my heart. All the reasons I am the way I am are inextricably linked to it, including my need to constantly survive in the present.

Without looking away from his phone, Rought settles his hand on my lower back again. And that tiny glimmer of understanding, of my own psyche, settles within me. It's difficult to be concerned about a past, about *the* past, when you don't realize you're missing a massive chunk of it. Maybe ignoring that disconnect as thoroughly as I did was self-preservation.

But now ... now I need to *know*.

"Coda?" I prompt. The tech awry isn't ignoring me, just buried deeply in their essence-wielding. "Was this right before my aunt went missing?"

Coda grunts in the affirmative. "Tracking back from when you ... you know ... about seven days before that. In a border town on the edge of California. No sense of Disa being in the area, but I never could track her. I've only got you now when you've got the phone on you."

Coda is using the day that the powers of the Conduit transferred to me to build a timeline as they piece together my aunt's movements. As I am now, Disa was always obscured from Coda's sight. But tracking Devlin should be easier. Well, somewhat easier.

"Reck's obviously involved," Rought says, his tone dark edged and not at all surprised.

"I don't have your brother connected to any of this," Coda says, slightly cautious, which in and of itself is unusual. The awry tech doesn't generally worry about ramifications stemming from the truths they uncover.

"Fucker." Rought's phone vibrates in his hand with

multiple text messages flashing on-screen. "It's always him. I'm taking care of it." He steps across the trailer, opening the door and stepping down and out into the rainy late morning.

Actually, it might well be early afternoon by now. My sense of time is seriously skewed.

"Well, that seems like it's going in a bad direction," Coda says quietly.

"Do you care?" I ask, suddenly weary.

The tech actually turns from their monitors to eye me. Then they smirk. "Might be a good show."

"Can you tell me if this is the only meeting between the Authority agents and Devlin?"

"Not yet."

"Can you make any other connections between them? Any payoffs or ... indication that he was one of their informants? Was he a former agent and they're just keeping tabs on him?"

"No, Zaya," Coda says quietly. "If he's betraying your aunt here, I don't have any evidence of it. Or any evidence that he's an undercover agent or anything else you might be thinking."

My stomach sours. Could the Authority have embedded someone into my aunt's life? But if so, wouldn't the essence-based connection between my aunt and her chosen mean they couldn't have kept such secrets from each other? Wouldn't the universe have stepped in if Devlin wished Disa ill intent?

But the universe hadn't saved her from whatever death had been her final death either.

Coda is watching me, not the monitors. Actually facing away from the information still flashing across those screens. It's somewhat disconcerting. Coda would normally prefer to never look away, to be even minutely disconnected from their current traces and information gathering. It's like breathing for the tech. Essential.

"Devlin could be meeting with the agents by Disa's request," Coda says. A note of caution still threads through the tech's supposition.

"I don't see why," I say, feeling just a little helpless. Adrift. Again. This is why I don't like mucking around in the *why*. Plus, I can feel Rought pacing around outside the trailer, as if his concern is seeping through to me from the intersection point. Even without me purposefully reaching for it. "The Conduit doesn't answer to the Authority."

"A collaboration, maybe?"

I shake my head. "Again, why? Disa is the most powerful being in the world. Why would she need them?"

"You could go ask them," Coda says. "Since they're sitting on you right now."

Silence settles between us. Coda watches me for a moment. Then, seemingly satisfied that I'm not going to implode, or maybe even explode all over their precious tech, they turn back to their keyboards.

The light tapping of Coda's fingers — working on tracking the dire mage, I assume — fills the strange void swamping my mind. It's oddly comforting to be tucked away with Coda, and knowing that even if I'm taking this moment to process things, the investigation is still ongoing.

I feel the moment Rought shifts outside as he heads down the driveway. Presumably to confront the agents.

Perhaps I should be the one to interrogate them.

Perhaps I don't always have to do everything on my own.

Coda still has the live vid of the agents parked in the

SUV displayed on the upper right monitor. I could watch for Rought, see how he handles the situation.

"You should eat something, Coda," I say, turning away from the monitors. "Have a shower, a nap, maybe."

"In a few minutes. I just want to get this all set up and running. It'll drop a pin on any hint of the dire mage's movements to and from the salon and notify me. I'll have the rest of the feeds from Newport integrated within the hour. And I've got the border crossings all covered as well."

Nodding, still comfortably empty-headed, but with an almost aching awareness of Rought's movements, I decide to head to the house for some more food. Or a nap. Though maybe a thick vanilla milkshake —

"You ..." Coda says quietly, not looking at me. "You're the most powerful awry in the world. It's not Disa, not now."

"Yes," I say, speaking by rote but not belief.

I've been taught my entire life that the Conduit is the most powerful being in the world. That even living as a lesser Gage is the ultimate privilege, as well as a terrible burden. And not that Disa ever appreciated even the mere mention of my father, I've technically got the power of the slumbering gods running through both my primary bloodlines.

Unless my ancestors are seriously full of shit.

But I don't feel powerful at all.

I feel the power of the intersection point. I understand that the power of the universe flows through me — as it flowed through my Aunt Disa. But every other powerful awry I know controls the essence they wield. Even my aunt seemed so focused and formidable.

Maybe it's just the transition period and a lingering sense of all the conversations I never had with my aunt. I should have had decades, even a century, to have those conversations. Maybe I actually needed those decades to be mentally and physically ready to hold this much power.

Maybe it's everything I've unknowingly lost.

But I don't feel like the Conduit. I'm certainly not focused or formidable.

Coda doesn't speak again, and I have nothing constructive to say. So I jump down and out of the trailer and close the door behind me.

Taking five deliberate steps, I stand within the overgrown orchard. Bare branches twine all around and above me. The plums and peaches must be on the verge of budding, but it will be a few more weeks for the apples and pears. I think.

I lift my face to the rain, closing my eyes to the cloud-shrouded sky, and I just try to breathe. Only for a moment.

I don't have any choice but to be the Conduit now.

I could hide away, ride out this transition period. I could wait for the universe to nudge me into play. I could redirect Coda's investigations into my aunt's death and drop the pursuit of the dire mage until the universe makes it my business again.

I could ignore all the truths cracking open before me, ignore what has been stolen from me.

The phantom scars of Chains's life force — the life I ripped from him — feel permanently etched into the skin of my forearms. A punishment from the universe for stealing Precious away from her immediate future? Just like dying on the beach while trying to rescue the young awry was a punishment.

Just like having my soul-bound mates torn away from me was a punishment?

For what?

What could I possibly have done at age seventeen to deserve losing those connections? Then being banished from my own life, set adrift when I didn't even know it?

I take a shuddering breath, then another.

When I open my eyes, I know I'm not walking away from any part of my past or present.

I don't give a fuck that the Conduit exists only in the present, only moves at the universe's prompting.

I want answers.

I want what has been stolen from me.

THREE

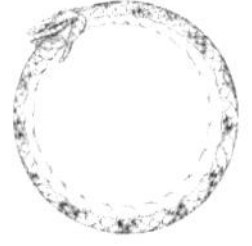

Precious is tightly curled up on the far side of my bed under a mound of blankets and duvets, just the top of her head visible, multicolored hair fanned out across the white pillow. DeVille, once again shirtless and with his left leg still splinted, is sprawled face down on top of the covers. A lack of clothing whenever possible, but especially while sleeping, is a shifter thing. They often run hot, and the healing DeVille's system is dealing with is also likely burning off a ton of energy.

Hovering in the doorway for fear of waking either of them, I catch the quiet rattle that underlies DeVille's sleep-heavy breath. He's ... purring? Instinctually trying to soothe Presh in her sleep in a way she'd never let him soothe her while awake?

I'm not surprised to see them both down again. Not only does grief come with an almost suffocating exhaustion, but Presh manifested streams of pure, unfettered power last night. Nearly enough to kill her. To possibly wipe the entire town of Newport from the face of the earth. I'm surprised she woke up long enough for hugs and a late breakfast.

"""

The two of them choosing my bed for a nap is interesting. Though at best guess, DeVille followed Precious in here after she fell asleep.

I don't step into the room. Simply lingering in the doorway to watch them both sleep — safe and somewhat sound — is its own kind of balm for my soul.

Just to assure myself that they'll both be okay — despite the fact that I completely failed Kris — I allow myself to look deeper than I normally like to delve.

Threads of essence flare all around Presh and DeVille, vibrant and strong.

Snipping Chains's threads, altering his fate, might have been the only choice in that moment — for me and the universe. Because losing Precious, and DeVille for that matter, clearly wasn't an option. Their threads are entangled, multicolored and multilayered. Both have a destiny. Or multiple destinies. And those possibilities will sharpen their focus — their draw — as Presh and DeVille each make choices and as they come into their full power.

From the intricate tapestry of fate I can now see blanketing my room, concentrated over my bed, a thin iridescent thread stretches toward me from Presh. A less vibrant connection ties DeVille to me as well.

I'm careful to not touch or interact with the energy that binds us. But I know these two are mine to protect. And not simply in the general way that all the souls inhabiting the earth are threaded through mine as the Conduit.

Presh and DeVille are mine. Me, Zaya. Not just me the Conduit.

But I knew that already, didn't I?

From that moment in the bathroom of the Choices Cafe with Precious. That soul-deep connection we seemed to form in the moment might have always been part of our combined destiny. Even though I also understand I wasn't supposed to rescue Precious just then. I wasn't supposed to die on the beach.

Nothing lasts forever, of course.

If I hadn't already known that as absolute truth, the missing, stolen, or severed soul bonds between Rought, Rath, Reck, and me make that fundamentally clear.

But Precious and DeVille are mine to protect for now. To mentor. Or to nurture? Am I capable of nurturing?

Such relationships are common among the awry. Purple-eyed essence-wielders protect other purple-eyed wielders — though my aunt only mentored me.

Prior to becoming the Conduit, I floated around the world, tugged this and that way by the universe and fixing things. Then walking away. I didn't even keep close tabs on those few who claim blood relations with me. No holiday cards or birthday celebrations unless I simply happened to be in town at the time. There were inheritances and bequests, but no one other than my aunt to turn to —

I never asked the Conduit for help. That wasn't my place.

She belonged to the universe.

Didn't she?

My head churning with too many unanswered questions, too many things I never slowed down enough to question before, I slip away, heading down the hall toward my aunt's bedroom.

But once there, I don't step past the doorway. Despite the massive plush bed and the easily lit fireplace, the room feels empty, unwelcoming, even for a simple nap.

People are still coming and going from the house, including Rought and Grinder seemingly swapping or coordinating vehicles, and Rath still prowling around.

Doing what, I have no idea. Gigi's in the kitchen, still interrogating anyone who crosses her path, and so subtly that they've no idea she's compiling profiles on each of them. Unless I want to get pulled into any of that — and I don't — a freshly churned milkshake isn't an option either.

I find myself drawn to the last door at the end of the hall instead. It's partially open, and I can't remember if I left it that way.

Just beyond that door, a dark-wood staircase spirals up into the tower where my aunt kept her office. Built-in dark-wood shelves line the walls, all strewn with books, some neatly stacked and some haphazardly piled as if abandoned in the middle of shelving.

In tidy stacks of three or four, Mack's black-metal-framed photographs are set around the base of the stairs, propped up against the lowest shelves with just enough space remaining to step through and ascend the staircase. Rath must have transferred the photos to the tower instead of my room, despite the fact that there isn't any space to hang them on the book-filled walls.

Though I knew of the tower, and that my aunt spent most of her time in her office at the top of it, this door was always obscured from my sight when I was younger. It only appeared when I was summoned by my aunt. In the first year or so that I lived on the estate, maybe longer, I occasionally perched in the large oak tree deeply rooted on this side of the house, gazing up at the tower windows, hoping for a glimpse of Disa.

I don't know if that's my own memory or just an implanted echo of the picture of me and Muta in the oak tree that Mack captured. Captured and turned into a memory? Or has the memory resurfaced because of the photograph?

I can feel the bark of the tree under the palms of my hands, and the way I needed to twist my leg around the thicker branches to anchor myself in its boughs ...

I wait, hovering at the base of the stairs with the photographs at my feet. I wait for more memories triggered by those images to surface. Memories of the friendship and love captured in black and white and ...

None do.

I shake free of the moment, crouching down next to the nearest stack of framed photographs, then glancing back at the still-open door.

If the door to the tower is still obscured by whatever weaving tied it to the Conduit, Rath can apparently see and walk through those protections. Though perhaps that casting has eroded with Disa's death.

At the front of the nearest stack is the last photo of all four of us together, on the beach by the fire with our fresh tattoos, in our late teens and early twenties. My tattoo was erased, along with the mating bite on my left hand, with my first death. And I'm just guessing that Reck is older than me by a few years.

Not really thinking about the why yet, I pick up and hold the surprisingly weighty photograph to my chest. Then I slowly climb the spiral stairs to the office at the top of the tower.

Though the cloudy sky valiantly attempts to filter through the upper windows, without the overhead lights on, the room is dimly lit. And desperately still. Quiet.

I grip the photo a bit tighter as my focus is once again instantly drawn from the top of the stairs to the massive curve-fronted, maple armoire set between the windows on the far right of the high-ceilinged circular room that tops the tower. Mahogany and rosewood glyphs line the armoire's double doors, concentrated around the two wooden handles. The metal of the picture frame digs into the flesh of my fingers, rubbing against my ribcage.

No keyhole has miraculously appeared on the sealed armoire since I was first drawn to it three days ago. Not that I've found any mysterious keys yet. The only clue to that nagging mystery is the note from my aunt I found with the ice-cream maker.

The armoire will open when you're ready.

Ready for what?

And how is whatever spell sealing the armoire meant to judge that readiness?

With the photo cradled in one arm, I press my hand against the smooth wood of the armoire — right where I'm certain an upper shelf stands within. A shelf that holds something that belongs to me. And as before, a strange, disconnected terror slides through me. My heart is suddenly hammering against my rib cage.

What could possibly be stored in the fucking armoire for it to be setting off my senses like this? The last time, this sense, this feeling, triggered a massive panic attack that left me gasping for breath on the floor.

Shaking as if merely remembering it is enough to relive it, I force myself to drop my hand, then to step back, to step away.

At some point, I'm going to have to face whatever is in the armoire. Whether it opens for me as my aunt indicated it would in her last note, or if I have to cut it open with a fucking essence-fueled chainsaw. Or maybe I'll just ask the gryphon to tear through the sealing spell stopping me from collecting what I know is mine.

If I have to destroy the exterior of the cabinet to retrieve what I know instinctively belongs to me, I will.

Just not right now.

Not with everything else I'm still struggling to process.

Actually, I'm not entirely certain the gryphon would fit in the office. And as silly as that thought is, it brings a smile to my face. The edge of panic triggered by the armoire and the memory of my earlier meltdown recedes.

I gently set the photograph on the dark-wood windowsill, facing it into the room. Then I circle to sit behind the desk centered within the space, flicking on the desk lamp as I do. My aunt's current notebook is still open on the forest-green blotter. Her favorite platinum fountain pen rests next to it.

The photograph of Disa surrounded by three huge shifters, which I found interred with unknown ashes and a blood-crusted dagger in the family mausoleum, rests on top of the journal.

I remember claiming the photograph and placing the dagger in its box back in the niche alongside the urn that was there. But I don't remember putting the photo on Disa's desk.

I settle into the wooden chair, rolling forward to peer down at the photo. I don't think it's one of Mack's. It's not shot in black and white, and it predates the other photos by almost two decades. That reminds me that I'm not even certain when Mack came to be my aunt's chosen. Was he the estate groundskeeper first? A shifter originally aligned with the Outcast MC?

Oh, fuck. I still haven't arranged transport for Mack's and Ingrid's bodies to a crematorium. Was that something the Outcast mage Harlee Larson was doing for me? Or Rath?

Should I ... start a to-do list? Or buy a planner?

How does the most powerful essence-wielder in the world stay organized? Yet another question I never asked my aunt. My aunt, who never seemed to have a schedule or even a phone. Why would I ask about those sorts of completely inane things? I had decades to figure out everything ...

No. I should have had more time. I didn't.

Seriously, my focus is all over the place. My mind is as disjointed as the power I'm still in the process of accepting, absorbing. And maybe for the same reason. Maybe I shouldn't even be trying to function yet.

Still, I'm starting to annoy myself.

I pick up the photo. It's faded, aged. But as before, I can't sense if it holds any special protections or preservation spells. It must, though, or the box it was tucked within must have had some sort of protections on it, because it's been interred for ...

I flip the photo over and make note of the date and names on the back. Again.

Oso, Ward, Disa, and Ari. Summer 1989.

Somewhere around thirty-four years.

Even without knowing exactly when Mack became my aunt's chosen, or why he was digging around the family plot when he died, I don't think I'm incorrect about this not being one of his photographs.

I suspect it was the blade, not the photo, that Mack was after. A blade with dried blood still somehow etched across its edge. A blade that seethed with dire-wrought malignancy, buried next to an urn with this photo. All three items are clearly connected.

I could give the photo to Coda, along with the names printed across the back. But despite my resolve to get the answers I need to move forward, it feels almost sacrilegious to dig into something that is really none of my business — something that firmly belongs to my aunt's past, not mine. Especially when my own present comes with more immediate problems.

I tuck the photo into my aunt's half-filled journal. I've already scanned the most recent entries in it for clues as to my aunt's disappearances and death, finding none. I'm not certain why I feel an instinctual need to hide the photo, or who I'm even hiding it from. Myself, I suspect.

Instead, I settle my gaze on the framed photograph I've brought upstairs with me, already knowing that I could stare at it for hours and still not absorb every detail. I'm actually slightly wary of how obsessed I might get about it.

The date — 2011 — printed alongside the caption 'Zaya and her boys' gives me a starting point to construct a timeline around the memories, people, and connections I'm missing.

I need, I ache, to gather as many answers as possible. For at least one of the mysteries threatening to overwhelm my present, my now. That painful desire threads through all the empty parts in me — the missing gaps in my soul?

And filling those gaps isn't something Coda can do for me. Even Rought's memories of that time might not be enough.

But that year, paired with Disa's journals that likely only I can access? That's something tangible.

I haven't read the centuries of journals collected on these shelves. Journals written by all the Conduits who came before me. It was never the right time for such things, according to Disa. Then I was banished, no matter that I didn't know it. Some of these journals even predate the Gage bloodline settling in North America as the self-appointed guardians of the intersection point.

My family history leans heavily on the core idea that it was the destiny for our bloodline to be the caretakers of the intersection point — rather than the literal colonization that claiming this site actually was. What with the Conduit being a goddess and all, as my aunts and uncles would have the world believe.

Now that I'm holding the power of the Conduit and the intersection point, I'm slowly becoming concerned — aware? — that the family history isn't as revisionary, or as self-aggrandizing, as I previously thought.

Speaking of gods, Muta stirs on my wrist. Transforming into his bushmaster aspect, he slides across the desk to curl around Disa's journal. It's not the sweet gesture it appears to be on the surface. Disa and Muta were not friendly. I'm almost certain that if my aunt could have countermanded whatever bond my mother invoked moments before her death — binding Muta to nine-year-old me — she would have.

Disa bought into the whole Gage god/goddess mythology, and she didn't think the future Conduit should be walking around with an inherently nefarious, exceedingly diminished death god on her wrist.

Muta's spiny tail whips across the desk, sending Disa's fountain pen spinning to the floor.

"Someone could turn their ankle on that," I say mildly.

He silently flicks his tongue at me, then curls into a tight coil. Deliberately turning away from me, facing the framed photograph.

"You could be down by the fire. No one is going to hurt me on the property."

The sulky death god ignores me. Always knowing better. Or rather, always just doing his own thing.

I quickly check the dates on the dozens of matching notebooks filled with Disa's handwriting on the nearest set of shelves. But after noting that the journals from halfway through 2003 into 2012 are missing and must be shelved elsewhere, I start exploring the desk.

The cabinets at the front of the desk yield a multitude of objects, most essence imbued and all randomly stuffed away, as if tucked somewhere for safekeeping but then forgotten. I pull out spellbooks and grimoires that need to be shelved, guessing that Disa hadn't gotten around to figuring out where they should go, stacking them on a corner of the desk. Muta hisses when I block his view of the window, abandoning Disa's journal to coil around the new stack of books — most of which quietly hum with varying levels of essence. Likely not as good as lounging by the fireplace from the bushmaster's perspective, but still good enough for a nap.

After half-heartedly sifting through its contents, I leave a wooden box filled with the greeting cards my aunt collected but never used where I found it. Though I have to tamp down a sharp spike of grief upon discovering the collection, and to quash a completely uncharacteristic urge to paw through the massive pile, looking for the cards I know she bought on our trips together.

I don't dwell in the past like that. I don't look through photos and reminisce. I don't actually have all that many photos at all.

I don't have as many memories as I thought I did.

I also ignore the plethora of financial documents filed in the bottom cabinet, though I'll need to double-check that I have digital copies of them all. Especially because I know there are alliances to renegotiate now that I'm the Conduit, specifically with the Outcast Motorcycle Club, whose territory borders the estate.

I set two of the essence-imbued objects on the desk, mindful of not blocking Muta's view. Both are used to identify and hone essence-weaving affinities. The first is set with various crystals and semiprecious stones, and the second with narrow bars of rare metals. I'll have Presh work with both as soon as she's ready for more focused training.

The three slim drawers on the other side of the desk were locked to me the first time I tried them, but they yield to my touch today. Perhaps my connection to the intersection point, and therefore the protections threaded through the house, is strengthening.

The narrow top drawer is filled with writing implements, loose-leaf paper, and bottled inks. An empty space to the side is presumably where Disa tucked away her current journal. A pile of seemingly random antique keys fill the central drawer. I note their location for when I have occasion to need one, notwithstanding that none of these will unlock the armoire taunting me from across the tower office unless a keyhole appears in its doors.

The bottom drawer is literally filled with gold, along with some platinum. Mostly coins of various vintages and currencies, but mixed with numerous bars and a few heavy chain necklaces. Though the Conduit rarely trades in worldly currency, sometimes paper money or credit cards aren't what a situation calls for.

The desk doesn't yield the missing notebooks. So I head back to the shelves. Though the journals of previous Conduits are usually grouped together, most of the other shelving is organized by year rather than categorized by subject or title. This was super annoying for young me.

Whenever I was allowed entry to the office, or had to wait for my aunt's attention even after being summoned, I generally just plucked random things off the shelves to read.

Not that I was much of a reader. Nor have I ever kept a journal. Though I think Disa might have encouraged me to do so … at some point …

That idea, those random thoughts stretch around me as if I've somehow manifested them as pure essence, shoving every other thought away. I press my hand against the nearest shelf to ground myself in the *now*.

Still, my chest tightens with anxiety.

I try to breathe through it.

Muta bristles his tail spines, presumably more pissed that I'm partially blocking his view than concerned with trying to pull me from the numbness once again spreading through my system.

Because I don't actually know, do I?

I don't know if I was much of a reader.

I don't know why I was never interested in keeping a journal.

I have an understanding of the portions of my childhood spent on the estate, and sense memories of the house and grounds, but it's nebulous.

Just like the trinkets — the treasures, perhaps — that were sitting on my bedroom windowsill. The jar of notes, the handmade wooden box holding the broken bracelet and spent protection stone. I have no idea where I got them, why I kept them, or really, who —

"How the fuck is this library organized?" a voice grumbles quietly behind me, the speaker talking to himself, not me. "It's fucking ridiculous. *Shifter Mythology* beside *A Book of Charms, Vol. 21*. Where are the other volumes? And that's next to *An Abridged History of the Awry in the Sixteenth Century*. Which is next to ... Zaya ...?"

I blink.

My back is pressed against the bookshelf next to the window, hands clenching the shelf on either side of my hips. I'm frozen there. Stuck. Trapped ...

Rath fills the space at the top of the stairs. He's made it almost all the way up without me sensing him. A frown etches across his face, aimed directly at me. But he's not angry. He's ... concerned?

"Zaya!" he says sharply, dropping the half-dozen books he's carrying onto the desk and crossing to me. "Zaya?" He's so big that he blocks out the rest of the office, including the armoire that keeps triggering these panic attacks.

He's so big that all I can see is him.

He touches my cheek, just the lightest brush of his fingers. Essence ... energy shifts between us. And now all I can sense is him.

My heart kicks against my ribs, as if it had ceased beating and suddenly started again.

I draw air into my lungs ... so much air that they might have been completely depleted. Had I stopped breathing? Was this another of those moments, though inside my head this time, where I somehow moved into that pocket of suffocating, inexplicable numbness? As when I'd first seen the objects on the windowsill of my bedroom, or when crossing up the path toward Rath on the front patio of the beach house.

"I was looking for Disa's journals," I say, my voice surprisingly steady though everything else still feels numb.

"Right," Rath says quietly. His hand falls to his side.

Then, before I even realize he's doing it, he somehow

herds me back into the desk chair without actually touching me. As if he can move me on an essence level, but in a completely noninvasive way.

I sit down, and he crouches before me. Even with him crouched, he's so huge, we're practically eye-to-eye.

"I didn't know this library existed," he says, his gaze running over me as if searching for a mortal wound.

"Disa's office," I say. "This is where she spent most of her time." I frown. "Didn't she?"

Rath chuckles quietly, though it sounds a bit forced. "I avoided Aunt Disa, so I'm not the one to ask."

"Did I ... did I like reading?" I'm still feeling shaky inside and not at all certain why it matters to me, matters enough to ask Rath.

He swallows, dropping my gaze and running a hand over his head. "I ... I always liked reading."

I frown. That wasn't an answer. "You don't know?"

He huffs. "You read. We read. Together. Yes."

"Do you still have the tattoo?" Okay, that was random. And way too intimate a question. And not specific at all, because Rath clearly has a lot of tattoos, though I've only seen hints of them on his wrists and collarbone.

But he knows exactly what I'm asking. Tension runs through his jaw. "Yes."

"You kept it."

"Why would I get rid of it? I thought you were dead. Not that you'd just ..."

"Just what? Forgot you?"

He doesn't answer.

That silence stretches between us, thick and tension-filled.

"You knew me," I say, anger slowly igniting through the residual nothingness that had me pinned in place by the window. And anger is so much better than that fucking numb shit. Anger gets things done. The numbness is fucking useless. So I embrace the anger. Eagerly.

"You knew me."

"Yes," he says, not looking at me.

I stand up, abruptly enough that the chair goes spinning away on its wheels behind me, smashing into the bookshelves. Rath flinches, dropping a hand to the ground to steady himself.

"You knew me!" I shout down at him.

"Yes," he says, steady and sure but still not meeting my eyes.

"You knew me ..." I sob. But only once. I'm still so angry I can't seem to move past this point, this moment.

He slowly stands, hands clenched into fists at his sides. "I knew you."

"When I heard your voice ... on the phone ... with Precious in the car ..." I shake my head in disbelief. "You felt ... you felt ..."

"I felt what?" His tone is soft, verging on gentle.

Utterly irrationally, that pisses me off. "Fuck you, Rath," I snarl, slamming my open palm to his chest, right over where I suspect he has an anatomical heart inked into his skin. An identical anatomical heart that we four all had tattooed, and which I lost ...

I lost the fucking heart when I died.

Rath takes a step back from me, from my vitriol.

"Fuck you, Rath. Fuck you for hearing me on that fucking phone. For seeing me in the motel, for coming here to my house, and fucking pretending you didn't know me."

"You didn't know me, Zaya!" Rath shouts, jabbing a finger toward the window. "You were fucking dead. I watched you get your fucking neck snapped! I heard it ... I heard it … and felt it slash through my fucking chest as if it … sundered my fucking soul."

Slightly thrown by that revelation — the specifics of how I died, even with no mention of who was responsible — my hand flies to my throat.

"I barely fucking survived without you!" Rath's chest heaves, visibly pained. "And you didn't fucking know me. You didn't know me, Zaya."

I try to hold onto my anger, to shore myself up against the pain, the agony evident in his recollection. None of that is an actual legitimate reason for his behavior the past few days. "So you thought playing games with me —"

"It wasn't a game." Rath tries to calm his tone. "It was never a game —"

"There are no threads between us," I say, quiet but resolute. "How was I supposed to know I didn't remember you?"

"I … I don't know … I don't understand what you mean by —"

"You have your memories," I insist. "You knew me."

He takes a shaky breath. "Yes. I knew you. I know … I know you liked to read … mysteries mostly … we'd meet in the treehouse, and you'd … we'd …" He scrubs another hand over his head. "What does it matter now, Zaya?"

"It doesn't," I say hollowly. "It didn't matter. It obviously never mattered."

"What the fuck are you saying?"

I look him in the eyes then, having to seriously tilt my head to do so. This uber powerful, dreadfully sexy male who was supposed to be mine. Maybe was mine. For a little while. "I … I'm saying that if you were truly meant to be … if you knew you were mine, that I was yours … that we were soul bound …"

"Then what?" he growls, amber edging his hazel eyes now.

"Just that. It obviously never mattered to you, or you never would have pretended you didn't know me."

He rears back. "You don't fucking know me —"

"Exactly."

He stands there, just staring at me with thoughts obviously whirling through his mind. And the longer we look at each other, the more the numbness starts creeping around all my edges again.

Forcing myself to look elsewhere, I cast my gaze over the books on the desk, on Muta watching us intently with his body tightly curled and head raised alertly. I settle my attention on the photograph I've set on the windowsill.

"The pictures are a lie," I whisper into that numbness coating my chest, my heart. "Just random moments captured in black and white —"

"The pictures are not a fucking lie!" Rath takes a ragged breath. "Zaya, please. This is just ... bad communication and minor mistakes. You are fucking exhausted. I can fucking feel how drained you are. It's just too much right now. Too much all at once. But we can move through this —"

The door bangs open at the base of the stairs. "Oh, nasty," Coda grumbles. Loudly. "So much fucking paper. Ugh, it smells fucking terrible in here ... like books. And old leather."

Footsteps clomp up the stairs.

Rath's shoulders sag.

"It's bad," I whisper, speaking more to myself than Rath. "If Coda is willing to leave their tech lair behind and report in person."

"So many fucking stairs," Coda grumbles from below.

"Do you know how much money you have, Zaya? Try putting in a fucking elevator. Or better yet, keep your fucking phone on you."

I turn to face the landing. Rath steps back to retrieve the chair — the only actual evidence of our fight — tucking it in place behind the desk. I'm pretty certain I dented the shelf with it. I'll have to figure out how to fix that later.

Coda makes it to the top of the stairs, glaring daggers at me, leaning on the top of the newel post, and clearly trying not to pant. "I've been texting," the awry tech snaps, a large laptop in their hands.

"I'm sorry," I say, because apologizing is the quickest way to move forward with whatever info Coda has deemed explosive enough that they needed to come to me in person. "I actually don't know where my phone is."

Coda pushes off the railing, practically stumbling around the desk after eyeing Rath and skirting in a direction where they avoid interacting with the massive shifter. The tech falls into the desk chair, placing the laptop down on the desk and opening it. The screen is black.

"Don't bite me, asshole," Coda says, eyeing Muta over the top of the screen.

Muta disappears.

"What the fuck!" Coda shouts, freezing with their fingers hovering over the keyboard.

Preceded by the weight of his robust essence, the bushmaster reappears, draped over my shoulders.

Coda shakes their head. "New tricks for the death god? That isn't fucking terrifying at all."

"He's always been able to teleport," Rath rumbles, sounding just a little too glib for my liking. "To protect Zaya."

I narrow my eyes at the shifter. "Coda is not a threat."

Blatantly ignoring me, Rath crosses his arms, then says imperiously, "Show us what you deem so important, awry."

Coda snorts. "Okay, Daddy Dragon."

Despite the sarcasm, Coda's fingers fly over the keyboard of the laptop. The screen remains black, but presumably the password or protections they're activating are similar to the ones installed on the phone I'm terrible at carrying around with me.

"I'm going to imbed a chip in your ass, Zaya," Coda says, as if reading my mind.

"Doesn't work," Rath says matter-of-factly. "Her essence fries it."

I throw him another narrow-eyed look. Muta shifts, trying to get comfortable on my shoulders.

Coda chuckles darkly. "Not my tech."

Rath takes a step closer, so he's within Coda's peripheral sight. "Remember, awry. Zaya is the fucking Conduit now."

"The name is Coda," the tech says sourly. They don't otherwise argue Rath's point.

Various programs open on Coda's laptop screen, arrayed in small boxes. Coda clicks on one of the boxes, enlarging and pulling it forward. It appears to be a new still shot of the person we spotted with Kris at the salon.

Bellamy.

"Is that the dire mage?" Rath asks.

"I think so," I say. "Hard to confirm without being near her."

"You don't need to be near her," he says with a note of warning.

I ignore him, settling my hand down on the corner of the desk and peering at the still frame on the screen.

Bellamy's eyes are hidden behind sunglasses. Her skin is

paler than before. But in a photo, I have no idea if that's a side effect of the corrupted power she wields or just her natural complexion. Her lips are outlined in blood red, then glossed over in a pale pink.

She's looking directly toward whatever camera or vid feed Coda caught her on.

"Where is this?" Rath asks, his phone in his hand and already texting.

"Newport," Coda says. "I've texted Zaya the coordinates."

"Send them to me as well," Rath says.

"What's the magic word, Daddy Dragon?"

"When?" I ask, interrupting the argument sparking between Coda and Rath. The tech does not, and will not, answer to a shifter. Not even an Outcast lieutenant. Also, I'm a little creeped out by the 'Daddy' moniker. Rath is only a couple of years older than Coda, if that.

"Ten minutes ago."

I straighten. "Where's my phone?"

"Wait!" Coda says. "That's not the important part."

"What could be more important?" Rath snaps.

Coda toggles a key on the laptop. And the image of Bellamy shifts, rewinding a few seconds. So not a screenshot, but a paused vid. "The dire mage was occluding all the other vid I found between the salon yesterday afternoon and this ten minutes ago."

"What? How?" Rath asks.

Coda flicks their long fingers toward the screen, as if all three of us aren't already riveted to the footage playing out on it. "Until this ..."

On the laptop, Bellamy looks directly at the camera, then raises her hand into frame with her red-polish-tipped forefinger and middle finger extended in a V. Or like scissors. Because she then pantomimes snipping something, straight at the camera.

The vid glitches, then the camera feed disconnects or goes dead.

"What the fuck?" Rath murmurs. "Did you lose the connection?"

"No," Coda says, sour to even be asked that.

"She showed herself deliberately," I say, slightly shocked that a dire mage can snip the energy flow of tech in that fashion, like Coda can manipulate such things.

Coda rewinds the vid and plays it through again. "Yep."

"Proving she can walk where she wants," I say, "go where she wants. All without us being able to track her."

Coda minimizes the vid, which is running on a loop, then pulls forward the footage from the salon that the tech found earlier of Kris and the so-called seer. "Same person. Skin color is off, different makeup. Or a glamour, maybe. But the angle of the camera clearly isn't optimized, so I can't get a hundred-percent match."

"Knocked out of alignment," I murmur. I already noted that. "And the paler skin color ... might have something to do with how much power she burned to manipulate and kill Kris remotely."

"She doesn't want us to see her full face," Coda says, nodding in agreement. "Same with wearing the sunglasses in the more recent footage. Plus the vid was partially occluded until you cleared it up for us, Zaya."

"She showed herself deliberately in the salon as well," I say. "But ... like it's a game."

"She wants to get caught?" Rath asks incredulously.

"No," I say, knowing I'm correct even as the assertion falls from my lips. "She wants an in-person confrontation."

"She's luring you," Coda says.

"Zaya specifically?" Rath sounds a little disconcerted. "She can't know that anyone is tracking her, or that Zaya even ... exists."

"She saw me ..." I say quietly. "Through Kris. While possessing Kris. During the confrontation with Chains."

"Might not be Zaya specifically," Coda interjects. "She could know that Rought is a hacker, could assume that's who she's playing with." They add snottily, "Unfortunately for her, she's got me on her tail."

"You don't fuck around with a dire mage," Rath all but snarls, clearly feeling out of the loop. Perhaps Rought is still dealing with the Authority agents or tracking down their other brother, Reck, and hasn't reported back to Rath yet.

Coda shrugs, snapping the laptop closed and standing. "The dire mage can't reach me. It's your asses they're about to ream."

"Try," Rath says. "Try to ream."

"That mage buggered you hard and fast last night, shifter," Coda says nastily, heading down the stairs without waiting for another retort.

I'm on the tech's heels.

"Zaya," Rath growls behind me.

"Have you eaten, Coda?" I ask, ignoring the presumptuous, controlling shifter.

"All good," Coda says, which isn't actually an answer. "Keep your fucking phone on you, Zaya. Better yet, send the shifters after the dire mage and stay on the property with me."

"You know I'll be fine."

Coda spins around at the base of the stairs, the open door at their back. The movement is swift enough to give me pause. "One of these fucking days, it will be your last death, Zaya. I don't want to be the one desperately searching for evidence of it. Of what happened to you. Like you're doing with fucking Disa."

I open my mouth to speak, not quite certain what to say.

Shoulders hunched, head bowed, Coda turns their back on me, swiftly heading down the upper hall.

"So I'm not the only one," Rath says quietly behind me.

When I don't answer him either, he steps around me, brushing his big body against me because there isn't enough room on the stairs.

Inexplicably — for someone who pretended they didn't know me, denying our previous connection, playing some game — he brushes his lips across my temple as he passes, not otherwise touching me.

Essence gently shifts between us, warm and sweet.

It's hard to lie through pure essence like that.

To me, at least.

FOUR

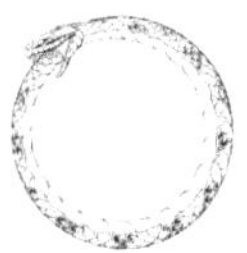

A most determined Presh and an equally grumpy DeVille are waiting for us at the top of the second-floor stairs, both glowering at Coda's back as the tech heads down to the main floor. DeVille is fully clothed, and his splint has been removed, but he's clearly still favoring his leg. Doc Z must have stopped in to check on the teens at some point during Rath's and my argument. Or I lost more time to that nothingness that keeps trying to —

Presh waves a phone in her hand, presumably indicating it's my device. I must have left it in my room at some point. Though as I think about it, I'm pretty sure it was charging downstairs earlier.

I definitely don't like this forgetful thing I've got going on. At what point do I become a liability to those around me?

I'm also not too pleased with the expression on the young awry's face. She's geared for an argument. I might have Coda to thank for that.

"I need some pants," I say, heading it all off. For a moment, at least. The sweater I'm wearing is fine, though the fair isle yoke and drop sleeves are a little restrictive. But the ankle-length gathered silk skirt I'm wearing is really not meant for early March.

I veer into my bedroom, Presh on my heels, then Rath after her. I narrow my eyes in warning at Rath over my shoulder, and he miraculously realizes he doesn't have my permission to enter my personal space. He steps back to hover in the open doorway instead.

DeVille leans against the hall across from the door, eyes shut, head back, as if he's going to attempt to nap upright.

My bed has been made, which is sweet of Presh. She's abandoned her cocoon of blankets somewhere, swapping it out for black leggings and a black-printed T-shirt under a lilac hoodie. The print on the shirt is a faded Outcast MC logo. The hoodie matches one of the washed-out stripes in her pastel rainbow hair.

Already fairly certain that I don't have anything appropriate to wear that's clean — otherwise I wouldn't have been traipsing around in a silk skirt all morning — I stumble over my suitcase in the entrance of the shallow walk-in closet.

Presh peers over my shoulder. "Pinky dropped it off at the gate earlier. Doc Z brought it up when she checked in."

A note is taped to the suitcase. I pull it off to read it.

Thank you, Conduit.
For protecting my Grinder.
I'm in your debt.
— Patricia 'Pinky' Wood

Essence stirs around my hands, then settles into my skin.

Ah, fuck. That's ... not good.

Pinky, aka Patricia Wood, is the mage who oversees the Outcast MC's cleaning — both for their legitimate business and their bloodier dealings. She and Grinder are chosen mates. She and I haven't even met yet, but despite my death-induced hazy memory, I know exactly what the mage is accepting a debt for.

At the Crescent Moon Inn on the outskirts of Cannon Beach, the morning after dying while doing a terrible job of rescuing Presh from the Cataclysm bikers, I was nudged by the universe with a glimmer of a *knowing*. From that nudge, I had Grinder take off his cut and leave his motorcycle behind the motel — allowing us to avoid an altercation with a group of unaffiliated shifter bikers. That's the protection Pinky is referring to in her note. But it's the declaration of being in my *debt* that bothers me.

Given the deliberate use of both her full name and biker handle, it's obvious that Pinky knew what she was doing with this note. Grinder is aware of who my aunt was, and seems to be a believer in the whole goddess/worship/religious connection that occasionally comes with being the Conduit.

I don't like people owing me favors that I haven't earned. Or that I don't intend to collect. It's dangerous. For them. Because the universe can randomly decide to call in that chit whenever it pleases.

Admittedly, anthropomorphizing the universe might not be that rational on my part. But when your entire life is randomly fucked with by a power outside anyone's control — even my own — it can come off as incredibly mercurial.

Focusing on my concern over Pinky's now-sworn favor, rather than obsessing over the unfathomable *why* of the universe, I crouch to open the suitcase. It's neatly packed, including all new cosmetics and skin creams. Mage brewed, though not my usual brand. Such things aren't easy to obtain on short notice, but I have no doubt these are almost as good as my own.

The suitcase also holds clothing and belongings I never expected to see again. After shedding my mostly ruined clothes at the beach where Breaker had died — where I had died — I left everything else at the motel, neatly bundled with all the towels Presh and I had used to clean up. My suitcase thankfully held enough clean clothing for both of us. I have an indistinct memory of Grinder grabbing that bundle, expecting him to have it burned because that's the most efficient way to deal with residual blood or essence.

Instead, Pinky spent a lot of time and essence to scour all of it clean. Including my favorite boots, my unlabeled designer bag, and my knitting. Those last two, I left behind because I was fairly certain the Outcast MC had planted tracking bugs on them. Or that Rought had, specifically.

Since it's pretty clear that all of the Outcast now know where I live, that isn't much of a concern anymore. Plus, tracking me is next to impossible. Unless, of course, the universe wants me found.

"Thank you," I whisper into the aether. Then, deliberately holding the note between my fingers, I press my hands over the clothing in the open suitcase and murmur a second time, "Thank you, Pinky," in the hopes it will void the debt the mage foisted on me with her note.

No essence stirs under or around my hands. Or the note.

Apparently, saving Grinder from whatever would have befallen him had the unaffiliated shifters happened upon him at the motel isn't offset by clean clothing.

"Shit." I sigh.

"Those are your favorite boots," Presh says, watching me intently.

I chuckle, looking up at her. "Did I say that?"

"More than once."

I hum quietly, quickly unpacking all my favorite clothing from the suitcase, including my once-again-pristine vegan-leather, merino-lined black leggings, and a thin-knit cashmere sweater that hangs perfectly off one of my shoulders. I left both, along with my boots, behind at the beach after I killed Breaker. After I stupidly left Chains alive, because it wasn't his time to die then. No more so than it was last night.

I change quickly, though for some reason, I don't swap the unusually sexy camisole-and-panty set that I found in the drawer earlier this morning for my simple sports bra.

Okay, I know why I'm suddenly interested in pretty, lacy things. The timing is just a little inappropriate.

I tuck my necklace under the sweater and the camisole. The large pink diamond caged in its golden threads rests between my breasts, neither warm nor cold against my skin.

"Coda found Bellamy," Presh says in a rush, as if she's been holding it in and can't wait a moment longer, not even for me to finish tying my boots.

"Yes," I say, slinging the designer bag over my shoulder and double-checking that I have a backup pair of sunglasses. Running a brush through my hair would also be a good idea, but not wanting to delay any longer, I settle on a quick finger-combing-and-ear-tuck combo.

Presh slides my phone into a side pocket in my bag, as if I can't be trusted to do so myself.

She's not wrong.

"I'm coming with you," the young awry says firmly.

From outside the bedroom, Rath shouts, "Absolutely fucking not!"

Shifters have excellent hearing, not that Precious was being quiet about her demands. Annoying shifters also have bothersome opinions and seem intent on foisting their demands off on me.

Yes, I'm apparently still mad at Rath.

I grab a clearly hand-knit brioche rib scarf in a pretty gradient — a light gray through a few shades of purple to black — off a hanger near the door, then step out into the bedroom as I wrap it around my neck. Even looped twice and with a fringe, it's long enough to fall to midthigh. But delightfully lightweight.

I have no idea who would have knit such a beautiful piece of art for me to wear. But this time, I allow myself to simply be pleased by the idea that someone cared enough for me to do so, rather than disconcerted.

Presh follows so closely that she's practically pressed against me, speaking earnestly. She blatantly ignores her older brother hovering in the doorway. "She killed my best friend. I deserve to go."

Rath crosses his arms, completely blocking our exit into the hall. "You will not set one foot off this property —"

"Fine." I walk right up to Rath, forcing him to cede the way. He does. "Let's go."

"What the fuck?! No!" Rath snarls at my back as I step out into the hall. Presh glances over her shoulder, chewing her lip worriedly. "This isn't some fucking game, Zaya. Some way to get back at me for some ridiculous grudge or perceived slight."

Passing DeVille, whose wary gaze flicks between Presh and the dragon shifter at my heels, we continue down the corridor.

"Rath ..." Presh whispers, now caught between her brother and me.

"The last time I trusted you, Zaya," Rath says. "You nearly got Precious killed."

"Whoa!" Presh pivots, pressing her palms against Rath's chest. Well, his lower rib cage. The young awry is tiny next to her overprotective brother. Though he's not entirely wrong. "That's not —"

I whirl back at the top of the stairs, gripping the post of the walnut handrail. Because I suddenly feel like punching the massive asshole, and I'm slightly thrown by that extreme reaction.

"If you were doing your universe-decreed duty," I say, speaking without really thinking, "I never would have been put in the position of choosing between your unhinged brother nearly murdering dozens of souls, or trusting Presh and her destined mate for five minutes on a clearly defined path to fucking safety!"

Rath reels back, nearly knocking DeVille across the hall. The younger shifter catches his balance, favoring his still healing leg.

"Wait ... my mate?" Presh squeaks. "What?"

"Just go, Zaya," Rath snaps, hands fisted at his sides. "That's what you're good at. Doing whatever you fucking want no matter the fucking cost."

"You're such a blind fucking fool, Rath." I sneer his biker name because I don't know his real fucking name. I don't even know if he uses the surname he shares with his siblings — Guerra. And that pisses me off. All of this, with him, pisses me off. And I'd rather be pissed than numb and overwhelmed right now. "There aren't any choices for me. Whatever illusion I had of choosing anything was always just that — wishful thinking. All I have is duty and destiny."

Presh grabs hold of my arm, forcing my gaze to her. "What are you saying? Was Kris my mate?! Is my mate dead?"

I blink at her, unclear about what she's asking.

Then I recall my slip.

In the incendiary exchange with her brother, I've inadvertently revealed information that isn't mine to reveal. Nor is it something I even consciously discerned.

Rath chuckles darkly, presumably at me getting derailed.

"Get the fuck out of my house," I snarl at him over Presh's shoulder.

"Still such a child."

Something goes dark and dead inside me. All my energy contracts, then practically explodes through the hallway and down the stairs.

"Oh no. Oh no! Zaya ..." Presh whispers, her own concerns set aside as she clings to my arm.

Rath takes another step back from me, all the anger and frustration draining from him.

"I was still a child when you knew me," I whisper. "Privileged and protected. Until I wasn't. I haven't been since I died for the first time."

"Zaya ..." Rath whispers, raising his hands to me, placating me. And not for the first time.

"You have no right to be angry at me," I say dully, my essence tightening all around me as if trying to protect me, as if prepared to defend me. "You have no say in how I choose to fulfill my fucking duty to the fucking universe."

The intersection point shudders beneath me, reacting

to ... well, me. To me reacting to Rath clawing at the soul-deep wound I didn't even know I was suffering from.

I want to press my hand against my chest. It hurts. It hurts. That soul-based wound radiates agony through my system, as if it was cauterized once but is now raw and bleeding.

But I don't. I don't press my hand to that wound. I don't stumble or sway under the onslaught. I stand tall and strong. I face my so-called soul-bound mate, and I don't allow any of that weakness to show.

Rath shifts, reacting to the energy practically boiling around us now — a combination of me, the intersection point, and darling Presh, who feels as though she's trying to calm me, calm both of us.

But her sweet, gentle healing energy is no match for my own power.

Shouts sound out from below. In the kitchen, then the entranceway.

"You have no right to walk around my property, my home, as if you own it," I say, still steadily holding Rath's wild-eyed gaze. There's no hint of his beast in his eyes.

"You're overreacting," he says. "You're tired and —"

"You have no position here," I say. "We do not know each other. We are not soul bound."

Rath grabs his chest as if I've knifed him, clenching his T-shirt as if trying to yank a sharp blade from his heart. "Tempest ... please ..."

I open my mouth to banish him from the property. I can feel the firmer connection I have to the intersection point now, and I have no doubt it would actually work this time. I could eject him. I could protect myself from —

"What the fuck is going on here?" Rought shouts as he

charges up the stairs, heedless of the energy writhing all around me and Rath.

DeVille is behind him, stopping to hover halfway up, his skin ashy with concern ... or maybe terror? I didn't see or feel him descend past me. Gigi and Coda peer up from the base of the stairs, wide-eyed and clearly overwhelmed.

By me.

I consider ejecting all of them from the property.

I am the fucking Conduit. I don't answer to —

Presh wraps her arms around me, hugging me tightly.

Rought steps between me and his brother in the hall, snarling at Rath. "Step back, step away."

"Don't get between us," Rath snarls back. "It's not your place to —"

"I'm Zaya's fucking guardian," Rought declares. "I step between her and anything or anyone with ill intent. Especially you, brother. Not only should you know better, but it should be impossible for you to hurt her."

"That's not ... I would never ..." Rath cuts himself off with a noise, a moan, that I can't easily identify. Anguish?

The pain in my chest eases just a bit.

Rought steps closer to Rath, lowering his voice to a murmur. "I think you need to take some time and figure out what the fuck you want."

Presh blinks up at me, and I rub my hand down her back. My essence and the energy from the intersection point both ebb, though they don't completely dissipate.

"I don't need time," Rath quietly insists. "I'm just —"

"Take it anyway." Rought pivots to me and his baby sister, stepping close enough to block our sight of Rath. Taking in our hug, he smiles warmly. "I hear there's a dire mage wandering around Newport, looking to stir up shit."

I meet his steady gaze, then glance down at Presh.

"Seems like the perfect opportunity for an essence training session."

"Really?" Presh asks.

I glance at DeVille.

The younger shifter looks away from Presh just long enough to nod at me, steady and sure now. "I'm up for it."

Rought presses a kiss to Presh's head, holding my gaze. "I'll come with you three."

"I'd like that," I say, just a bit stiffly. Because I can feel Rath looking at me, and I'm not interested in seeing his judgement. Again.

Presh slips away from my hold. But instead of following Rought and me as we head to the stairs, she turns and hugs Rath.

He holds her gently, inhaling deeply and closing his eyes.

I look away. I walk away.

Doing whatever the fuck I want.

According to Rath, that's what I'm good at, after all. I might as well fulfill his expectations.

THE QUAINT STREETS OF NEWPORT AROUND THE Nail Bar salon are quiet, making me realize I don't actually know what day of the week it is. Though that isn't completely unusual for me, especially when I'm traveling internationally, it feels like another symptom of the disconnect I'm still —

Rought, talking quietly on his phone while continually surveying the immediate area, slides his warm, large hand across my lower back. And just like that, my surroundings solidify around me. As if I had actually been drifting partially in the aether. I understand that just because I'm the Conduit now, that doesn't mean my physical body is up for containing all that power yet. Especially given that I was dead only a couple of days ago.

Still, the drift is annoying.

"Good," Rought says into the phone. "Just waiting on Grinder. If we're in town long enough, we'll grab dinner for everyone on our way back. Who have you got tailing the Authority assholes?"

The two agents weren't staked out at the entrance as we left the estate. Of course, had they been there but the universe didn't want them to see me — as when I left to pick up Presh at the rave — then they somehow wouldn't have noticed when we left. I'm not surprised that the Outcast MC has one or more members tailing them. Despite the agents' ties to Reck and his ties to the motor-cycle club, the Authority isn't exactly welcome to wander around claimed territory.

"Have her send me updates every thirty minutes until we get back? Good." Rought listens for a beat, his gaze sliding to me. "Yep, the Nail Bar. Ask Cay if she needs ... no? Okay."

Presh rocks on her feet just a little, pulling my attention to her. Then she smiles at me, gently.

Right. Training.

DeVille leans back against the huge crew-cab pickup Rought commandeered to take us into town, pulling a crushed pack of cigarettes from the pocket of his faded black hoodie and sticking one in his mouth as he searches his pockets for matches or a lighter. DeVille technically isn't patched into the club yet, presumably having to wait until his beast form is revealed. Or maybe there's an age requirement? But his oversized hoodie has the Outcast emblem emblazoned across the back. A hand-me-down, maybe. Or stolen from his brother Rought's closet.

Presh follows my gaze, curling her lip at her self-appointed bodyguard. DeVille flashes her a cocky grin. His natural dark gray hair falls around his cheekbones, artfully framing his green eyes.

In a few more years, the teen is going to be a heartbreaker — and he won't even notice his effect on people. Because his fixation with Presh will only deepen as the bond between them strengthens.

Presh snaps her gaze back to me. Deliberately. Clearly annoyed, but also clearly attempting to ignore that her exasperation is mostly directed inward. Losing Kris, almost losing herself in the process, but having DeVille steady and sure at her side is no doubt confusing. Only a few days ago, Presh proclaimed that she wasn't 'a fan' of male lovers.

"You were saying something about essence resonance?" the young awry prompts, forcing me to focus on the here and now and not dwell on the intricacies of soul bonds. Specifically, whether or not those bonds have to be sexual in nature, especially if a person's sexual preferences are ascribed elsewhere.

Those connections don't have to be sexual. But most are.

"You said I might be able to pick up trails?" Presh touches the back of my hand.

Right. I'd been in the middle of explaining why I dragged Presh with me, away from the protection of the estate, despite Rath's protests. I nod, sweeping my gaze up the street in both directions again. "There will be a lot of those trails here."

Except for the nearly collapsed Outcast clubhouse three blocks up, the MC has cleaned every trace of the brawl with Chains, the berserkers, and the other unaffiliated shifters from the immediate area. In this particular block, the boarded-up windows are the only lingering evidence. Though most of the stores are closed for business and the foot traffic is minimal, the restaurant on the corner appears to be pumping out take-out — most of it likely for the shifters who've spent the day cleaning up the area — and the grocery store has fruit and vegetables displayed outside their plywood-covered windows, under a front awning.

The streets are still damp, but the rain has eased.

"Because of what happened last night?" Presh asks, swallowing. Her attention has shifted westward toward the ocean, as if she's recalling or visualizing where Bellamy lured her, then killed Kris. Where I murdered Chains before his time.

"Yes. We don't need to follow any of those trails from last night. But despite the circumstances, it's a good opportunity for you to practice picking out different resonances."

"If I can," Presh says quietly.

"You can," I say firmly. "All of the awry can sense essence, even if they don't see it. It's our fundamental nature. We pull, or weave, essence from ourselves and our environment."

DeVille's lighter isn't working. He shakes it and clicks it a few more times. His gaze is intent on Presh though, and I have no doubt he's listening.

Rought pivots, phone still pressed to his ear, snatches the unlit cigarette dangling from DeVille's mouth, and crushes it into tiny flakes of paper and tobacco. DeVille shoves away from the truck, seemingly ready to fight for his right to slowly poison himself. Shifters don't easily die from carcinogens, but they can make themselves sick if they try hard enough.

Rought silences his younger half-brother with a sharp jab of his forefinger and middle finger against his chest.

DeVille loses his breath with a pained gasp, then wheezes on his next compromised inhalation.

Rought's tone is low. "You're standing in the presence of a fucking goddess, who has more power in her little finger than you'll ever access or see in your lifetime. Pay fucking attention. Learn something."

Well, that makes it clear where Rought stands on the Conduit-as-a-divinity issue. Thankfully, his beliefs don't seem to deter him from making out with me. Though with his beast a mythical creature, maybe that dampens the whole intimidation factor.

"I'm not awry," DeVille protests weakly.

"You have no idea what you're capable of yet," Rought says.

"We don't share that bloodline," DeVille says, frustration edging his words.

"I should hope not," Rought says with a hint of a threat. "Since you've been following my sister around like a lost puppy ever since you first laid eyes on her."

DeVille goes very still, deliberately not looking at any of us.

Precious flicks her eyes up to meet mine, her gaze filled with questions that I know she's not ready to have answered. Despite my unfortunate slip during my argument with Rath.

"Though we obviously share commonalities, every awry is different," I say, ignoring Presh's look and keeping us on track. It's one thing to take a moment to educate the young awry, and another thing to let a dire mage get bored with their hide-and-seek game and start wreaking havoc again. "I don't generally see residual essence trails. I can feel essence, say in spells or charms, though it has to be extremely robust for me to pick up on it. But what I can see when I take a moment to look are the threads of fate, the essence-forged connections if you prefer, that weave us all together, between each other but also within our world."

Presh's eyes widen. She blinks a few times.

I pause, only partway through my explanation. It's possible I'm imparting too much information to be useful. I've been worried from the start that mentoring with me might not be the right experience for Presh.

"Threads of fate ..." she murmurs. "And sometimes you just know you're supposed to do something ..."

"Like go to the beach." DeVille, now listening intently, steps closer. Though his gaze still rests on Presh not me. " 'The path leads directly to the beach,' you said."

"Yes." I sigh. Last night's failure lies with me, though. Not the teens.

Presh closes her eyes, swallowing. "Kris said ... she said that we should turn up the street. That there was a better place to hide ..."

"Maybe this is too much," I say. "Why don't we go back to —"

Presh's eyes snap open. "No, Zaya. I'm here ... I want to do this ... please?"

DeVille exhales a heavy breath. "I shouldn't have listened."

"It's not like you could have carried both of us, Andy," Presh says, firmly maintaining the prickly walls she's erected between them.

"I could have," he insists.

"It was not your fault!" Presh snaps, hands clenched at

her sides. "I listened. I listened ... to Kris. And you ... you tried to protect ... me."

They stare at each other for a moment, DeVille towering over the tiny awry, both of them presumably reliving the events of last night, replaying the terror and confusion in their heads.

"Why the beach, Zaya?" Presh asks with a croak, pulling her gaze from DeVille to look at me. "Was that one of the things you just know?"

"Yes."

"Because ... you can see the future?" DeVille asks.

"No."

"Fate," Rought interjects, though he doesn't look up from texting on his phone. "Zaya just told you. She can see, or feel, the threads of fate."

That's the easiest answer, so I don't elaborate further. Especially because this is about focusing Presh's power, whatever that power might turn out to be. She almost self-combusted last night through the terror and pain of losing Kris, during which I got a look at the depths of the essence she will eventually wield. That much access to essence, paired with the multistrand, multicolored threads of fate that surround Precious, needs focus.

For any number of reasons.

Many awry don't survive the full manifestation of their power, and one awry can take a lot of people with them if they implode.

"Fate," DeVille scoffs, shaking his head. "There's always a reason. Something tangible."

"In the aftermath," I say, incapable of fully disguising the smirk his doubt evokes. Because I've seen his threads and who he is undoubtedly fated to already. "There's usually a reason, yes."

"So the beach?" Presh prompts. "What reason would there be to send us there?"

I think about that for a moment. "Logically ... depending on the dire mage's skill set, there's a good chance that salt and water would have interfered with their castings. Maybe even stopped the mage from ..."

I realize what I'm saying, too late.

Presh visibly deflates.

DeVille grimaces, then scrubs a hand over his face. "So if I had gotten Kris to the beach, the mage might not have been able to ..." His gaze flicks to Presh, taking in the anguished look on her face. He doesn't finish his thought either.

Not at all certain whether I'm even capable of bringing comfort to anyone, I pull Presh against me in a one-armed hug, even while reaching for DeVille and laying my hand across the back of his neck. He instantly tucks next to Presh, bowing his head so I can reach him easier.

I never reached for my aunt like that. Never sought physical comfort from her. She offered all her knowledge and all her support, but hugs just weren't a thing. She'd been the Conduit for over seventy-five years by the time I was born. There are very few people comfortable coming into any contact with that level of energy, even with the necklace currently hanging around my neck to help mitigate it.

Still holding the teens, I meet Rought's gaze. His phone is forgotten in his hand, his expression tender but not sad.

He looks at the three of us as if we're everything he's ever wanted.

My chest floods with that internal sunshine, that steadying warmth, that Rought seems to lend me effortlessly. Presh relaxes against me. DeVille closes his eyes with an inaudible sigh, curling his fingers around Precious's wrist. She doesn't brush him away.

A familiar green pickup truck pulls up to the curb, parking alongside us. Rought tears his gaze away from our huddle. DeVille steps back from the loose embrace as well, pivoting to straighten to his full height.

Not because the massive, grizzled, dark-skinned shifter who steps out of the truck's cab is a threat, but because he's a lieutenant in the Outcast MC. By his own admission, he's ranked even higher than Rought, and DeVille is only a club prospect.

Grinder, wearing his full cut with his beard neatly trimmed, claps his hand on Rought's shoulder hard enough that the gryphon shifter stumbles slightly. They're a similar height — both of them giants compared to Presh — but Grinder carries the weight of age in his broad shoulders and massive chest.

"Glad to see you all unscathed with my own eyes," he says in his deep, gravelly tone. His gaze flicks to me still cuddling Presh as he crosses to us, ignoring DeVille in that shifter hierarchy way. Meaning he likely knows everything he needs to know about the young shifter's health and welfare without a single word or glance exchanged between them.

Presh peeks up at Grinder with a sad smile as he pauses before us. Then he levels his gaze on me and deliberately taps his chest with the first three fingers of his left hand, over his heart.

"*As the weaver wills*," he says reverently.

He means me. Never mind that in my opinion, it's the universe doing the actual weaving, generally before each soul is reborn into this plane of existence. I — which is to say, the Conduit — just mess around with the individual threads while on the earthly plane.

I huff belligerently. "I wish."

A broad grin overtakes his deference. His slightly crooked teeth are white against his dark skin. His brown eyes are warm, welcoming. I still have no idea what his beast is. I would have thought a bear, due to his sheer size. But since he's an Outcast — a mixed-clan shifter club — he could be an exceedingly rare shifter breed, like Doc Z and Cay. Or even mythological like Rought and Rath.

"As you say, little goddess." Grinder chuckles. "We'll follow wherever you lead."

I side-eye him for that declaration as well, but let it slide without comment.

Presh scrubs her hands over her face, then steps away from me, as if forcing herself to stand on her own. Her shoulder brushes against DeVille's arm. He makes a visible effort to not react.

I meet Rought's gaze and instantly know that DeVille isn't the only shifter struggling with personal boundaries. The gryphon shifter simply hides it better.

Two surprisingly quiet motorcycles slide around the corner, heading our way. Despite being deliberately muffled, the heavy bikes are clearly powerful and dangerous rides, though neither Outcast biker wears a helmet. Stealth outweighs safety for these shifters, apparently.

"Pepper and Piston," Grinder says, stepping toward the newcomers. They could be twins, though the female has darker-hair than her sandy-haired brother. Both are sharp-featured and slim, for shifters, at least. "Good. We're set."

I throw a look at Rought.

He laughs. "Did you think I'd let you wander around looking for a dire mage without extra backup?"

"I wasn't planning on much wandering," I snap, though without heat. I'm actually having trouble not just grinning at Rought like a lovelorn idiot whenever he so much as glances in my direction. Being so enamored with anyone is a first for me.

At least as far as I remember.

That thought wipes even the hint of a smile from my face.

Right. "Essence trails," I say brusquely, shoving away the black-and-white echoes of my lost memories that dully reverberate through my mind. Memories captured in Mack's photographs and imprinted on my brain, with none of the nuances of the before and after to mitigate them. "Sometimes it's about feeling, and sometimes it's about sight."

"Okay." Presh bobs her head determinedly. "I'm ready."

I step around her so I'm at her back, completely out of her peripheral vision. Then I hold onto my essence and the essence that radiates from my necklace as tightly as I can. "You can feel ... or see ... the essence that twines around Grinder, yes?"

Presh takes a deep breath, then closes her eyes.

"Remember what it felt like to walk around the property," I murmur. "How it felt while we were dancing and you could follow, even anticipate, my moves ..."

"Yes ..." Presh murmurs. Both of her hands float up in Grinder's direction.

The burly shifter holds still, not wary but trying to be helpful. Behind him, Pepper and Piston remove their sunglasses in unison, revealing black eyes so dark against the white sclera that they appear to have no pupil.

Everyone's attention is riveted to Precious.

Except for Rought. He's watching me.

"Grinder's essence is substantial," I say, not needing to reach for it myself to know that. "There's no question that he is powerful."

"Deeply rooted," Presh whispers.

"Yes," I agree, surprised that the young awry has picked up that much on her first try. But then, she's known Grinder for a long time. "Stable."

"Yes." Presh smiles, quietly pleased.

"Now your brother," I prompt.

Presh's hands flare to the sides, palms partly facing upward as she pivots to assess Rought's essence. "Oh ..." she whispers. "This is ... different."

"Yes," I say, trying to not just gaze at Rought adoringly myself. "Rought is a ... presence."

"With a capital *P*?" Rought asks playfully.

"The gryphon?" Presh tilts her head to the side. Thoughtfully, I assume. Not that she's hearing something I can't.

I start to elaborate, to prompt Presh to focus on what feels different when reading her brother's essence, but the descriptive words that want to tumble out — that Rought feels like the sun dancing across my skin on a chilly, windy day, like being cuddled next to a bonfire and gazing up at the endless universe spread across the starlit sky but knowing I'm not alone — won't be at all helpful for Presh's assessment.

Still, Presh says, "Starlight ..." questioningly. She opens one eye, peeking at me over her shoulder. "Or maybe the ... cosmos? Rought feels a little like the intersection point. I'm not ... I don't know how to explain it."

"He does," I say. "And the exact words aren't important because it's a feeling. Dozens of shapeshifters left residual trails up and down these streets. They will have some commonalities, but they're all fundamentally unique."

"Especially the berserkers," DeVille mutters.

"Exactly," I say. "But there's nothing darkly tainted about the shifters' essence. Nothing malignant. Nothing that makes you want to clench your teeth, or that runs cold down your back. And the dire mage's power will feel different than the berserkers as well. Though now that I think about it, whatever spell Chains used last night had a lot in common with the corrupted energy the berserkers give off."

Presh frowns. "So I'm looking for corrupted energy?"

"No," I say, "because you probably won't know it, not until faced with the actual source. You're looking for a tenor that's not the shifters. Or mine. Though I won't have left any trail. I can't be tracked like that."

Grinder and Rought share a glance.

Then Grinder clears his throat. "Not to be that guy, but any of us would be able to smell a dire mage from blocks away."

I offer him a knowing smile. "You'd think so, wouldn't you? But the mage has been out and about in Newport this morning while you were cleaning and fixing windows."

Grinder glances at Rought again, sharp and questioningly. Pepper and Piston share a similar glance, and I catch a hint of essence shifting between them. The shifter siblings are telepathic. That, paired with their unusual eye color, and with them being mixed-clan shifters in a pack that occupies territory along a coastline, narrows down their species sharply. Both are exceedingly rare marine shifters. Well, rare in that they're choosing to dwell on land. Likely dolphins.

Rought grimaces. "Seems the dire mage is highly skilled

in obfuscation spells. We've only picked her up when she's wanted to be seen."

Grinder scratches his beard. "But ... the possession ..." He clears his throat, glancing at Presh and DeVille with concern.

"Yes," I say, not making the elder shifter elaborate. "Either this dire mage has an unusual skill set, or she's —"

"Too skilled," Rought mutters.

"Or ..." I continue, slightly more pointedly, "we're dealing with multiple mages."

"Motherfucker," Grinder snarls. "They don't usually work together, do they?"

"They don't usually live long enough," Rought says. "After going dark."

"Neither do berserkers," I say mildly. "Usually."

Silence falls between us. Grinder pulls out his phone and starts texting. Likely checking in with the rest of the Outcast lieutenants — or warning them all, including Pinky.

"Okay," Presh says determinedly, though her voice remains a much-needed sweetness. "I'm looking for ... feeling for energy that doesn't match the shifters."

I smile at her. Bellamy's path is easy to distinguish from the vibrant, natural energy of the shifters. For me, at least. The dire mage's residual is smudged — oily and weirdly cloying — all around us, as if she's been walking these streets recently. "I'll give you a hint, shall I?"

"Toward the beach," she says, with just a hint of a question threaded through the declaration. "Again?"

"Yes. But to the south this time."

I step up beside Presh, not touching her but near enough. She starts off down the block, keeping to the cleared sidewalk. Rought, Grinder, and DeVille array themselves behind us, near enough to grab us or dart in front of us if needed. Piston and Pepper start their motorcycles, then begin to navigate an outer perimeter, circling a block ahead, then back around.

Together, we go dire mage hunting.

Though I find myself wondering if there's an ice-cream place nearby. Actually, the grocery store should have —

"Zaya?" Presh twines her fingers through mine. Her voice is gentle, as it was in the motel room when I was barely functioning. Or rather, functioning just enough to get the young awry to safety.

"I'm with you, Precious. Always."

"I know. Thank you for letting me come with you."

I laugh quietly. "With this posse of shifters? It doesn't get much more secure."

"And with you," Presh murmurs reverently.

Just this one time, I don't brush that whispered bene-diction away. I share a glance with Rought over my shoulder and let this feeling merge with the tiny ball of light, of warmth, that's taken up residence in my chest. Then I ease my hand away from Precious's hold so her senses aren't overwhelmed, and I focus back where I know I'm supposed to be. Here in the *now*.

FIVE

RECK

ZAYA FUCKING GAGE IS SITTING AT THE FUCKING bar attached to the fucking hotel the Outcast MC has commandeered as a temporary clubhouse, since fucking Rath took the fucking roof off their regular local last night.

The bane of my fucking existence and the object of all my beast's desires is playing on her phone, sipping some pinkish-orange slushy drink in a martini glass, legs crossed and swinging one foot. Seemingly permanently attached to her drink via her fucking straw, cheeks hollowing with every pull of those lush fucking lips. Just like at the club last night.

Zaya. Drinking. In the middle of the fucking day. As if she isn't the one responsible for the chaos unleashed on this town last night, fucking destroying most of Main and First Streets. And shredding another hunk of my tattered soul right along with the other destruction.

Less than twenty-four hours ago, I would have sworn

that my soul didn't have a shred remaining to be sundered. But Zaya fucking Gage is on the loose, and she's going to destroy all of us stupid enough to stumble into her path.

The Outcast MC pledge still setting up the bar keeps stealing glances at Zaya like he might try to shoot his load. He probably saw her dancing last night at the clubhouse. Like her privileged fucking cunt is obtainable for anyone in this backwater town, let alone some shit barely out of his teens. He probably shifts into a fucking donkey or muskrat.

I hover like a moonstruck moron in the doorway of the corridor leading back into the office spaces and then into the hotel itself — even as I blame my fucking beast for getting caught up at the mere sight of our duplicitous bond. The Outcast MC have leased out the entire hotel for the next couple of months, bar and laundromat included. I doubt it was busy in the offseason anyway. The main building is set back from the ocean's edge, but still close enough to hear the surf and catch a glimpse of the beach through any west-facing windows.

After having been unusually active all day, infusing power through me that I haven't felt in years, my beast is oddly quiet in Zaya's presence. Even now, with her in our sight, the cu-sith is pressed into the back of my mind. It was so present even after I wrestled control of my body back from it right before dawn that I've been fighting its instincts all day. Mostly instincts to maim or outright slaughter anyone standing between us and her. Zaya fucking Gage.

The only thing currently keeping me away from the estate property is the two Authority agents, Shaw and Wilson, I've got posted there. Those corrupt assholes are a most effective deterrent to me storming the house — and, if the cu-sith had its way, prostrating myself at her fucking feet.

My reawakened beast loathes both Shaw and Wilson, but that's not the only reason I don't want them knowing anything about Zaya or my connection to her. They — the Authority — don't need more leverage with which to cage me.

Once again, Zaya has left the estate without those fuckers noticing or notifying me.

I'm not sure why I'm fucking bothering involving Shaw and Wilson, or with even feigning that any of this surveillance is officially sanctioned. Not on the Outcast or on Zaya.

Except ... I know.

I fucking know the Authority is always working both sides of anything having to do with me. Ever since I blasted through their academy in record time and requested Cascadia and the Federation for my official placement. Leveraging what remained of my ... my what? My morality? My worth? The last vestiges of anything good within me?

Fuck me. I just wanted to keep eyes on my family — those who need my protection and those who deserve my vengeance — so I took any and all assignments, no matter how corrupt, no matter what I had to do, to gain position and authority.

As such, while Shaw and Wilson might officially be assigned to me, I'm continually aware that they're also my watchers.

The cu-sith that makes up one half of my permanently destroyed soul presses its claws into my brain. Metaphorically, obviously. But it still hurts like fuck. The beast is trying to get me to focus on something specific.

I sweep my gaze across the room, not getting the hint.

Last night, the cu-sith ceded my human form to me only after Zaya was carted off by my brother Rought. She passed out — again — from whatever the fuck she did to cut down Chains like he wasn't a senior shifter in the Cataclysm MC, with all the power that comes with such a position within the structure of an essence-tied pack. Each shifter essence-bound through fidelity oaths or blood or bitten bonds. Through that web of bonds, the more powerful filter strength to the lessers, and the lessers provide stability to leaders far more powerful — and more likely to be unhinged.

Zaya didn't even have to touch Chains to drop him.

My memory of last night, after being nearly suffocated by a spell so fucking malignant that my beast voluntarily rose to save my undeserving ass, is hazy as fuck. I might not have been in control of the cu-sith's actions, but even pressed into the background of my own mind, I can see and sense what my beast can.

Zaya cutting Chains's strings and him dropping to the pavement, dead before he hit, is clear as fuck.

I don't know what kind of power that is, but I know there's no fucking way someone as fundamentally irresponsible as Zaya should be the one to wield it. Not unchecked.

I mean, just walking away from the three people pulled from the primordial ooze, shaped by the fundamental energy that fuels the fucking universe, and destined to be yours to protect, to cherish? Who the fuck does that?

Zaya fucking Gage does that. Did that.

Not that I believe any of that 'soul bound' shit. She might have hoodwinked me as a child, manipulated all three of us as teenagers until we could barely stand to be out of her presence. But I'm not that naive now. I'm not that easily coerced. Her essence-twisted tricks won't work on me. Not again.

The pledge saunters over to Zaya, sliding a new slushy

drink toward her across the bar without asking if she wants a refill. From my perspective, she barely acknowledges him. As it should be.

He shouldn't even be breathing the same air as her, let alone looking at her like he's ready to beg for scraps. She could burn him through with a mere look, smirking while she leeches every last drop of —

My beast presses forward. Not enough to move me, but enough to exert pressure against my skin. Still, the typical red haze of the cu-sith's consciousness, the need to destroy and fuck everything and everyone up, doesn't flood through me.

With the cu-sith's reawakening, my truth-seeking abilities are back in full force. I've also got this weird sense — currently lodged at the back of my throat like a malignant tumor — that I might be able to speak with the beast's voice. Except the cu-sith only ever says one thing: *die, die, die.*

That's new.

And I hate new shit.

After Zaya unleashed hell on the unwitting Outcast shifters, all because she wanted an excuse to flaunt herself in front of the entire clubhouse, I got maybe a couple of hours of sleep in my SUV. After transforming back into my human self, I couldn't stand to be around people. At all. The lies — even if meant to be simple platitudes or minor twists of the truth — that flow freely from every human I get within a few feet of are a constant stabbing to my already beleaguered brain.

I couldn't block that deluge of thoughts — or more specifically, of intent — all through the early-morning hours. Too many people were already up and fucking yammering to each other while I was still trying to get some sleep. I had to abandon my suite — in this very fucking hotel — and retreat to my SUV in the parking lot like some fucking novice.

That extreme sensitivity — walking around like a lie detector riddled with live wires — finally eased a couple of hours ago. Though I'm still avoiding people in general. And my fucking phone. One check-in call with fucking Shaw this a.m. and I thought my brain was going to explode from the shit he constantly spews. Both Rought and Rath have been all up in my messages, but I'm just deleting them unread.

The beast shifts back within me again, finally freeing my limbs and my mind enough that I push myself toward Zaya. Weaving through all the empty tables between us and heading for the bar. She's wearing a dramatically long black dress painted with dark-red flowers and green leaves. Roses, maybe. The long sleeves cover her arms. Her light-brown hair is loose and wavy over her shoulders, and the blue of her veins are a sharp contrast to the pale skin of her neck.

She's still too slim.

And something is off about the outfit.

The cu-sith's claws prickle across my mind. Again.

A warning? A wariness?

I shove the beast back hard, fucking pissed that I have to do so. I'm not some newly manifested shifter. I've held this beast at bay for thirteen years now.

Zaya's back is to me, and there's no mirror behind the bar, but it's still odd that I step right up beside her without her noticing. I don't think she's faking it. Even though I can't normally sense an awry's lies from the truth, I'm adept at reading body language.

Zaya is playing a word game on her phone.

That is so utterly mundane, it gives me pause.

The beast is shoved down deep within me, but I can still feel the ghost of its claws prickling against my brain warily. What could possibly concern the death god that inhabits me? The beast thinks Zaya is its mate. Soul bound by the universe and all that shit. It doesn't give a fuck that she abandoned us, then ignored us for over a decade. So its cautious quiescence is disconcerting.

"Reck," Zaya purrs, straw in her mouth, face angled slightly toward me. "Fancy meeting you here."

I can't see her eyes through the dark-tinted black sunglasses she's wearing. Indoors.

I unbutton my suit jacket and slide onto the stool next to her, forcing myself to maintain my distance when I want to lean into her intimidatingly. I'm wearing my typical black suit over a white shirt and black tie. It marks me as an agent of the Authority almost as much as the badge in my pocket does.

Stupidly, I can still recall the contemptuous energy that emanated from Zaya outside the room at the Crescent Moon Inn — at the suit, at the badge, at her classifying me solely by those things. "Your type ..." she said.

The awry have always sneered at authority in any form — and the Gage family even more so. As if they're above it all. Better than the rest of us. They don't need to follow the rules that govern all of those, all of us, with immense power.

"Don't you have better things to be doing, Zaya?" I ask scathingly. "Day drinking? That's beneath even you."

"Even me ..." Zaya murmurs, sounding oddly amused as she takes a long, slow sip, draining the last of her first drink.

The donkey or marmot shifter-fuck sidles up to the bar

between us. His gaze is on Zaya as he asks me, "What can I get you, brother?"

"I'm not your fucking brother," I snap, resisting the urge to reach over and slam his face into the bar. He's flexing Outcast affiliation. But no matter what my uncle wants, even after all these years, I'm not an Outcast. I never will be. I made other choices. Choices I can never walk away from.

I'll die with this Authority badge in my pocket.

I just want to take my fucker of a father with me when I do.

"Step back," I growl. "Even better, go double-check your inventory for tonight. In the stockroom."

The pledge stumbles back from the bar, from me. Then he takes off like I've just threatened to murder him. It's possible that the steady presence of the cu-sith is making me come off even more unhinged than usual.

Zaya smirks at me, totally fucking delighted at my unintentionally aggressive display. "Nasty boy, Reck."

"I asked you what the fuck you're doing here, Zaya."

"You didn't, actually."

I lean closer, trying to intimidate her. I can't scent her at all or feel the energy that usually pours off her. She's masking both somehow, even though she didn't at the motel. More lies. More fucking games. "Take off your sunglasses."

Zaya giggles. Then she plucks her straw out of her empty glass, pushes that glass away, and stabs the straw into the newer slushy drink.

The sound of that laugh creeps up my spine.

The cu-sith presses forward, just for a moment, and sloughs that sensation off as it would a malignant spell. Why would the beast react to —

Zaya's grin widens. "When was the last time we fucked?"

I rear back from her, completely thrown and weirdly disconcerted. My stomach sours. And unlike my response to her mere presence in the clubhouse last night, I swear my dick shrivels at the question.

Zaya and I never fucked. We fooled around those last couple of months together. But the three-year age gap between us had previously, and firmly, kept our friendship purely platonic. I was such a simp for her that anything else wasn't even a thought in my mind when she was underage. Not until she climbed into my lap, in full view of my brothers, and kissed me. A switch flicked then. All the desire I'd been channeling elsewhere homed in on …

I kill the thought. It's all just more concrete evidence of Zaya's manipulative abilities.

She continues undeterred. "We should fuck. You're completely on edge. And I think this conversation will go better if we fuck."

It's not unlike Zaya to initiate. I would have happily continued in my older-best-friend role until we were both in our twenties, even knowing that she and Rought had consummated their relationship, and that she and Rath had been fooling around for a couple of years as well. I was perfectly fine fucking other people. Just using any warm and willing body to get off, not even remotely serious about any of it.

Though … only when Zaya wasn't in town, and never with any of the locals or Outcast members. Not until after … after Zaya died.

Supposedly died.

Maybe even faked her death to get away from all of us.

To get away from me.

Zaya giggles again.

And again, the sound is irksome. I've never found anything about Zaya remotely displeasing before —

Pure, unfettered relief floods my system. The cu-sith retreats even further back in my mind, as if in denial.

I've been released. Or I've overcome the terrifyingly intense attraction, the desperate need to belong to Zaya.

I'm free of her. Free of the obligation of the bond.

I have no idea what happened last night to trigger that disintegration. But I'm fucking free. Free to just sink into the darkness, to wallow within the depravity that I confront every day in my job. Even free of the retribution, the revenge, I've worked toward for the last thirteen years.

Zaya Gage didn't die.

I'm not responsible for the death of my soul-bound mate.

I don't need to avenge that death.

No bond lingers between us. No obligation.

I'm fucking free.

I throw my head back and laugh. I laugh and laugh, ignoring the tears edging the corners of my eyes and the cu-sith's claws once again digging into my brain.

Zaya laughs as well, sounding as completely unhinged as I know I do.

I grasp her wrist. A shock of energy shudders between us. But it's just another layer of disturbance across my already fucked-up senses. So I tighten my hold, dragging her off her stool and pulling her with me back toward the hall and the empty offices.

Still laughing, she follows me willingly.

My beast scrapes sharp claws against my psyche, against my insides. Hard enough to bleed me out, to bruise. Mentally, at least.

I ignore it. I keep the beast at bay. I have enough practice to withstand anything. Zaya Gage insured that with the sharp crack of her neck and her lifeless body hitting granite.

If I ignore it for long enough, the cu-sith will fade away again, smothered in the vast emptiness of my soul.

Just like it did after Zaya died.

"Not dead," I say, laughing again. My chest aches like my heart has been ripped asunder. My head aches as if my brain is bleeding, my sight too sharp and hazy at the edges at the same time.

My body aches as if I'm dying. It's possible I'm having a stroke. Or a heart attack.

I'm gripping Zaya too tightly. She'll have bruises on her wrist.

But she doesn't pull away.

Skin-to-skin, I can feel the lie of her. I have no idea how she ever fooled me before. The abilities lent to me by my unusual beast usually don't work in the presence of awry. They never worked with Disa, around Disa. Though perhaps Zaya's aunt never outright lied to my face. But now, somehow, for some reason, my beast offers me protection against all of Zaya's manipulations, even inadvertently.

The soul bond was a fucking lie.

A trick.

Even as a child, Zaya had abilities beyond what a nine-year-old should wield. She could twist luck, occasionally even knowing the outcomes of minor incidents ahead of time. Games we would play — no player ever bested Zaya fucking Gage in a game of chance — or things like running out of gas or a dramatic switch in the weather.

How didn't I know, even then, that those abilities were some sort of mental manipulation? Catching the youngest of us three — Rought — in her snare so easily. Then Rath ... then —

Zaya grabs my face with her free hand, lifting up on her tiptoes to bite my bottom lip. Hard. "Pay attention," she snaps. "You have a room?"

"The office," I grunt, licking blood off my lip. Nausea roils through my stomach. The bones of my face ache, especially where she's touching. I twist out of her grasp.

"Fuck the office," Zaya says, looking up and down the empty corridor. "Do it here. I like an easy exit."

"What?"

She backs up against the wall, hiking up her dress, grabbing my hand and yanking it between her legs.

She isn't wearing any underwear.

She's also smooth shaven.

I feel like I'm functioning, barely, on some sort of time delay. My mind is struggling to catch up as Zaya grinds against my hand, panting dramatically.

Wrong. Wrong. Wrong.

Lie. Lie. Lie.

"Take off your glasses," I demand, trying to find her clit. And failing. She's acting like she wants me, but her flesh isn't as capable of lying. She's not wet, not even damp.

Zaya laughs nastily. "Want to look me in the eye when you fuck me? So romantic, Reck."

"Every fucking word out of your mouth tastes like poison."

She giggles as if I've just complimented her, yanking at my belt and then my zipper. "That doesn't stop you from wanting to fuck me," she says. "All three of you cunt-struck idiots. You were just the easy target."

"What?"

She shoves her hand in my boxers. I'm soft. So soft that I'm surprised she finds my dick at all.

I grunt.

She pouts, tugging on my limp dick hard and fast. "Really? I expected more."

I snarl, getting seriously pissed off. It's not like she's ready for me either.

I jam my dry fingers into her. She mews, arching off the wall and shoving her breasts forward. As if she's actually enjoying being fingered, but ...

I still can't smell her, still can't —

"Reck!" she snarls. "Stop fucking around. I want your dick in me. I want your come dripping from me."

Under her slightly-too-tight grip — and the image she's shoved into my head — my dick finally starts to harden.

She hums contentedly. The noise slithers down my spine. The cu-sith has retreated deep into my mind. That should be a relief. But I look down at Zaya's upturned face, pumping my fingers in and out of her and making swipes at what I'm hoping is her seriously uninterested clit with my thumb, and I can't reconcile any of what is happening with what I actually want.

This is not the Zaya I want.

This is not the Zaya who ruined me for all other potential hookups, and for any other intimacy, the first time she slid her tongue between my lips.

The first time she ground down on my ridiculously hard cock with only our shorts between us.

The first time I slipped my fingers into her bikini and watched her come on my hand, nearly fucking coming myself just from the press of her energy.

This isn't the Zaya from the picture I've hoarded all these years — covered in layers of decryption so the

Authority techs couldn't accidentally stumble upon it during their biannual mandated sweeps — because when my fucked-up life was too much to bear, I just needed to look into the eyes of my dead soul-bound mate.

Each time I gave in to that need, I swore I'd never do it again ... yet I never could bring myself to outright delete the photo of my Larkspur looking at me as she orgasmed.

Zaya yanks me by the dick, lifting her leg up over my hip and trying to line me up. "Lift me," she commands. "Fuck me against this wall."

Moving with intent before I even make the decision, I fucking tear her sunglasses off.

The purple eyes that meet mine are so pale they're practically white. Zaya's irises are ringed in darker purple, almost black, but then abruptly fade into a light lavender barely indistinguishable from the outer whites. The severely bloodshot whites. Her pupils are sharp pinpoints, not blown out with any level of desire.

"What the fuck is wrong with your eyes?" I snarl.

Zaya twists my rapidly deflating dick in her hand harshly, though I barely feel anything. "This is what you want," she insists. "This is what you've always wanted."

I start to pull away, knocking her leg off my hip.

Straightening against the wall, she clenches both legs tightly around my hand to stop my retreat, partly trapping my fingers in her barely damp cunt.

"You don't want me," I say, trying to regain some control. "You never wanted me, Zaya."

My own lie slithers over me, cutting deep.

My ... lie?

Zaya grabs the back of my neck, using it and my dick as twin levers as she yanks me against her. As if she's going to try to stuff my soft dick inside her despite my unwilling body.

She's way too strong.

I grunt, rearing back and shoving her harshly against the wall to get her off me.

Her sharp nails dig into my skin, deep enough to draw blood. Essence slithers over the back of my neck, over those wounds. Malignant, cloying essence that ...

Is she trying to push me? Compel me?

"What the fuck!?"

The cu-sith suddenly presses forward, sloughing off whatever the fuck this cunt is trying to do to me. That's the second or third time she's tried that trick.

"You've been fucking manipulating me?" I snarl, grabbing her by the neck and slamming her head against the wall.

Zaya moans dramatically. Then she deliberately sucks the blood — my blood — from her sharply pointed fingernails. She writhes against me with my deadened dick still clasped in her hand, as if in the throes of passion.

Lie. Lie. Lie.

"Um ... Reck?" A sweet, Southern-tinted voice emanates from farther up the corridor, from the direction of the hotel lobby. "What are you doing?"

Heart suddenly pounding, I jerk my head toward the newcomer, having already recognized the voice but completely thrown by the context.

Precious stands at the end of the hall. "Who is that? Reck?"

My little sister is not alone.

Zaya fucking Gage stands next to Presh. I know she's Zaya because she slowly lowers her sunglasses, and her eyes are blazing purple nebulas. The same as they were in the room at the motel.

And I can feel her ... I can feel that desperate draw to her. That terrible connection that I hoped was truly gone.

I can feel the cu-sith trying to tear through my skin to get to its mate.

Just like in the motel room, the real Zaya completely ignores me.

She cocks her head, leveling her gaze on the impostor. The impostor with my shriveled dick in her hand and with my hand wrapped around her neck, choking her. Lightly, but still.

Zaya Gage ignores me as if I'm completely unworthy of any acknowledgment.

And I am.

I am unworthy.

I always have been.

Precious's eyes narrow with accusation. Her chin quivers as she clearly catalogs the many levels of my current betrayal. The depths of my depravity.

The malignant creature pinned by my hand to the wall cackles, incredibly pleased. Her gaze is riveted down the hall, as if I also suddenly don't matter in the least, even with her neck in my bruising grip.

"Hello, little awry," she croaks, grinning madly. The smile is too wide, cheeks stretched. "Or should I say ... hello, sister. Nice to finally meet you in person. I've been waiting for you, so patiently, all day."

She means Presh.

She's claiming a blood relation with Precious?

I'm nothing ... I'm just ... bait?

I wrench my hand and my dick away from her. Then,

stumbling a couple of feet, I spew blackened vomit all over the wall and floor.

SIX

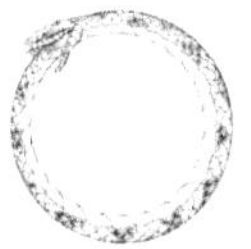

ZAYA

"It's a good likeness." My voice is weirdly calm even as I defensively slip my sunglasses back up to cover my eyes. My gaze is locked to the dire mage wearing my face ... and body. All while trying to ignore Reck propped up against the wall and vomiting all over his shiny shoes. Shirt and suit jacket rumpled, his belt and pants still undone. Though thankfully, his cock is tucked within his boxers. For his sister Presh's sake, at least.

And apparently the dire mage Reck has just been fucking up against the wall, the dire mage working for the Cataclysm and stirring up shit in Outcast territory, is now claiming that sibling relationship as well.

Bellamy ... Guerra? Or is she blood related through Precious's mother?

Having someone he was trying to fuck suddenly declare she is his sister — truthfully or otherwise — might explain Reck's extreme reaction. Though it doesn't explain the rather concerning black bile he's purging. Perhaps the cusith held barely skin deep within Reck ate something it shouldn't have last night after I passed out. Such as one of the berserkers.

"The outfit is wrong," Presh says, her lower lip quivering despite her forced bravado. "But ... she might have fooled me too."

My heart squelches a little. Out of love, I think, because the sensation is entirely new for me. The young awry is already gearing up to defend her brother despite finding him trying to fuck a dire mage with my face.

Though, with all the idyllic past captured in Mack's photographs still floating fancifully, hauntingly, in my mind, that might be more disconcerting for me.

Reck Guerra. Half-brother to Presh, Rath, and Rought. Ridiculously pretty, dark-olive skin, dark eyes, jutting cheekbones, sharp jawline and all. Even while puking up blackened bile all over the wall and carpeted floor.

Reck. Another of my destined mates, according to Mack's photographs.

But I feel only a strange sense of disconcertion around the eldest of the Guerra siblings. No pull, no attraction. No unusual emotional response. Not like the perpetual, soul-aching pull toward Rought, who I can feel even now all the way through the walls and out onto the front sidewalk. Not like the need to continually push back against Rath — possibly so I don't simply succumb to the security of his embrace, losing what remains of my sense of self to his almost-desperate need to protect me.

And yes, I'm not so irrational that I can't understand my own reactions. I just need a little time, and a lot of space, to get to the obvious conclusions.

"Wrong?" Bellamy smooths her hand down her floral dress, frowning. She narrows her eyes on me, exaggeratedly tilting her head. "You try cobbling together a glamour based on a shit-for-brains teenager's impressions."

She means Kris. Kris, whose mind and body she possessed to get to Presh.

Precious flinches.

I lay my hand on the young awry's shoulder, because I'm fairly certain she's a moment away from throwing herself down the hall at the dire mage. And we definitely don't need a repeat of last night, ending this time with Presh's essence lashing out or me trying to snip Bellamy's threads before her time. Not that I knew I had that ability as the Conduit before last night.

I don't have to look any closer to know that the dire mage's robust energy isn't being snuffed out anytime soon.

Rought is outside only because he stopped to take a call from his uncle — the Outcast himself. As far as I could discern, anyway. Based on Rought's suddenly stiff body language and the use of 'sir' in his initial greeting, the Outcast is peeved.

DeVille is at the front desk, charming the clerk for information. Unnecessary information now, given that we followed the dire mage's foul essence trail through the hotel easily enough.

Well, I followed it easily enough, coaxing Presh along with me. Bellamy is exceedingly skilled at cloaking herself. She's just no match for me. Nowhere near a match.

Reck straightens, wiping his face with his shirt. His dark-eyed gaze settles on me, then flicks to the dire mage, then back to me. Presumably noting the differences between us.

Feeling uncharacteristically considerate, given that Reck

hasn't yet zipped up his pants and was attempting to fuck an impostor wearing my face, I slowly tug my necklace free from my sweater and scarf, allowing it to settle against my chest. The massive uncut pink diamond yawns with power, as if sleepily stretching after a nap.

Bellamy's gaze shoots to the necklace. An uneasy avarice edges the fake smile she's still holding.

"Fuck ..." Reck groans, scrubbing his face.

"This is how you know," I say, almost gently, but speaking to Presh. "If you can't read or scent essence. I'm surprised a mage can hold any sort of glamour that looks remotely like me, no matter how much blood was spilled in the spelling of it. But this is how you know."

I'm even more concerned now about the dire mage's skill set. The potion from last night that incapacitated the shifters and locked them in their animal forms. Invading Kris's mind thoroughly enough to pilot her body and kill her remotely. All the tech obfuscation, and now a highly realistic glamour.

While some simple spells or charms might be accessible to most essence-wielders, mages typically specialize in one, maybe two areas. Two compatible areas. Potions, mind manipulation, obfuscation, and glamour are not compatible in the least.

Reck, looking grim and depleted, slides his hand into his suit jacket pocket. Either going for a weapon or his phone.

Bellamy flicks her gaze in his direction, completely dismissing him. She hasn't reached for any sort of weapon yet or drawn on any of her power.

Holding Kris's mind last night, then cloaking herself all of today, has to have been a huge essence drain. I'm surprised she's able to maintain the glamour. Perhaps fucking Reck was meant to provide some sort of energy boost that we interrupted?

"So all I have to do is steal a trinket?" Bellamy asks mockingly, still fixated on my necklace.

"Come and take it," I say, flashing her my own sharp-edged grin.

The dire mage chuckles darkly.

"The eyes are wrong," Presh says, rubbing her arms and shivering as if Bellamy's laugh might have affected her on a physical level. "She can't fake an awry's eyes."

Bellamy's smile widens, turning manic. "They're not fake, youngest."

I blink.

Awry?

She's claiming that she's awry?

A … dire awry?

I blink again, deliberately this time as I try to get a look at Bellamy's threads.

"The fuck you say," Reck snarls. Pivoting to face off with the dire mage, he takes a few steps back. Far enough to get between her and Presh.

Bellamy clicks her tongue chastisingly. "Come, come, brother —"

"Don't fucking call me that!" He pulls an essence-enhanced stun gun from his pocket. It's no bigger than his palm, but as it's Authority issued, I have no doubt it's nasty. Probably deadly to most targets.

And yes, Bellamy is claiming to be a Guerra sibling.

"Goodness." The self-proclaimed dire awry presses her hand against her chest dramatically. "Is that because you couldn't fuck me properly but still wanted to?"

"I wanted Zaya," Reck says. "You knew what you were doing when —"

"What's going on here?" Rought, trailed by DeVille, is suddenly crowding up against our backs.

The hallway really isn't wide enough for three people to stand shoulder to shoulder. Especially not with the width of the gryphon shifter's shoulders factored in. Rought snags Presh gently by the arm and pulls her back behind him, taking her place at my side. Reck is still ahead of us, between us and Bellamy.

"Oh good!" Bellamy cries with false brightness, clasping her hands in front of her. "We're almost all here."

"You don't have to hold my hand, Andy," Presh grumbles behind us, shifting so she can peer between Rought and me at the dire awry.

Dire awry? That just doesn't make any sense ...

"I'll put you over my shoulder again," DeVille mutters in a warning tone.

"You won't," Presh says.

"Don't make me."

"Where's the dragon?" Bellamy asks, grinning madly as we all ignore the teenagers bickering. "On his way? You can't have a family reunion without all of the family ... I mean, all of us in this particular country, that is. Daddy will be so pleased to have us together again."

"We don't fucking know you, mage," Rought says caustically.

"I know enough," Reck says. The dark-tinged energy of the cu-sith roils around him. "Enough to lock her up and forget the paperwork."

"Oh, yes!" Bellamy talks over both brothers as if they're inconsequential. "Let's do proper introductions." Making a show of it, she combs her sharp-tipped red nails through her hair, then down her face and across her shoulders, snagging layers of essence as she goes.

The glamour coating her cracks and crumbles. More of that foul-tainted essence writhes around her.

Rought huffs a few breaths as if clearing his senses.

Behind me, Presh gags and DeVille snorts.

Reck doesn't outwardly react.

Bellamy's clothing remains the same, and our heights must already be similar. Either that or the heels she wears make it close enough. But the dire awry's hair and skin are darker than my own — a dark olive similar to Reck's coloring.

She does a cute curtsy. "Bellamy Guerra."

In truth, Bellamy looks more than just similar to Reck, though her facial features are slightly more rounded than his. They could be full-blood siblings. Or twins.

"No," Reck says, sounding utterly sick. He's close enough that I can see a trail of blood drying on his neck and staining the back of his collar. The dire awry scratched him, badly. "This is just another fucking trick."

I take a step closer. Rought flinches as if intending to pull me back, then stops himself. I don't need to move nearer to the dire awry to confirm what I'm looking at, so I pause in deference to his caution.

Bellamy's eyes are the same as before. A light lavender, practically white-gray, around her contracted pupils, with a thin dark-purple rim around the irises.

"Not a dire mage," I say. "A dire ... awry."

"That's not ..." Reck says. "That's just part of the ..."

"Why ... ?" I ask Bellamy.

She blinks, thrown by my question. "What?"

"Why?" I tilt my head, deliberately looking at her threads. Trying to untangle the nasty knot of essence all around her, for a glimpse of her life force, of her fate. But those threads are shadowed, even muddy, some of them a deep red verging on black. And though black usually indicates deadened lines of fate, these are somehow still emanating energy.

Even odder, not all those threads are attached directly to her. As if some have been snipped, then tangled up with the lines of destiny or life force that remain.

"What are you looking at?" Bellamy snaps, trying and failing to hide her uncertainty.

I blink away the confusing twist and churn of the dire awry's essence threads. Though not before I glimpse the blackened gossamer threads connecting to each Guerra sibling she claims. The thread between her and Reck is slightly thicker, indicating a direct blood connection.

"Why reach for the essence in your blood?" I ask. "In the blood of others?"

"Why the fuck not?" she snaps.

"You've polluted your —"

"You know nothing," Bellamy snarls.

I slowly remove my sunglasses. Again.

Bellamy, who might have been too occupied trying to stuff Reck's cock inside her to fully notice my eyes when we first came upon them in the hall, takes an involuntary step back.

Apparently I'm still having an issue with seeing someone who was destined to be mine in that ... situation. Position? Hence my unusual posturing, and whatever is currently radiating from my eyes intensely enough to make the dire awry hesitate.

And that's not even addressing the sibling connection. Which Bellamy knew about, even if Reck didn't.

Bellamy is the type of awry who earned us all the name, the designation. A name that, even after centuries of us reclaiming it for ourselves, is used to reinforce our otherness and everything that's wrong with how we wield essence.

The twisted awry.

Unstable enough to try to fuck our blood relations. Sadistic enough to mentally manipulate a sibling into that act. Triggering some sort of blood-based spell — judging by the scratches on Reck's neck and the blackened bile his system was attempting to disgorge — to counter any resistance.

I raise an eyebrow, feigning an assuredness I certainly don't feel. "I thought you got a good look at me last night. Through Kris's eyes."

Presh sucks in a breath behind me.

"Apparently those impressions weren't reliable," Bellamy murmurs, gaze riveted to me.

"We can chat easier with her in a cage, Zaya," Reck says, not looking away from the dire awry. If he were wearing the fur of his cu-sith right now, his hackles would have been all the way up. "Standing around in a hall just puts Presh and DeVille at risk."

Bellamy laughs. "It's a good thing you're so pretty, brother, because you're fucking stupid. You think you can cage me?"

"Because you claim to be awry, you're all powerful?" Reck scoffs.

"I am awry," Bellamy snaps.

"Then why the blood casting?" I ask again, genuinely confused and still just a little thrown by it. "And all the sacrifices, I assume?"

"For power!" Bellamy thrusts her hands upward dramatically, apparently also somewhat thrown by my fixation on how she accesses and wields her essence. "Why the fuck else?"

"You're awry," I say. "You have all the power you would ever need. You can pull from anything, everywhere. That's what it means to be awry. Only pulling from your own blood or the blood of others ... that life force is fleeting, temporary even, when removed from its living, breathing host."

Bellamy just stares at me, not answering but listening intently.

"That's limiting. Limited," I continue. "Which forces you to kill again and again, shredding your own soul, your own life force, in the process." I have to stop myself from rubbing my forearms, even though the echo of Chains's life force etched across my skin has faded. "Or to drain yourself with every cut. Tying your castings to —"

"Why the fuck are you giving her pointers right now?" Reck snarls.

Rought clears his throat. "I have to agree, Zaya. This doesn't seem like —"

I huff. "Fine."

"Back to the cage?" Bellamy asks mockingly, sneering at Reck. "Like father, like son. You couldn't even fuck me properly. You think you're powerful enough to cage me?"

"What the fuck?" Rought mutters quietly.

"I'll tell you later," Presh whispers.

"If I can't cage you," Reck says malevolently, though his shoulders have stiffened at his siblings' commentary, "then the most powerful awry in the fucking world certainly can. And you just killed someone she took responsibility for."

My stomach sours at the reminder that I was responsible for Kris — prompted by the universe, in fact — and failed her. That I almost failed Presh and DeVille as well.

Bellamy snorts. "You've got this awry on retainer for the Authority?"

Reck gestures toward me. "You were just impersonating her. Badly."

"Good enough to fool you," Presh mutters behind us.

Reck's jaw tightens, veins straining in his neck, but he ignores Presh's jab.

"I'm not putting anyone in a cage," I say mildly, uncomfortable at being included in Reck's posturing. We aren't working together. We barely know each other. And there is no fucking way I'm helping the Authority with anything, no matter how dangerous the awry currently standing before me is. "The upkeep alone is a nightmare."

Reck throws a look my way. "You're making fucking jokes? Now?"

Bellamy's gaze swings back to me, the movement seeming unhinged. Though perhaps that's just the energy writhing around her. "I'm here for the littlest of us. Daddy wants her home." Her uncanny eyes flick over Reck and Rought dismissively. "You boys can pout and play at being scary beasts, but Daddy knows we girls are where the real power lies." She fixes her gaze over my shoulder, on Presh. "Come now, baby sis. I'll show you all the power that runs in your veins."

"I'm not going back!" Presh insists. "Zaya is mentoring me."

"Her? She couldn't even stop me from taking your pretty friend's mind." Bellamy licks her lips, then grins. "Couldn't stop me from siphoning all that little shifter's power, pathetic as it was."

Presh tries to lunge between Rought and me. But DeVille must still be holding her hand, because he yanks her back. Shrieking, she tries to wrench free of him.

As promised, DeVille unceremoniously lifts her over his

shoulder, pivots, and starts back down the hall. Presh beats his back with both fists, snarling.

I watch them for a moment. We all do. But fortunately, Presh's fledgling power doesn't spike. Not as it did last night.

"To Grinder," Rought calls over his shoulder. "Then straight to Rath."

Not looking back, DeVille waves in acknowledgment, then nearly loses hold of Presh when she throws her body to the side in an attempt to roll off his shoulder.

"See you soon, baby sister!" Bellamy calls down the hall, drawing all our attention to her again. Though I don't think Reck has looked away from her once.

"Explain this all to me," I say to her.

"Ugh," she groans affectedly. "All talk and no play makes Bellamy a bored and bloody awry. The last awry I saw wearing that necklace roiled with power." She laughs darkly, taunting. "Speaking of cages ..."

I blink, my stomach bottoming out.

That ... she means ...

She's seen ... my aunt? In a cage?

No one cages the Conduit. She has to be lying. But why would —

Reck lunges for Bellamy, stun gun thrust forward. He's fast, even in his human form, even for my eyes. Though that could be because I'm suddenly and completely numb. Again.

Unfortunately for him, Bellamy has more than enough time to smirk, step slightly to the side, and pull a wicked-looking athame dagger from the pocket of her dress.

I blink.

The dire awry's wrist is already dripping with blood. I

missed her cutting herself. Or she did it on the sly with the dagger tucked under her sleeve, not in her pocket at all.

Bellamy flicks a few drops of that blood toward Reck. Borne on a twist of her essence, the blood splatters across the stun gun, searing into Reck's hand. The essence sparking around the gun fizzes, then smokes.

Reck grunts in pain, dropping the gun. But without hesitation, he wraps his other hand around Bellamy's neck, pivoting to slam her against the wall.

She slits his throat with the athame, already muttering under her breath. A bastardized form of Latin, maybe. As if she needs actual words to cast. She doesn't.

I blink a third time.

Rought surges forward, grabbing Bellamy's wrist to twist it and the athame over her head — even while grabbing Reck's shoulder and yanking him away from the dire awry.

Bellamy shrieks indignantly, slamming the palm of her free hand against Rought's chest — along with an utterly foul spell. A curse so malignant it smells like burnt flesh.

All the blood dripping from her wrist and Reck's blood on the edge of the blade sparks, then crumbles into ash.

Rought takes the direct hit of that combined power, stumbling back just enough for Bellamy to wrench her wrist free, then — oddly — drop to the ground.

I reach for her threads through the numbness. Though only seconds have passed, my mind is still lagging after Bellamy alluded to knowing or having seen my aunt. Logically, I know that feeling is purely psychological, not at all physically impairing, but it's slowed me nonetheless.

Through a gap between Rought's legs and Reck's prone body, Bellamy looks up and meets my gaze. She smears her hand through the blood still pumping from Reck's neck, spreading over the floor.

A red-tainted shadow coils up her arm.

A thread of essence.

She's casting again. Using the life force contained in Reck's blood to —

Rought makes a grab for Bellamy, snagging her by the hair and jerking her head sharply back.

"No!" I shout. Panicked, I lunge the last few steps between us. "Don't touch her!"

At my command, Rought instantly releases Bellamy, reeling back with his hands up, slamming his back against the wall so I can get by him.

Bellamy's power snaps out around her, then more of those red-shadowed threads try to grab Reck — and Rought. They slide right over me, barely registering to my senses.

I reach, getting hold of the strands tracing over the two shifters, entangling my two destined mates as if Bellamy is trying to compel them, or ... transport them?

I cinch my hands around all of it. Then I yank. Hard.

Firmly attached to her own casting, Bellamy is dragged partly over Reck with a shriek. Instantly up again, kneeling on him, she pulls back against me.

For the briefest of moments, she tests her strength against mine.

I'm the stronger. By far.

But I still don't expect her to drop everything I'm holding.

I don't stumble, but under my hold, the malignant essence the dire awry has called forth and twisted from Reck's blood dies, turning into more ash.

The remaining essence twines around Bellamy's hands

and arms. Thus anchored to her body, it ignites. She screams. The stench of her casting fills the tight hallway, creating a sensation like I'm suffocating.

She screams again, seemingly in utter agony.

Then Bellamy disappears.

"What the fuck?" Rought shouts.

Reck groans, then starts coughing. His throat has already started to heal despite his blood loss being substantial enough to fuel a teleportation spell. Though that might point to the power of the cu-sith shifter more than the strength of the spell or the dire awry who cast it.

I stare at the space that formerly held Bellamy. I don't understand how she wields essence at all. And I certainly wasn't expecting her to teleport. Still, the way she tried to twist the energy she stole from Reck's blood around Rought and Reck felt as though she might be trying to contain or even move them. Chains had demanded as much from her when she possessed Kris's body the night before.

For a mage, teleportation is a complicated spell, typically requiring multiple casters. Even for a telekinetically inclined awry, teleportation is a rare affinity.

Rought touches my cheek lightly, calling my attention back to the present. The thought of Bellamy having seen my aunt tumbles around in my mind again, instantly intensifying my focus. There's no more time for training sessions. Two problems have seemingly become one — the dire awry and my aunt's disappearance — unless Bellamy is bluffing about my necklace.

"Presh?" I ask. "And DeVille?"

Rought's got his phone in hand. "With Grinder and Pinky, well protected and heading back to the estate. Piston and Pepper are escorting them."

I nod, mind whirling, sorting through all the fragments

of revelation that don't remotely add up. "Would you let Coda know we need a new trail?"

"Do you have any idea how far she could have gone?" Rought asks, already texting. "Can you ... sense that?"

I shake my head. "I have no idea."

He nods. "Rath's called in more of the Outcast crew, widening our patrol area."

"She's oddly powerful," I murmur thoughtfully.

"I got that." Rought rubs his chest. Bellamy hit him hard with that malignant curse.

"I should look at that," I say.

He smirks at me. "It will barely bruise. But I'll happily strip down for you later."

Still sprawled at our feet, Reck huffs dismissively.

Both of us turn our attention on him.

"You're a piece of fucking work," Rought snarls.

"I'm not the bad guy here," Reck croaks.

Rought leans over, teeth bared in a clear challenge. "We're going to have words about your fucking Authority agents, who I had to run off Zaya's estate. And if I'm not happy with those words, I'm going to beat the fuck out of you."

Reck appears completely confused by his brother's vitriol, just for a moment. Then his gaze flicks to me, and his expression hardens, crystalizing into a pure loathing. "You just let her go." His words come out mangled through his still-healing throat.

"Don't interfere next time," I say coolly.

He snorts, then coughs. "I can't stand the chatter."

I eye the ashes that have replaced the pool of Reck's blood. Even looking for it deliberately, I see no trace of the essence Bellamy used to fuel her teleportation spell. And the way she screamed ...

Reck props himself up on one hand, following my gaze with a frown. "She ... immolated herself? Just to get away from us?"

"The Authority has no jurisdiction over anything having to do with the Conduit," I say.

"What?"

"There is no 'us.' "

Reck flinches as if I've slapped him. But he quickly recovers, baring his teeth in a nasty grin as he slowly stands. "Keep fucking around in my business and you're going to have to deal with me."

Rought shifts as if to step between us, then checks himself.

"No," I say. "You're going to have to deal with me. Run that past your superiors and see where it gets you, Reck."

He opens his mouth to continue arguing, but I turn my back on him and walk away. Rought lingers behind for a moment, but I don't bother trying to hear what else passes between the brothers. Instead, I pull my phone out of my bag to fill Coda in on the new info we've stumbled upon. Stumbled through?

My first month of being the Conduit — the most powerful awry in the fucking world, according to a sneering Reck — isn't going particularly smoothly. And I don't have anyone to blame but myself, and the weird delay I'm operating within.

I still have all the same people to protect. Plus the mystery of my aunt's death, even though technically I'm supposed to simply move forward from that without much ado. And now I've got a dire awry to quell — a designation that is completely unknown to me and therefore capable of even more chaos than a normal awry.

Though 'normal' and 'awry' really shouldn't be used in the same sentence.

I TEXT CODA AS I WANDER OUT OF THE HOTEL lobby without paying much attention to my surroundings. It's not like anyone can sneak up on me these days, even when I'm distracted. Beyond all the other revelations of the last ten minutes, all of which I dutifully report to Coda, the way that Bellamy reaches for and twists essence is still bothering me. It's an entirely internal nagging, but it's verging on a … *knowing*.

I pause, looking up from my phone and finding myself on the edge of a small parking lot at the side of the hotel.

My aunt would get obsessed about things too. Bits of history or some essence theory, and she'd lock herself away in her tower …

Dire mages are pure destruction incarnate. At least for the short time they wield power without self-combusting or being taken down by a stronger essence-wielder. Or, more likely, a collective of essence-wielders. But I've never come face-to-face with one and not had them turn away, abruptly and definitively, just at the sight of my eyes.

A dire awry, though …

Bellamy has restricted her power by only drawing it from her own blood or the life force of others …

My phone buzzes in my hand.

I've gotten distracted again. In the middle of a fucking thought. Whirling the problem, the quandary that is Bellamy around in my mind.

Why didn't I intercede earlier?

Was I thrown by seeing Bellamy wearing my face and attempting to fuck Reck?

Was it the reveal of her awry designation, or her true face and blood-tie claims?

No. When I need to move, when I need to intercede, I always do. Without hesitation and even without a prompting from the universe. But I didn't move this time. I asked questions.

I never ask questions.

I've also never had a knowing sneak up on me as it did with Precious, even though I also *know* I wasn't supposed to intercede in that moment at the cafe. I've done lots of things seemingly on a whim, like traveling to Tokyo three months before being called to rescue Kiki and the other young shifters from a trafficking ring.

But I'm the Conduit now ... and my aunt used to get obsessed about things as well. Maybe there's a lead-up to a full knowing, or a sensitivity that builds —

The two Authority agents formerly stationed at the entrance to the estate, Clara Wilson and Brett Shaw, are parked next to the truck that I thought Rought parked outside the Nail Bar salon. Someone apparently moved it while we were in the hotel, or while we were walking in this direction.

Maybe Grinder and Pinky dropped it off when they picked up DeVille and Precious?

I look down at my phone to find a text message from Coda. The first is an acknowledgment of the update I sent.

>*Got most of that through your and the baby girl's phones.*

Then, a moment later,

>*The kids are back.*

Their eyes fixed on me, the Authority agents slowly exit their hulking SUV. There's an identical vehicle parked a few lanes over, farther away from the hotel. Otherwise the lot is mostly empty. Presumably the matching vehicle is Reck's.

Is Reck staying at the hotel? And if so, why? Why not stay with his family at the main pack house? Where does he normally live?

Right.

None of that is my business.

The Authority agents flash their badges at me in perfect unison. As if they've practiced the move. It would be adorable if they weren't suit-swathed serial killers.

I have a hazy recollection of already proving my diplomatic immunity to some Authority agent in the last seventy-two hours, so these two shouldn't be attempting to approach me at all. But then, they shouldn't have been parked on the edge of my estate either. Based on Rought's reaction, I have Reck to thank for that illegal surveillance.

"Ms. Gage?" Wilson loosely clasps her hands in front of her. It's combat mage shorthand for 'I come in peace' — as if I didn't already know she keeps her wand, through which she channels essence, up her sleeve. "We'd appreciate a moment of your time."

Shaw, shoulder to shoulder with his partner, stuffs his hands in the pockets of his pants, rucking up his suit jacket and slumping slightly to seem more casual, more approachable. As if he didn't try to shoot me and the teens under my protection last night.

I have the weirdest urge to put both of them in their place.

It's completely childish of me because I don't wield power like that. It's not my place to punish people for sheer stupidity. I simply step in when the universe directs me to do so.

Unless I'm rescuing a pastel-rainbow-haired young awry from asshole bikers. Then I apparently do a bit of fate-twisting all on my own. And pay for it.

"Yeah," Shaw says, grinning widely and laying on some accent — New England, maybe — that I didn't catch before. Presumably because I've simply ignored him every other time he's spoken. "We can be friends, right?"

Energy shifts behind me, and though I'm expecting Rought and maybe Reck, it's Cayley and Doc Z who step around the building, moving with that almost lazy shifter swiftness until they're flanking me.

Doc Z is in her full Outcast cut. Strawberry-blond hair pulled back in a sleek ponytail, generous curves swathed in leather. Cayley's wearing her envy-inducing leather jacket with all its kinky merit badges. I catch sight of the large badge on her shoulder, taking a moment to discern the intricate text-based design. *Fuck the Authority*. It looks brand new.

I wouldn't mind that printed on an oversized hoodie, and I never wear printed clothing. I'm also supposed to maintain a certain level of neutrality, so ...

"Ugh," Cay says, curling her lip at the Authority agents. "There goes my appetite."

Shaw narrows his eyes, shoulders tensing. "This has nothing to do with you, kitsune." He uses Cay's beast designation like it's an insult. Which is an odd take for another canine shifter.

Cay huffs, then makes a show of angling her body toward me — thereby dismissing the agents. "We've been tasked to pick up dinner."

"And me?" I ask, slightly amused. Grinder, or maybe

Rath, assigned Cay to watch over me. Though it's possible that's more for the Outcast MC's safety than my own. I'm still not certain that Cay is officially patched to the club, as she doesn't wear the cut. Though the Outcast is her pack alpha, maybe the kitsune is more valuable to the Outcast as a freelancer.

"Any time, any place," Cay all but purrs. "Just give me a wink, and I'll make it worth your while. Or, more accurately, worth your wild. Emphasis on the wild."

"I'm completely certain I couldn't handle you, Cay," I say, laughing at her wordplay.

Doc Z breaks her stoic silence, though not her focus on the Authority agents, to murmur to me, "The Outcast has called a meeting with his lieutenants. Rath pulled me off patrol, so I circled around to meet up with you."

Rought, Rath, and Grinder are all Outcast lieutenants, but I don't know how many others there might be.

My phone buzzes with a text. It's from Rought.

>*Got called in. Surprised it took this long. I'll meet you back at the estate? Text me if you need anything.*

"We discussed me not needing a bodyguard, right?" I ask rhetorically.

Cay and Doc Z both ignore me.

As expected.

Not bothering to argue my point, since getting back to the estate to check on Precious and waiting for the next Bellamy sighting is where I should be focused, I start toward Rought's truck.

"We would all benefit from a conversation," Wilson says. Her hands are no longer folded in front of her, but she hasn't pulled her wand yet. Her gaze flicks between me and the two Outcast shifters. "All of us."

"Is that a threat?" Cay asks, almost jovially. "Because I'd love a reason to kick your ass over the border."

"You don't have that kind of authorization, bitch." Shaw's already ruddy cheeks flush. "Just because you occasionally ride Guerra's dick doesn't mean —"

"That's not a thing," Cay says quickly, glancing at me.

"None of my business," I say steadily, though I'm not sure which Guerra is being referred to. Reck, most likely, since Shaw is his agent.

Wilson throws Shaw a quelling look. Her gaze is still cold, deadened, but apparently she's not so willing to ignore what little bit of policy the Authority actually follows. Specifically, that its agents can't operate in claimed territory — in this case, Outcast territory — without oversight by the local powers.

Cay might not be patched into the Club, but Doc Z is.

It's an easy guess that the agents are using Reck's familial connections to the Outcast as a loophole and following his orders to surveil me.

"Ms. Gage." Wilson tries again as I reach for the driver's-side door handle of the truck.

Energy shifts around me. I pause, just for a moment, to look around the parking lot.

Strands of life force are suddenly woven all around me, threading through and around Cay and Doc Z, then to a lesser degree around Wilson and Shaw.

I focus on the Authority agents.

They instantly scramble back from me, reaching for weapons. Their lines of fate are blunted. Sickly, even. And short —

Cay steps in front of me, yanking the truck door open, then practically picking me up and tossing me into the cab. She climbs into the truck after me, forcing me farther over on the seat and wedging me against Doc Z, who has somehow already entered on the passenger side.

Shifters just move that fast, especially while I'm distracted.

I blink a few times, trying to clear my sight, but the lines of Cay's and Doc Z's life force are abundant, distractingly filling the cab of the truck.

"Don't test me, assholes," Cay snarls out the door right before she slams it shut and presses the start button. The keys must be somewhere in the console.

Wilson has her phone to her ear. Her deadened gaze is riveted to us as Cay hits the accelerator and peels out of the parking lot.

Doc Z throws her arm across my chest. "Slow the fuck down, Cay!"

"I'm ready to tear their throats out," Cay seethes, clenching the steering wheel as she speeds up the main road away from the motel. "Would you prefer that?"

"That would be ... messy," Doc Z says cautiously, lowering her arm. Her gaze is fixed to the side-view mirror.

"Exactly!" Cay snaps.

Silence falls in the cab. I should probably be angry at being moved without permission, but I'm still a little discombobulated.

Plus, I'm used to being suddenly moved, to a certain extent. Though usually it's the universe doing the moving. The energy roiling off Cay gradually quiets. Doc Z is as steady as ever, though she shifts her attention from the side mirror to the back window.

I blink away the last of the steadily fading threads twined around us. I experienced a similar visual overlay, for lack of a better way to put it, when walking through

Cannon Beach with Grinder. I'm not certain that it means anything at all. Other than how much I need a good nap.

"So we aren't picking up dinner?" I ask.

"Fuck!" Cay shouts.

"We'll get it delivered," Doc Z says mildly.

"It'll be cold," Cay grumbles.

"They aren't following us." Doc Z shifts, facing forward again.

I laugh. "They know where I live."

Neither of the shifters finds me amusing.

I remember to send a text back to Rought, recognizing that checking in, that communication, is something regular people do when in a relationship. As new as all of this is for me, if not for him.

Heading back to the estate.

Then I text Coda. *Bellamy?*

Coda sends me a series of icons that I can't decipher except that I think it might be the hacker's version of, *I'm on it, fuck the fuck off.*

Cay glances down at my phone, then up at the road, worrying her lip. "So ... it's not a thing?" she asks tentatively. "That I used to fuck Reck? On occasion."

"It's not a thing," I say, ignoring a pinch of something in my gut. I'm probably just hungry. Breakfast might have turned into early lunch, but getting antsy partway through meant I missed out on most of it.

"But all three of the brothers ..." Doc Z murmurs quietly. "All three are your mates?"

I let that question linger between us for a moment, but not because I'm uncomfortable or upset. I'm not certain what claims might be pending or what expectations come with —

"Because ..." Doc Z rushes to fill the silence. "I'm ... I've fucked Rath. And I thought ... I thought ..."

"Okay." My stomach really sours now. I'm an adult. I'm not possessive. Or jealous. Though I've never had a committed relationship, or any sort of relationship, for that matter. "That's not my business either."

"So ... you're not claiming them?" Cay asks. "You'd be fine with Rath fucking Zephyr?"

"Hey," Doc Z huffs. "Don't put yourself outside of this, Cay."

The kitsune shifter shrugs. "I didn't follow Reck across the continent, then pledge the Outcast when I could have become a snooty, rich-as-fuck surgeon —"

"None of this is my business," I say sharply. Both Cay and Doc Z flinch away from me. "I've had something stolen from me, stripped from me. And I didn't even know it. All four of us have. I don't ... I don't judge anything that has happened in the in-between. And I can't predict what will happen moving forward."

Cay shares a glance with Doc Z over my head. Then they let the subject drop.

We drive in silence for easily ten minutes, until the edge of the estate comes into view. I finally turn toward Doc Z, facing the confrontation I've managed to avoid all day.

Coward that I am, I never have to deal with the aftermath of my actions. Other than occasionally dying, of course.

"I'm sorry about Kris," I say, steady and firm. "I should have ... I made a choice, and it ended with her death."

"I got your note," Doc Z says, swallowing whatever emotion — sadness, anger, grief, disbelief — seems as if it wants to clog her throat. "I didn't understand it until a few hours ago."

It takes me a moment to remember the note I left Doc in the motel. A thank you for the mage energy brews she'd given me, which twisted into a *knowing*, channeled through me but not for me to necessarily understand.

"Choice, not fate, not love or devotion, twists the path," Doc murmurs as she tugs a crumpled piece of paper from her jacket pocket and smooths it over her knee. *"And not always in the way intended."* Head bowed, she takes a deep, shaky breath. "You tried to take Kris with you, when you ran with Precious and DeVille. I knew then. I could feel it, instantly. A heavy doom weighted in my heart. I tried to twist the path back, by bringing her to you … but Kris made her own choices."

"Bellamy made those choices," I say.

Doc Z nods, then carefully folds the note and tucks it back in her pocket.

Cay pulls onto the estate drive.

We remain quiet all the way into the house, stuck in our own heads. And I don't think about the oddity, the weird synergy, of being flanked by these two women, and of the three brothers we're all linked to.

One for each of us … that would be the more generally acceptable sexual pairing.

If all three didn't belong to me.

<h1 style="text-align:center">SEVEN</h1>

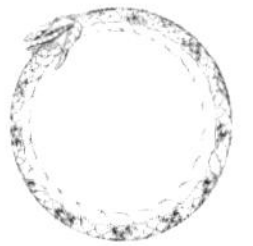

ROUGHT

I WAIT TO BLEND THE MILKSHAKES UNTIL I HEAR Zaya's footfalls on the stairs. She's been upstairs checking on Presh and Deville in that quiet way of hers, trying to not hover or even impose. Even though all the shifters who've taken over her home have done so completely uninvited.

Cay and Doc Z have gone back to town, but Rath is still here, having locked himself away in Disa's tower office, scouring the books there for who-the-fuck-knows-what while running patrols via his phone. Despite the ongoing tension between the two of them — they didn't acknowledge each other even once over dinner earlier — Zaya hasn't outright banished him from the estate.

On the other hand, Reck and his Authority grunts have gone radio silent. Neither the Outcast network nor Coda has picked up Bellamy's trail. There's a chance that the dire awry claiming kinship with the Guerra siblings might have actually managed to off herself with that teleportation spell.

Though Precious is the only one among us siblings giving any consideration to Bellamy's claims.

Not that I don't believe it. Especially since Zaya hasn't outright denied it, and I'm fairly certain my soul-bound mate would know. Know and want to protect us, both from Bellamy and from doing something we might regret to one of our own. I just don't give a fuck.

Zaya's reserve is new. This keeping her distance from everyone but Precious — and even then, I catch the beat of hesitation any time my sister reaches for her. Though she was quiet for the first few months we knew each other, still healing from the trauma of witnessing her mother's murder, Zaya Gage was always full of laughter and light. Forthright, sarcastic, she dominated me and my brothers with a mere look. Then she would soothe our unmanifested inner beasts with a playful quirk of her lips or a brush of her fingers against our own.

This Zaya is remote. And I already know that's not out of self-preservation. She holds herself back from fear of what she can do. And though watching her do that hurts, aching through that half-healed wound still lodged deeply in my chest, in my soul, I understand.

I understand what it's like to be more powerful than everyone else.

The violet of Zaya's eyes is new as well. Even I have to steel myself when those eyes shift and I'm suddenly caught in her otherworldly secondary gaze. The weight of the ancient power she now wields aches in my bones even when not directed toward me. She wears sunglasses near constantly, though that does nothing to hide the sheer power that radiates from her. Power, energy, that I don't think has anything to do with the essence-artifact necklace she now wears.

Hence Zaya hovering in doorways to check on the still-healing DeVille and Presh instead of stepping easily into the room with them. Hence the careful way she avoids accidental touch. Hence not pushing back at Rath as much as she might have done before. Though I don't really remember them ever being at odds enough to warrant more than playful teasing from Zaya to keep him focused on the bigger picture, rather than overwhelmed by the minute details.

I've never had a problem with focus, with seeing the grand scale. Not from the moment I met Zaya and understood my place in the world. More so even after the gryphon manifested.

That energy that continuously radiates from Zaya shifts when she's partway down the stairs, as if her attention has turned toward me. Her essence, the fundamental core of her being, has been reaching for me like that since she allowed herself to believe the truth of our pasts, as captured in Mack's photographs. I felt that same energy brush against me when I brought Precious to the property for the first time, pulling me out of the car and all the way to the house, where I barely stopped myself from crushing my lips to hers on the patio.

At the time, that tentative touch of Zaya's essence hurt. Not physically, but as if it ripped open that soul-deep wound within me. Because she was unsure of her welcome, is unsure. After our kiss and throughout the day, during which we've been annoyingly pulled apart by outside sources — and by fucking Reck, fucking, fucking Reck — I've just accepted that tentativeness as my soul-bound mate trying to find her way back to me.

My own disconcertion ... or sense of displacement,

maybe ... eases each time I touch the small of Zaya's back or brush my fingers against her hand.

Maybe we're already slowly re-creating those threads that she says are missing between us.

Zaya slips almost silently down the corridor leading to the kitchen, her questioning smile widening as she lays eyes on me.

Okay, let's be real. When she lays eyes on the milkshakes churning in the blender.

"Is there enough for two?" she asks.

"Always," I say, keeping my body language sedate and nonthreatening even while barely stopping myself from lunging over the counter, sweeping her into my arms, and blurting all the declarations that want to fall from my lips every time I catch sight of her.

I'm way out of my comfort zone. Zaya and I just fit together all throughout our childhoods and our teenage years. I didn't have to figure out what to say or do ahead of time. We simply experienced each moment together.

She crosses around the counter into the kitchen, head tilting back to keep meeting me eye to eye. My beast shifts inside me, pressing forward to gaze out of my eyes. The gryphon is utterly fucking possessive and has absolutely no interest in hiding that from our newly found mate.

That's new as well. Another point of disconcertion. The beast being so present. But I keep my body relaxed, and I don't fight it.

Our mate is wearing one of those sweaters that drapes across her shoulders, exposing her collarbone. The beast likes the bare expanse of her long neck. It likes that she looks us in the eye. And that sometimes we can see the section of the universe from which our souls were carved in that gaze.

But while that visual might also be new, the connection isn't. For me, it's still deeply cemented, woven through every breath I've taken since I first saw nine-year-old Zaya. Every breath I tried not to take when I thought I lost her.

The blender goes quiet.

We've just been staring at each other, suspended in this moment. And I don't give a fuck if that makes me some sort of lovelorn sap, because Zaya is staring right back.

"What flavor?"

The rasp in her voice shivers over me, taking my half-hard cock — its perpetual state when I'm around Zaya — to fully erect. Some of that might be a side effect of all her power, all her essence, now being focused solely on me. Or it's our severed souls brushing up against each other, seeking purchase? Those threads that Zaya says are missing between us.

"Double chocolate," I say, managing to ignore my compressed cock and thankful I'm wearing jeans with a bit of stretch rather than sweat pants. I flip up the sound baffle on the blender, pouring our shakes into the waiting, previously chilled glasses. "I added chilled hot fudge sauce to your dark chocolate ice cream."

"Yum," Zaya says. Then, indicating the blender, "Fancy."

"It was still in the box in the cupboard," I say, pouring the second glass. "When did Disa get the kitchen renovated? I don't think even half these appliances have been used. The counter configuration is new, and at least one wall has been removed."

A thicker clump of melted ice cream slides over the rim of the blender jar, causing the milkshake to overflow. I set down the jar, reaching for a tea towel to —

Zaya leans forward and licks the oozing, creamy chocolate ice cream up the side of the glass. More overflows the rim, and her pink tongue darts out — twice more — to stop the flow.

I'm utterly mesmerized, clenching the tea towel in one hand as if a scrap of fabric has any chance of anchoring me. My balls tighten so abruptly I nearly fucking come in my fucking jeans.

Zaya, still not touching the glass with more than her mouth, takes a long, slow sip of the milkshake. "I guess I've claimed this glass now?" she says, laughing quietly, flicking her gaze up to meet mine for a brief moment before returning it to the milkshake. She runs her tongue around the rim, clearing every errant drip. "Tasty."

I don't answer. I can't fucking answer. All the fucking blood that should be circulating through my brain, fueling higher functions like speech, has diverted into my ridiculously hard cock.

I attempt to keep it, to keep all of this under control.

The atmosphere doesn't help. The low lighting in the kitchen. The blankets I've already thrown over the sectional couch in the TV niche in the adjacent family room. A couch that's more than big enough, with a few cushions removed, for me to fuck Zaya properly, the two of us stretched out over and tangled together on it.

I've been living a half-life. My cock only stirring when I reached for it in the lonely dark, the stale nothingness, the void that stretched within and without me since losing Zaya. Jerking off to memories that wouldn't fade.

Zaya glances at me, brow pursed adorably in an unvoiced question.

I let my head fall back, groaning slightly.

"Is everything ..." She inhales sharply.

I risk peeking at her.

She's staring at my straining erection. Fixedly. Then she tongues the corner of her fucking mouth. Maybe licking off a remnant of the milkshake, but ...

"Looking at it isn't going to help," I mutter.

Zaya's eyes shoot up to mine.

And thank fuck, there's nothing wary or fucking tentative in that look.

A playful, knowing smile quirks the edges of Zaya's lush lips. Still holding my gaze, she reaches over, picks up her milkshake, and takes a large sip, easily draining a third of it. Then, like an utter brat, she tops her glass up with the remaining milkshake in the blender.

"It's like that, is it?" My voice rasps with suppressed desire, though Zaya's playfulness actually eases the intensity literally grabbing me by the balls.

"Most definitely." She flashes a grin my way, settling her hip against the counter to take in the space around us. "I'm not certain when Disa renovated. Nor why."

Right. I was talking about the kitchen. "These used to be multiple rooms," I say, reaching for my own milkshake.

"The rest of the house hasn't been touched."

That's voiced with a hint of a question, though it's more a snag in her energy than anything uttered out loud.

Zaya doesn't remember the house. Not well, at any rate.

My chest pinches. For her, for us. Ignoring it, I sip my shake. Despite my still-jutting erection, I lean deliberately back against the counter, stretching my legs out. Open, relaxed, easy. Steady and true, for my mate. "And the furniture isn't ..."

"Dusty and old?"

I laugh. Nothing was ever dusty in Disa's house, though I suspect it was Ingrid's magecraft that kept it that way. But it was as far from modern as a house with running water and electricity could get. On the North American continent, at least.

"Was it always like that?" Zaya asks quietly, still looking at the open-concept great room instead of at me. "Between us?"

Then, just in case I've missed her meaning — and I haven't — she reaches to the side and, almost gently, cups my still-erect cock. I slide closer along the counter so she doesn't have to reach quite so far. Understanding that despite her hand placement, Zaya isn't coming on to me. She's figuring a fuck-load of things out. But still, I need to be closer to her.

"We were just kids together," I say carefully, drawing in the subtle wild-mint-and-creamy-vanilla scent of her that has nothing to do with her shampoo or creams. I know I need to be utterly honest. Always, but especially in this moment with her hand resting lightly over my denim-bound cock. Her trust is woven through that gesture and the question.

I'd love to just say yes, then press Zaya back over the counter and eat her out until she's screaming my name, weak limbed and utterly satisfied. But a half-truth is not what she needs. Not what either of us needs. "So at first, no ... just inseparable, enough to bother our caretakers."

"Then ...?"

"Then my cock started getting hard around you."

She laughs quietly, taking a tiny sip of her shake. "And ..."

"You wanted kisses."

"Then cuddles?"

"Yes." I can feel my heart beating. It's still steady, but each beat feels deliberate, intent.

"Then ..." She looks up at me, deliberately catching my

gaze. Those violet eyes that practically weep with power rake over my face, memorizing me, taking me into her. "We figured out how to make each other come?"

I laugh, pleased it doesn't come out at all shaky. "We figured out if we kissed and cuddled ... vigorously ... that it felt really, really good, and I had to change my shorts."

She laughs, utterly delighted.

That joy aches through my chest, pained in the absolute best way. "We mostly did a lot of that ... until we figured out how to sneak away long enough to remove clothing and pleasure each other deliberately."

She blinks up at me for a long moment, perhaps absorbing the picture of a past I've tried to present as playfully as possible.

I lean forward slowly until I'm close enough to press my forehead gently against hers. "Your milkshake is melting."

Her gaze flicks to my lips. Her hand tightens around my cock. "It tastes good that way too."

I wait, perfectly ready to shift in whatever direction Zaya wants to go. I can't imagine how fucking overwhelmed she must be, but I'm also so fucking thankful for Mack and his photographs. The younger Zaya might have taken anything I brought to her on pure faith, any scenario I spun, any game I wanted to play. But adult Zaya — both the fixer who roved the globe helping some people, destroying others, and collecting favors along the way, and now the Conduit ... that Zaya isn't going to trust so easily.

Not even me.

Not without those threads that Zaya expected to see connecting her to her soul-bound mate.

I can see it in her interactions with Rath. Other than at dinner tonight, they can't be in the same room without sniping at each other. Rath, to my senses, clearly regrets every fucked-up thing he says. Those words, demands, spoken out of the unfettered fear of losing Zaya again. All three of us already know what that feels like. And all the while, Zaya collects each stupid demand my brother makes, building a shield from them to be used against him.

Then there's her almost painful indifference to Reck. Not that I'm currently a fan of my eldest half-brother. My own hero worship first fizzled when he abandoned us for the Authority. Then that admiration completely died when I uncovered his role in the death of our soul-bound mate.

Her apparent death.

Zaya releases my cock, tentatively touching my face instead. "Rought ..."

"I'm fine," I croak. "Sorry. I'm here. I'm fine. I'm never leaving you again."

"You saw me die," she says, as if she can read my mind. Or sense my thoughts. Maybe she can. "You said you were half-dead yourself."

"I should have fucking crawled to your grave on shattered bones and with my fucking soul shredded," I snarl, still so fucking pissed at myself. "I should have —"

"Gages are cremated," she says, all matter-of-fact about it. "So ... I suppose you could have stalked my body, then immolated yourself alongside it."

"That's the plan," I growl, catching her gaze and holding it, even though I know she's trying to lighten the mood.

She opens her mouth as if to protest, then just shakes her head at the promise she sees, maybe even feels, etched across my face.

"Milkshakes," she murmurs, keeping us focused on the now. "And ..." She tilts her head toward the TV niche. "A movie?"

"If you're not too tired," I say gruffly, not quite able to bounce back to pure levity so quickly. Even though I was the one to set the playful tone first, with the milkshake and the movie. I was the one who said I would exist in the now with her, utterly fucking contented.

"I'm not." She takes my hand and tugs me toward the couch. "Coda finally collapsed, creeping up on forty-eight hours without sleep according to Gigi. If Bellamy is in the country, she's shielding herself better than ... expected."

"Dire awry ..." I murmur, setting my milkshake down on the coffee table and reaching for the blanket draped over the back of the sectional.

"Apparently," Zaya says sourly, settling on the couch and curling her legs underneath her. She's still clutching her milkshake. "She can't get to Presh on the estate, though. And there's a good chance that teleportation spell knocked her right out. She doesn't wield her magic properly."

I shake my head at her, sitting down next to her and drawing the blanket over both our laps.

"What? It might be important," Zaya protests.

"Bellamy is a raging psycho."

"Or ... she's a tool. Meant for fine crafting but being wielded like a blunt machete."

I snort.

Zaya slaps me on the arm. "You know what I'm trying to say."

A tiny missing section of our shared past, our soul connection — or maybe that's what a minute shift in the universe feels like — settles on my chest. Because this is my Zaya ... my Zaya ... here with me.

I reach for her without checking myself, my reaction, and thankfully she sweetly snuggles against my chest, under my arm. Had she not, I don't think I could have stopped myself from hauling her into my lap, kissing her until she melted into me, then fucking her hard right here and now.

"It was never like this," I whisper to her, tucking the blanket around her legs. "Never quite as intense."

"That's okay, right?"

"It's ... perfect."

In an effort to keep it easy between us, I reach for the remote, pulling up the movies I've already queued so Zaya can pick one.

"I was thinking ..."

I glance over at Zaya, who's holding her now-empty glass against her chest while hungrily eyeing my milkshake currently melting on the coffee table.

I laugh, grabbing my glass and offering it to her. She grins at me, not bothering to even play at protesting the exchange when I take her empty glass from her.

"You were thinking about my milkshake?"

She laughs. "No. Instead of a movie, I thought ... you could tell me something I don't know ... not ... not anything from the photos or how we ... got separated."

"I don't actually know that part," I say quietly. That conversation is the opposite of keeping it easy between us, keeping it in the now. I'll go there with Zaya, of course, but ...

"Not something that we shared previously, I mean. Not a memory of ... us. Just something that ..." Zaya looks at me, open but with a hint of tentativeness. "That's ... that's something people do, right? Exchange stories from their recent past that they ... think ... might ... help forge more intimacy?"

"I don't know," I say. "I've ... never done that."

"Me either."

"All right." I settle back on the couch, thinking but still

trying to hold on to some of the playfulness that keeps sparking up between us. "Like, what level of intimacy are we talking about? Do you have a story queued up for me?"

"What do you want to know?" She bites her lip, then covers whatever is going on in her head with a sip of milkshake.

I want everything, of course. But I suspect that will take a lifetime. And even if Zaya, in this current incarnation, and I don't know each other well yet? Even if we're missing the threads she needs to see, to feel, to agree that we're connected by the universe? I already know I want that lifetime.

"Tokyo," I say. "We almost crossed paths about eighteen months ago."

Zaya nods, slightly hesitant. "It's not ..."

"A good bedtime story?"

"I die. Muta gets pissy. The edges of it all are really hazy. That happens ..."

"When you die and come back?" My chest aches. Again. But this time, instead of ignoring it, I embrace it. I need all these parts of Zaya. I need to know that we would have found our way back to each other — always and forever, despite whatever fucking divine intervention tore us apart.

"Yes."

"I want it."

"It's yours."

"What can I give you?"

"The gryphon," she says without any of her earlier hesitation.

I swallow, my stomach abruptly hollow. "It's not ..."

"A good bedtime story?"

"No. And it will ... make you look at me differently."

She stills, just looking at me for a moment. I hold her gaze even though I want to shy away from the intensity of what she's asking, whether she knows that or not. Then she drinks the last of the shake, sets the glass on the coffee table, and turns, legs tucked under her, body partly propped up on the back of the couch. So she can keep watching me as I tell my tale.

I shift the blanket around, keeping it mostly on Zaya and propping a few more pillows behind her so she can lean back, taking a moment to settle everything roiling around inside me. She doesn't push or prompt me. She doesn't even smirk knowingly.

"I've never told anyone the full story before," I finally say, not certain why I need the disclaimer. "But Rath suspects some of it."

"Then you should pick another story in exchange," she says easily. "Because Cayley knows some of what I have to tell you about Tokyo. And Coda too."

My chest tightens with another of those emotionally borne pains that are everything I desperately want to feel in one tight tangle, everything I lost for thirteen years. I knew I loved Zaya as a friend, absolutely adored her and relished how it felt so simple to just be with her. To be her friend. To make her laugh. Only then, years later, to realize that I loved making her pant and gasp with pleasure even more. Still later, when I knew unequivocally that I was deeply in love with her. Friends and lovers, and wanting to bind myself to her forever in the shifter way with bites despite the soul bond that already existed between us.

But none of that love ever hurt like this before I lost her.

My voice is thin, a little ragged, but I force the words

nonetheless. I would endure more pain than this for Zaya. I have, actually. And I have no doubt that I will again.

"Our beasts all manifested late. Later than most shifters, who manifest in their mid to late teens …"

"Maybe the mythical needs more time to bake," Zaya says, grinning at me.

A bit of tension eases from me under that grin, under her attention. Maybe her own essence has settled — she's weary but not sleeping well. Yet.

I have plans to help her out with that — help her empty her mind enough to sleep — in any way she'll let me.

"Maybe …" I chuckle, settling my gaze on the empty milkshake-stained glasses on the coffee table. "I can't speak for Rath and Reck …"

"That's okay," she whispers. "I understand that … part of it all."

The part about being soul bound to multiple people, I think she means. The balance in those relationships. It's precarious right now between we three half-brothers. Rath will work his shit out, then Zaya and he will find some sort of equilibrium. But Reck … with Reck, I have to stop myself from interceding whenever he's anywhere near Zaya. Well, from interceding any more than I already have.

Ultimately, even as overwhelmed as she currently is, Zaya can handle Reck. And how she handles him is none of my business. It never was.

"For me …" I push through all the clamoring thoughts, trying to ease into the story that Zaya has asked of me. Though I'm certain she's just now getting an idea that what might have seemed a simple request — how I ended up with a gryphon for a beast — isn't. "I think … because we bite-bonded that summer, and then you died … I think it might have … damaged my connection to my beast. Or somehow put it into a sort of stasis. I'd been feeling the stirrings of the beast from around my birthday that year, and specifically whenever we were intimate."

"Hence the exchange of bites."

I glance at her. Her expression is open, interested. Engaged. She's leaning toward me with her right arm along the back of the couch, fingertips only inches from my shoulder. If I were to lean back …

I lean back. So she can touch me if she wants to, though I keep my head turned slightly away from her. For focus, not out of shame. At least that's what I tell myself.

"The gryphon went dormant," she prompts. "After you watched me die?"

"I didn't know the gryphon part then, at seventeen. But yes." I lean forward again, setting my elbows on my knees, hands clasped. But I force myself to shift slightly closer to Zaya. Now is not the time to shut down. I'm making too big a deal about all of this. I push through. "On your twenty-first birthday … I …" I rub my thumb over the scar on the meat of my thumb. "I decided I needed to … move on …"

"That was a long time to wait, Rought," Zaya says, like the fucking goddess she is. "Especially for a teenager."

I huff, then justify myself. Just a little. "The bite mark didn't fade. It silvered …" I open my palm toward her. "But it didn't blacken like a rejected bond would, and it didn't fade like a broken bond."

She leans forward just enough to take my hand, inspecting the bite mark but not touching it. Thankfully, because I already know that would be far too distracting.

"I was … severely hurt. It took me about six months to walk without assistance."

Zaya sighs, pained.

I don't give her space to interject though. I need to barrel forward now. "Rath will tell you that the only reason he was on his feet earlier was that the dragon saved his fucking life. Not quickly enough to save you as well, but …" I swallow that part of the story down. Zaya doesn't want to hear about that yet. "Anyway … I went to school, took online courses, got into the tech thing. I was already into cars."

"The gold Camaro coupe you restored," she murmurs with a hint of contentment. Maybe she's pleased that she already knows that little bit about me?

"Right." I take a breath. "I patched into the Outcast MC at eighteen. Too young, but I think my uncle, the Outcast, was worried. I figured out pretty quickly that I had to hide it. But he saw, I think. Or felt it, maybe. The void … the need to follow you into it … I … couldn't do that …"

"Of course not. For your family."

"No, Zaya." I look at her. "Because the bite mark hadn't faded. Everyone said it would fade in time. I waited, part of me desperately hoping it wouldn't. Part of me hoping to just be released from it. But Rath, Reck, they were convinced that …"

"I was dead. That was the logical conclusion."

I huff again. At her logic. It was never logical between us. It was friendship, then passion. A deep abiding love.

"I was … living in that void too," she confesses quietly. "Partly in it, maybe. But I didn't know it."

Grief shudders through me. I rest my bowed head in my hands and simply weather it. "That's done now," I croak.

"Yes," she echoes, as if testing out the idea. "That's done now."

I take a deep breath. I'm laboring the point, trying to come at it around the edges so I don't have to reveal the core. "I took off a couple of days before your twenty-first birthday, just got on my bike and rode south. Crossed the California border, tried to get arrested. Or better yet, beaten down or even killed, for some petty fucking shit ..."

"Unsuccessfully?" she asks playfully. "You weren't trying very hard."

I snort an involuntary laugh. "On your birthday, I sought out this underground shifter club on the outskirts of San Francisco, took every drug and drink offered to me. Then followed a girl ... a woman ... wolf shifter out back ..." I take a deep breath, glancing over to see if Zaya is still with me.

"Do you think I didn't have sex with anyone in the last thirteen years?" she says, matter-of-fact about it.

I blow out another breath, focusing on my hands again. On the bite mark. "I thought that if I could be intimate with someone, even just to get off ... I picked someone your opposite in every way, light-blond curly hair, deeply tanned skin. Tattoos. Brown eyes. She wanted to kiss, but I ... couldn't. But I could ... touch her. If I kept my eyes open. That was okay. She got off on my fingers, then dropped to her knees. And that was okay too. But I couldn't stay hard. She was ..." I laugh hollowly. "She was sweet about it. She blamed all the shit that was in my system and asked me back to her place to sober up. I can't even remember her name. Maybe I never knew it. I told her I'd get my bike and meet her around front. She left to tell her friends or go to the bathroom. I really have no idea."

I finally look over to meet Zaya's gaze. Not a hint of judgement in her eyes. "I'd heard the train coming. Even the light rail track they have in California has this buzz to it when the train is near. I took off my cut, left it with my bike. I climbed onto the tracks. They're above ground even through the less populated areas. I watched the train coming."

Still holding my gaze, Zaya takes a breath. I watch her chest rise, then fall.

"I ... those trains are automated, so I was careful to stay out of sensor range until it was too late. I ..."

My chest feels as though it's cracking open. Weirdly painful tears flood my eyes.

"I couldn't exist without you. I knew ... I knew you were waiting for me in the aether. That's why the bite hadn't faded." I take a shuddering breath. "I timed it perfectly ..."

Silence settles between us.

Zaya smooths her thumb over the bite mark on my hand. "And then ..."

"And then the gryphon tore through me, from me. And I woke up three days later on the beach, as close as I could get to the boundary wards keeping me from the Gage estate without alerting anyone."

Zaya reaches for me. And this time, I can't stop myself from pulling her into my arms, into my lap. She twines her arms around my neck, legs straddling mine.

"I knew then," I whisper into her neck. "Without a doubt, I knew you were still alive."

"Because the gryphon knew."

"Yeah." I press my face alongside hers, just breathing for a moment. "I picked myself up, walked the entire fucking way back to the main pack house, avoiding everyone. Got online and figured out what had happened. The gryphon fucking derailed that train. No one was badly injured, but there was a massive investigation. Even I couldn't find any uncompromised footage. Just a bright flare of essence whiting out the entire area, then flickering back on to the derailed train in all its crumpled glory."

Zaya presses her face into my neck, breathing me in. "And then ..."

I tighten my hold on her. "I started searching for you. I couldn't get anywhere fucking close to Disa, not that she would have answered my questions. But I could have —"

Zaya's fingers thread through my hair, and her mouth is on mine before I've even registered that's she shifted in my lap. The kiss is all encompassing, desperate. Her tongue in my mouth. Jaws, lips, all tense. Teeth almost biting.

Instantly hard again, I grab her hips and grind against her core. Too much clothing between us.

Zaya gasps into my mouth, then groans and melts into me. The kiss softens, easing into passion instead of being edged in terror. The terror of almost losing each other.

Even if Zaya doesn't remember our foundation, her body knows me. Trusts me to take care of her, to give her what she needs. That connection.

She tugs at my shirt, so I yank it off. Her mouth is on mine again the moment it's clear. Her hands are all over my chest, gripping my shoulders, as she grinds down on my cock.

The residual spell flare from Bellamy's curse — blackened lines radiating across my chest, muddling all my tattoos — retreats under Zaya's hands, dissipating under her touch. As if that lingering bit of foul essence can't stand even a brush of Zaya's heady power.

"Please ... please ..." Zaya whispers, sucking on my bottom lip.

I palm her breasts. She's not wearing a bra, maybe just a camisole. Her nipples are erect. I groan into her mouth.

Her essence snaps out, flooding the room, then twining

loosely around us. Her kisses and caresses become almost frenzied.

"What's happening?" she gasps, still trying to keep quiet though both of us would sense if anyone was near. Before I can articulate a response or try to slow us down, she adds, as if chastising herself, "What's happening doesn't fucking matter right now. I need your cock in me."

"Oh, fuck," I moan. "Is this ... too fast?"

"Am I currently coming on your cock?" she asks.

"Fuck, not yet."

"Then it's not too fast ..." Zaya reaches between us for the buttons of my jeans. Then she takes a shuddering breath and hesitates for a moment, meeting my eyes. "It's not too fast, is it? We can ... we can ..."

Her pupils are blown out, swallowing most of the violet of her eyes. Her lips are slightly swollen, flushed, from our fierce kisses.

Keeping my gaze locked to hers, I slide my hand up her thighs and under her skirt, which is already rucked up. With a gentle swipe of my talons against the sides, I tear off her underwear. The partial transformation of my fingernails is effortless, triggered with barely a thought, as if the gryphon is pressed against the insides of my skin as eager to touch, to fuck, Zaya as I am.

She laughs, breathless and relieved — and not at all concerned about me suddenly manifesting aspects of my beast. Then she shifts back to free my cock from my jeans.

"No underwear ..." She flashes a wicked grin at me.

I laugh, helpfully sliding my hips forward and leaning back so she has more room to maneuver on me.

Hand ringing my cock, holding me in place, Zaya rises on her knees —

Trying to slow us down just a bit, to savor the

moment, I slip my fingers between her legs, seeking her warmth, teasing through her wetness. She shudders, closing her eyes and groaning quietly as I rub her clit in light little circles.

"I haven't gone home yet," I murmur in answer to her question about my going commando, hoping my shop-worn callouses aren't too rough.

Something flashes in her eyes — and it might simply be the universe looking through her, just as the gryphon peers through me. With one hand still gripping my cock, she pins me by the neck against the couch with the other. "You aren't going anywhere."

Fuck me. My brain fucking melts. I'm already seriously fucking worried that I'm going to come too quickly, even though I jerked off after our morning make-out session.

Still teasing her clit, I raise my free hand, grinning in surrender. Because the only other option is to grab her hips and fucking impale her on my rigid fucking cock.

Zaya nods, perfectly serious.

Then she notches my waiting and willing cock into her entrance. With no other preamble. Bobbing her hips, she coats me with her wetness, takes me in inch by inch.

I would have happily eased into penetration. Teased her into coming on my fingers, then my tongue. But I'm also not saying no to anything Zaya wants, needs, from me.

I get that this isn't just sex.

It's primal, fundamental.

My soul-bound mate is claiming me. I'm already hers, but she needs to know it, feel it.

Zaya gets me fully seated within her, head lolling back to expose her neck as she pauses. Pauses and simply savors me buried deep inside her. I close my eyes for a moment, holding a groan and my climax at bay. Unable to watch her enjoying my cock without coming, without even a single full fucking stroke.

She slowly lifts herself up off me ... slowly, slowly sliding me out of her with a quiet groan. I chance a glance at my mate. Her head is still fallen back, chest thrust forward — eager nipples practically begging for my mouth.

I oblige, not bothering with trying to get her sweater off. Just shoving it up and yanking the camisole down to expose her tight, dark nipples, palming one and sucking on the other.

Zaya wraps her arms around my head, groaning and twisting her fingers through my hair. Then she fucking slams down on my cock.

Fuck, fuck.

Zaya grinds down. I glance to where we're joined, but happily — because the sight might actually do me in — her skirt covers us.

Zaya slides up me, quicker this time, then down. "Oh, fuck. Why ... why does this feel so good?"

"Condom," I gasp.

Angling her hips forward, she grinds against my base, bouncing on me shallowly.

Everything goes blurry around the edges.

I palm her face. "Zaya, love. Condom?"

"No," she gasps, violet eyes blinking open. "I don't ... I can't ... the Conduit ..." She blinks again, her expression clearing, forehead pinching.

But I get what she's saying. That isn't something we need to discuss right now. To keep her with me, because I'm already barreling toward the edge, I grasp her hips, find her clit with my thumb, and thrust up into her. Twice.

Zaya pins her hand around my neck again, shoving me back against the couch before she takes over, grinding into my hand while also gripping my cock in her warm, tight pussy.

"Fuck," I say through clenched teeth. "I'm going to come, my Marrow."

"I'm here," she gasps. "I'm here."

Her rhythm becomes erratic. Her hold on my neck tightens, then loosens completely as her forehead falls to my shoulder. As if she's lost control of her limbs, her body.

I vaguely hope I'm keeping pressure on her clit, because my balls tighten even further, pleasure prickles at the base of my spine, and then I'm fucking coming so hard my vision completely whites out.

Zaya buries her face and her shouted cry in my neck, shuddering and trembling, clenching tightly around my cock.

All her energy, all those twists of essence that have thickened around us, contract tightly. Chest to chest, that power from Zaya burrows through my skin, then expands.

I swear I feel all that essence fill the ever-present void, sealing over the mortal wound in my soul.

Zaya's tight pussy flutters around my still-rock-hard cock as she shudders against my chest, either riding residual shocks from her orgasm or tipping over a second time.

And all I can do in the moment is accept everything pouring from her, greedily clutch her to me, as I ejaculate again. Long, almost painful spurts. Even though I, too, have already come.

Both of us shout again, loudly. Though we've been trying to keep quiet out of deference to the sharp-eared shifters in the house.

Then Zaya collapses over me, limp and humming against my neck, completely content to just sprawl across me and breathe.

My heart is fucking beating its way out of my chest. I smooth my hand down her spine, opening my eyes to check on her.

Rath is hovering halfway into the family room.

His hair and skin are damp, as if he's come in from outside, maybe from patrolling grounds that don't need to be physically patrolled. His gaze is riveted to Zaya in my arms. His expression verges on desperate.

Zaya opens her eyes, tipping her head just enough to settle those purple orbs of blazing power on her untethered soul-bound mate.

I can actually see her power reflecting against the nearby windows.

As if the universe, peering through the Conduit, is interested in this moment.

In how Rath and the celestial dragon are going to react.

I run my hand down Zaya's spine again.

Rath's shoulders and his expression relax. He meets my gaze. Relieved. Then he steps back the way he must have entered, through the back patio doors. Presumably he was drawn to the house by all the energy, the press of essence that felt as if it bound Zaya and me together.

Perhaps even reforged our bond?

Zaya tips her head up, nose ghosting over my jaw as she easily dismisses Rath to whisper in my ear, "Again?"

I lift her off the couch, making sure my jeans are buttoned enough to not fall down while I carry her up the stairs and into her bed. With the door firmly closed and locked behind us.

The noise-canceling wards etched around Zaya's walls flare the moment after I throw my mate on the bed, yank off her skirt, and bury my face in her pussy. Gobbling up her gasps and moans, I lick up every drop of her sweet minty tang, all for myself.

EIGHT

ZAYA

THE FIRST HINTS OF SUNRISE HAVE LIGHTENED the gaps between the heavy drapes as I slowly surface from a deep, dreamless slumber. On my bed. In my bedroom. The estate is still and quiet around me. Even the simmer of the intersection point feels settled, content. I'm curled up on my side, facing the windows and tucked next to a warm, welcoming body.

Rought.

Our evening activities come back to me in a heady rush. My climbing into his lap. My pushing us past the kisses. The desperate need to connect to him after his confession that he had tried to kill himself, thinking I was waiting for him just beyond the veil.

But instead of being embarrassed or feeling hollow as I often do after a sexual encounter, I feel ... calm. Even ... happy? And maybe a little intoxicated.

I carefully roll over, blinking through the early-morning

dark that still shadows the bedroom to take in my lover's face. My soul-bound mate. Rought's expression is utterly relaxed, his breathing measured in sleep. He looks younger than thirty. The dark-blond hair long enough to curl at the ends falls wildly over his brow. He's mostly sprawled on his back, but curved slightly toward me. The arm nearest me is flung up over his head, resting along the headboard. One leg is splayed, foot hanging off the far side of the bed. His other knee is bent toward me as if he's just rolled away from holding me.

While I'm tangled in layered blankets, Rought is gloriously naked. Miles of naturally tan skin stretches over taut muscle, tattoos feathered — some of them literally — up his arms, his shoulders, kissing his neck.

I quash the urge to turn on the lights so I can take him all in, every minute detail.

The dense patch of curls around his softened cock is darker than his hair, and I suppress a quiet curl of desire and another sudden urge, this time to take him in my mouth and gently suck him to hardness.

I don't like giving blow jobs. That's really fucking intimate.

But ... how close could I get him to orgasm before he woke?

Okay. Being dick drunk is most definitely a thing.

Plus there's the matter of consent. Would I want to wake up on the verge of orgasm with Rought's tongue between my legs, lapping at my clit?

Desire pools between my legs, my nipples tighten, and I swear my aforementioned clit fucking twitches.

So ... that's a yes.

I laugh silently at myself, then carefully untangle my legs from the sheet and duvet that have been rearranged so they cover only me. I'm wearing a simple black silk night-gown with thin straps, which normally falls around midthigh though it's currently bunched around my hips.

Last night, Rought made me come twice more on his tongue, then pressed me to the bed and fucked me hard and fast before coming again himself. I can't remember the last time I came two or more times in succession, and even then that was mostly by my own hand or with the help of a shower wand. Sleep came easily after that release, even though I've never shared a bed with someone before.

We might have only been teens fooling around thirteen years ago, thinking we loved each other enough to try to bind ourselves together by exchanging bites. But it's becoming clear that the reason I can't remember ever really liking sex — other than when driven to it out of the sheer need to touch, to momentarily connect to another person — is because I can't remember all the years with my soul-bound mates.

My gaze rests on the partially curtained windows, recalling the items collected on the dark-wood windowsill. Items currently hidden from my sight. I know without asking Rought for clarification that those were, are, tokens of our friendship. Our love, plural. The broken bracelet, the jar of notes, and the handmade wooden box that I knew, even without a single memory of them, were from three separate people when I first tried to touch them.

No other trinkets are collected anywhere else in my rooms. So what else could they possibly be but gifts from my mates?

Except those gifts are now surrounded by that strange suffocating emptiness, felt when I first tried to examine them. Is that emptiness, that void, a side effect of our bonds being severed? Assuming that's even what happened. Or of my memories being wiped? Or maybe it's all a side effect of my dying that first time ...

Maybe I lost the soul bonds all on my own. Nothing nefarious about it. Just a tragic side effect of being Everlasting ...

Except if that were the case, the same would have happened to my aunt. She was Everlasting too. Did she have to renew her bonds with her chosen every time she died?

Of course, that line of thought brings up the ultimate unanswerable question ... does any Conduit ever truly die before the final time? Or do our bodies simply go into stasis until they are strong enough to once again house our souls?

The necklace now perpetually dangling around my neck feels heavy for a moment. Normally, I barely notice it. I wrap my hand around the cage of gold threads that encases the pink diamond. The essence contained in the diamond stretches, as if testing its boundaries. I know it's filled or fueled with my own essence, like some kind of extra storage or an extra battery ... or whatever is the best metaphor. Because my mortal body isn't strong enough to hold everything the universe needs me to hold, including the intersection point.

I slide my legs off the bed. I intended to close the curtains before slipping back in to snuggle and maybe even sleep. But now that's been overwritten by a pure need to check, to verify, whether I can now touch the tokens arrayed on the windowsill — now that I understand the connection to my three soul-bound mates.

A warm arm wraps across my ribs just below my breasts and gently tugs me back from leaving the bed.

I glance over my shoulder. My quiet laugh dies on my lips.

Because Rought isn't touching me.

Not with his hand, at least.

The arm that was flung over his head is stretched out across the bed toward me, yes. But his fingers — once again tipped with the sickle claws he manifested last night — are curled as if holding onto something ...

Open in slits, Rought's eyes blaze with a golden-tinged power. His features have sharpened, bones pressing against his skin. He's partially transformed?

He tugs me closer. Again. But still not touching me. Simply tightening his fingers around ... air ...

Not air. He's holding ... he's manipulating —

I blink, shocked and overwhelmed. All the essence blanketing the room comes into focus. Most of it is settled sleepily around both of us. Even Rought's complex, multi-layered twist of life force is currently gently twined around him, though a few of his threads stretch beyond the walls of the room. Likely his sibling bonds.

A thick rope of vibrant essence stretches between Rought and me, hooking into his rib cage right through the memorial anatomical heart tattoo etched across his actual beating heart. Sprigs of what I now know is wild mint and vanilla flowers radiate from the tattoo's valves and arteries — the scent of my essence.

Shimmering with power and sparkling with starlight, that bond is currently roped around my lower rib cage ... before then hooking into my heart ...

I curl my hand around the essence tie stretching between us. This is no ordinary thread that might form between us through extended intimacy.

That essence shifts under my hand, as if more energy is being channeled through it.

A fierce possessiveness pulses through my chest, fueled by a raging desire, and softened with ... adoration.

I can feel everything radiating from Rought.

It's overwhelming.

I inhale deeply, struggling to accept it, absorb it, because I'm not at all certain I can block it. I close my eyes for a moment, still holding the bond in my hand but trying to clear my eyesight, and my head.

The connection eases into a simmer of awareness.

I open my eyes.

Rought's eyes narrow, crinkling at the edges at my reactions. Smugly. Then he bares his teeth.

It isn't a smile.

This is the beast — the gryphon — who's awoken to drag me back to bed.

The gryphon who lassoed me with the bond.

All the unusual smugness, all that vehement possession, radiating through the connection — that's not Rought's either. At least not at this level of intensity.

I contemplate running, getting some space between us. An irrational response to any beast. But this connection, this revelation, is almost too much because ... because ...

"The soul bond," I whisper, needing to vocalize the realization, however quietly.

Energy shifted between Rought and me — new threads forged and anchored — when we made love, strengthening with every orgasm. Perhaps because of the trust and vulnerability inherent in the act of allowing someone to bring you to that pinnacle of pleasure.

But this bond, the bond the gryphon is holding, is otherworldly. This is our missing soul bond.

Or, more accurately, and assuming I'm actually managing to wrap my head around all of this ...

It's another soul bond.

I *know*. Just touching it, I *know*. This connection

couldn't have been easily taken from us. Not even through death. It's constructed out of the very energy that created the universe, that created our souls. The energy that creates our life force, our fate.

The gryphon controlling Rought's body abruptly lunges across the bed, grabbing me by the back of my neck and looming over me on his knees.

I relax into that hold, gazing up at him. I'm not prey. I cannot be dominated. But I relax so completely that he has to hold me aloft. I press my hand against his chest, laying my palm over the heart tattoo — over the anchor point of our soul bond. I hold his blazing golden gaze, not a hint of Rought's blue-green visible in those glowing orbs.

The gryphon, and therefore Rought himself, is a demigod. Not just a mythical beast. He wields too much power to be anything else. The beasts of his brothers and their ties to me — a goddess of sorts — are further evidence of that.

The gryphon stares back at me, fierce and determined.

Something cracks open deep in my chest — as if I've held all my need and desire and love walled off around my heart. It floods through my system with a weird, amped-up joy. I sob against the onslaught of my own emotions, my own acceptance. Just once.

"You held the bond?" I ask in a teary whisper.

"Mine," the gryphon rasps through not entirely human vocal cords. He raises his other hand, running the smooth back of a sickle claw up my neck, angling my head to give him all the access he wants. He tracks his nose across my skin, inhaling deeply.

My nipples tighten, almost painfully.

His ... his ... "Yours ..." I murmur. "Separate from Rought?"

He huffs, clearly not interested in exchanging words. "Yes. Mate."

Two soul bonds? One to the man and one to the beast? And the one between Rought and me was severed —

He hooks those claw-tipped fingers between my breasts, curling the sharp points carefully away from me. Then he shreds the front of my nightgown.

"Oh ... that's not —"

I'm shocked, apparently speechless, as he hooks my necklace in one finger, then tugs it around my neck so it hangs down my back instead. He shouldn't be able to touch it.

Still looming over me on his knees, he shifts his hold on the back of my neck, tugging my upper body into a deep arch to bring my breasts closer to his mouth. He licks around my left breast, then runs the flat of his hot, oddly rough tongue across my nipple.

A sharp spike of desire, verging on painful, rips through me. I moan, deep and needy. A noise I've never made in my life.

The gryphon switches breasts and repeats.

I twist my fingers through his hair, holding him with all my strength. Warmth pools between my legs. That raspy tongue does another pass over each breast.

I rub my thighs together, writhing against his hold. His grip tightens on me.

But I'm not fighting him.

"I want ... I want ..." I pant, feeling myself spiraling out of control. I was trying to figure out the bond, trying to focus, but my essence is now pouring out of me. Pouring through me, because I can feel the energy of the intersection point in the mix. I can feel it, but I can't seem to bring myself to stop it.

The gryphon tears the shredded nightgown from me, flinging it away as if it's offending him. He shoves me back on the bed, bends my knees and presses them open. Then he just stares down at my exposed and seriously needy pussy.

For way too fucking long.

I groan, wiggling against his firm hold as if I might entice him to just fuck me. "Rought —"

"No," the gryphon rumbles, still staring down at me as he slowly wraps his hand around his jutting cock and strokes it, almost experimentally. "Sleeping."

Oh, fuck. Okay. "That's ... maybe we should wake him before we go any further?"

The gryphon lunges over me, caging me in with his body, then lowering his face until his golden eyes are blazing into my soul. "You want gryphon instead?"

I blink, trying to think through the haze of desire ... does he mean ...? "I'm not fucking the gryphon," I say firmly.

The gryphon narrows his eyes, as if he's actually contemplating fully transforming and fucking me in his beast form.

I reach for the cock currently jabbing into my thigh rather forcefully.

The gryphon grumbles, lifting one hand to pin my arm back in place.

I quickly and firmly stroke his thick length, twisting my hand over the tip. Then I repeat that sequence. Every muscle in his body tenses as he freezes in place, hand still suspended.

Wiggling and shifting — while keeping him distracted by jerking him off — I manage to slide off the bed between his legs, just enough to get my mouth wrapped around the head of his cock.

His entire body jerks, nearly choking me. Then he snarls, holding himself completely still over me, head angled to watch me suck him off.

I'm so amped up that even though I really need two hands to hold him in this awkward position, I slip my fingers between my own legs, teasing my clit. My orgasm is right fucking there —

The gryphon abruptly yanks his cock out of my mouth and hand, grips my hips, and hauls me back up on the bed. He flips me, dragging me back into a kneeling position. Then, pinning his knees to the side of the bed to even up our heights, he fucking lifts me up into some sort of half-suspended downward-dog position — just my hands now planted on the bed. Then he licks my core from behind.

Licks me right from my clit and up, ending in a swirl around the pucker of my ass.

I shout, scrambling for handholds in the sheets.

He does it again. It's invasive. It's overwhelming. I've never had anyone do that, touch or lick me back there, and it's too intimate.

I open my mouth to tell him to stop.

The gryphon swirls his tongue over my clit again, then stuffs as much of his tongue into my entrance as he can, thrusting in and out.

His grip on my hips is punishing. All the blood not pulsing through my pussy is running to my head. I'm shaking, nerves on full alert even as my mind feels like mush.

He licks me again — the full flat of his tongue, no flicking or sucking — all the way from the top of my labia, over my clit, my entrance, and back to swirl up over my ass.

I fucking moan. Fucking wantonly. Like he's repro-grammed my brain and I …

"I want …" I pant, trying to get my forearms under me, my knees on the bed. "I want."

The gryphon lowers me as if he's actually going to listen. But then he curls over me with one hand still holding my hip, settles the other hand between my shoulder blades, and pins me to the bed.

I open my mouth to protest.

He thrusts into me from behind, fully sheathing himself.

I scream, only partially muffled by the bedding.

I don't intend to. I don't want to. I've never been a screamer, not in any situation. But it's torn from me.

The gryphon controlling Rought's body holds me down and fucks into me, pounding thrusts. It should hurt. It should be too much. But I take it, absorbing it. He bottoms out against my cervix, and I usually don't like that. But every inch of him going in and out of every inch of me is fucking glorious.

Because something else is shifting between us now. Beyond the primal claim that the gryphon is obviously enacting, and which I'm most uncharacteristically allowing.

All the essence that poured through me comes surging back now, doubled in intensity. Swollen, robust, as if my essence reached out and collected streams of extra energy — from the intersection point and from the gryphon.

That essence floods into me, filling me. The pink diamond that has fallen on the bed beside me blazes with it. The purple of my eyes is reflected from the walls, as it seemed to light up the clouds above the estate when I claimed the intersection point.

Absorbing every joule of that energy, I press down into

the bed with my hands and forearms. I arch my back against the gryphon's firm hold. He gives into my press, either ceding it willingly or unable to force me back down without hurting me.

I lift my head, realizing that we're reflected in the tall mirror on the back of the partially open closet door. I moan at the sight of the two of us. Rought all golden-skinned, taut muscle, and tattoos thrusting into me from behind. The golden gaze of the gryphon fixed to me, flicking between the mirror and down to where we're joined. And me on my hands and knees with the necklace swinging forward from my neck. My breasts, no matter that they're small, bounce with each thrust. And my eyes …

My eyes aren't my eyes anymore. Purple nebulas of sheer power practically swamp my face.

As if the universe is gazing through me and into this moment.

I press my hands and forearms against the bed, then start meeting the gryphon pounding into me from behind, thrust for thrust.

It quickly becomes too much to hold, all that energy, all this pleasure. Too much to contain. My body convulses with it — pleasure and pain crashing through me. That mind-altering combination crests, then tumbles over into sheer pleasure. My eyes close. I lose control of my limbs.

The gryphon snags me around the ribs, right where he held me with the soul bond, and pulls me back against his chest. He bites the junction where my neck meets my shoulder, but through the bliss I'm riding, I feel no pain.

Essence twists and snaps all around us — I'm feeding into him, and he into me.

He thrusts into me once more, stiffens, and stills. He

growls into my neck, into the bite. His hips stutter as he comes.

My heart pounds against my chest. My head feels light. And completely, blessedly empty.

The gryphon slowly withdraws his teeth from my shoulder. He hasn't broken the skin, though I might bruise. Then he holds me aloft, limp in his arms with his face pressed to my neck, even as his cock slowly softens inside me.

As if he can't bear to let me go.

I groan quietly in protest when he finally slides out of me, accompanied by a gush of come. But he just gathers me up into his arms, resettles us on the bed, and curls tightly around me.

Mate, he whispers in my mind. *Mine.*

I shiver from the press of that psychic touch, but I'm too fucking blissed out, too utterly content to worry about him apparently now having unfettered access to my mind.

We've fully bonded, I realize, with that immense exchange of essence. The demigod inhabiting my soul-bound mate must have telepathic abilities. Maybe fully realized only now, brought forth with the exchange of power, because he spoke out loud before, however begrudgingly.

"Mine." I voice my claim on him out loud, overwhelmingly possessive about a connection I never thought I'd have, never even dreamed of having. "Mate."

I understand that all of this — the soul bonds, the demigod mates — might simply be an extrapolation of being the Conduit. Of holding an intersection point. I understand that I'm still not really a person who is allowed desires and whims. Lovers. Anyone who I might place above my duty to the universe ... but ...

"My aunt didn't have soul-bound mates," I whisper.

Maybe my aunt's reality and everything she taught me, everything she made me become, doesn't hold true for me. Me, Zaya, as the Conduit now.

Maybe this moment is just for me to savor, to celebrate. A gift from a fickle and capricious universe.

The gryphon's chest rumbles behind me. It's not a purr. More of a rattling coo. But with that gentle comfort vibrating against my back, I'm asleep before I form another thought.

NINE

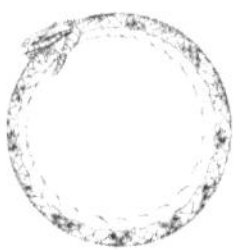

RATH

I wait until Rought gets Zaya behind the sound-barrier wards on her bedroom to sneak back into the house that I haven't actually been invited to enter. Walking the grounds in the middle of the night, soaking up the mist from the surf with the fog stirring around my feet, is like walking through a dream. Or a nightmare.

But each time the echoes of the past threaten to swallow me, I reach out for Zaya's energy. I can feel her from anywhere on the property now. Or more specifically, the dragon that makes up the other half of my soul — minus the sliver that belongs only to Zaya — can sense her, track her, scent her in the wind and from deep within the earth.

That's all from her claiming of the intersection point, I now know. But only because I've spent the last twelve hours locked away here in the library tower, surrounded by a trove of knowledge that I technically also don't have permission to consume.

I'm guarding the Gage estate, which needs no guardian, like some fucking dragon of lore.

Sleep would be a good idea. Except that with rest comes all the dreams, richer and more real than the snips of my past revealed in Mack's photographs.

I'm livid that Disa's chosen took those moments from us without consent. I'm also elated. Because without Zaya seeing them yesterday morning, I wouldn't have been drawn back into the house this evening to witness her coming so perfectly all over my brother's cock.

The relationship that took them years to transform from friendship to lovers to chosen mates has taken only a few days to rekindle — counting from when Rought discovered Zaya at the motel.

My chest cracked open at the sight of the two of them tangled together on the couch last night, with a terrible, painful ... hope.

I have to shift my own semihard cock at the recollection. Again. Because I've always been a glutton for that kind of pain. When it comes to worshiping Zaya from afar, at least.

I refocus on the leatherbound tome splayed open on the desk. I can't fucking beat off in the library. I can't jerk off anywhere near Zaya. I might be willing to hide away in the tower until she gets around to formally kicking me off the estate, but I'm not forcing myself on her any further, not even peripherally. This particular book, and the three I read before it, details exactly how connected Zaya is to the intersection point — she carries a fucking shard of it around her fucking neck now — so the last thing I want to do is make her sexually uncomfortable. Especially now that she's invited Rought back into her bed.

It was always easier between the two of them.

When we were young, Zaya nine and me eleven, I easily slipped into the same older-brother role that came naturally with Rought. As we aged, I tried to hold on to that self-appointed role. Desperately tried to not envision that it was Zaya's hand on my cock, not my own, every time I jerked off. Then later, that it was Zaya's throat swallowing my cock, not the mouth of whatever pack bunny pulled me into the washroom or storage area at the clubhouse.

Zaya put a stop to all of that the summer of her fifteenth year. Not that she needed to do anything more than pull my lips down to hers to trigger that response. I never even contemplated looking at another person sexually until at least a year after she left me. A year after she had her neck snapped, severing the intense connection between us.

I know now that connection wasn't completely severed. It's intermittent and full of static, though, as if something is blocking it, or it's trying to filter through me. As if our fucked-up soul bond is actually stronger when Zaya is pissed at me.

Not that I'm riling her up deliberately.

With an internal huff at the ridiculousness of rolling all this history through my head yet again, I tug my notebook toward me, peering down at the map I've copied and then modified twice. It details the intersection points. The information in the three books I've cross-referenced confirms the same locations, but each book differs on how the intersection points are connected around the globe.

Either the authors of the histories I've pulled from the appallingly catalogued estate bookshelves don't know — or those attachments can shift.

My mind has been hovering around a conclusion, helped along by the information I've been able to uncover about the necklace Zaya has inherited from Disa. How and when it was forged — and more importantly, why. I suspect the lines of essence, or life force as one of the histories open before me on the desk claims, shift whenever a new Conduit comes into power.

The main problem is, the books in the library appear to be organized by year. Not the year the book was published, which would at least offer some clarity. But the year the book was either purchased or last read, at best guess. Because within each year, the books are also vaguely clumped together by subject matter. As if they were collected out of interest before the interested party moved on to other areas of study.

I came to that conclusion because the shelves nearest the desk are covered in treatises about mythical creatures. Some of which I've never laid eyes on, even with my advanced degree in the mythos of essence with a rare-breed shifter focus. Not even in the few private collections I had to be invited to get access to. Notes are penciled into the margins of these collected essays, in what I suspect is Disa's neat but cramped hand, for any entries about celestial dragons, gryphons, and cu-siths. My, Rought's, and Reck's beasts.

Disa was keeping tabs on us, studying us. Even after banishing us from the estate and making us believe our soul-bound mate was dead.

I can't open any of the journals arrayed on any of the bookshelves to confirm what I suspect. My list of questions grows longer and longer even as some of the answers start filtering in. I have no idea if the journals are all from the previous Conduits, but I can't even shift the one currently sitting on the desk where Zaya left it.

I know most of this isn't technically any of my business.

But I also know that Zaya knows I'm in the tower, and she hasn't outright banished me.

I suspect she can't.

I suspect, based on the single tome I've uncovered about soul-bound mates on a shelf halfway up the stairs, that Zaya can't control us or hurt us like Disa could.

That should thrill me, except …

Except I suspect the reverse might not be true.

We might be able to hurt Zaya, or at least put her in harm's way. Not without destroying our own souls in the process, of course. But a pinpoint of fear has been lodged in my chest ever since I came to that conclusion. And not because of anything I would ever do, have ever done, to Zaya.

I laid down my life for my mate thirteen years ago, after watching my brother Rought fall before me. Only to be horribly surprised and utterly dismayed when I woke up in a hospital. Without her.

But Reck …

I'm not certain Reck has any soul remaining after that night. And Rought knows something, or suspects something, about Reck's involvement in what happened the night we lost Zaya.

I don't want to believe it of my elder brother. Reck put himself between our sperm donor and the rest of us, over and over again. He might still be doing it, trying to protect us, to this day.

Would Reck have sacrificed Zaya, however unintentionally, in some grand move to protect Rought and me?

And now this shit in Rought's report about the dire awry? With Bellamy claiming blood ties to us all, threatening to drag Precious back to our sperm donor? Never mind how any of that connects back to Reck, since he was the one trying to fuck her while she was wearing Zaya's face.

I ignore the irony that I tried to convince myself Zaya was an impostor when I first heard her over the phone, first saw her in the motel.

I don't write any of those thoughts or questions down in my notebook. I don't want those answers. Not yet.

Instead, I close my eyes, recalling the soft, needy noises Zaya makes when she's coming but trying to stay quiet. The way her energy contracts right before she crests, then pours out of her as she rides that pleasure. All of which I was privileged to witness only a few hours ago, brighter and more vibrant than any of the memories I hold of my soul-bound mate.

That recollection relaxes me enough that I can shift my attention to the next book on the pile precariously perched on the far corner of the desk — a series of essays on the awry. I've already flipped through it for mentions of soul-bound mates but found none. So I lean back with the intent of simply reading it, front to back. The chair creaks under my weight.

Focusing on Precious's extremely unusual manifestation as an awry, rather than on Zaya, is a much-needed reprieve from my ongoing obsession over my soul-bound mate.

THE MORNING HAS FULLY DAWNED, THOUGH NO one else yet stirs in the house, when the lightest brush of energy precedes her up the stairs.

I might have thought I'd imagined her into being, except she's always on my mind and has only now come to me. Approached me with no other reason but to see me.

She pauses at the base of the stairs. I close my eyes, angling my head toward her as if that will help me hear every nuance of her passage.

I'm utterly and completely obsessed with my lost mate. But it feels … right. It feels as it should. Even when I'm saying stupid shit to Zaya, I feel anchored here. Finally understanding how adrift I've been. Simply being here, on the estate, near Zaya, fills all the jagged wounds in my soul that I've tried in vain to patch with duties and devotion to the club and my family.

I hear something slide quietly and then a light click of metal on metal.

Zaya's looking at the pictures.

My own gaze falls on the photograph she's set in the window. Of the three of us and Zaya on the beach — the last moment we four gathered together with love and joy in our hearts. Only to have that joy ripped asunder — irrevocably, I had thought — not even a week later.

I'm not going to be able to ignore for much longer that Rought knows something — multiple somethings, and focused on Reck specifically — about the night we lost Zaya.

She climbs the steps, trailing her fingers along the thick railing.

I don't imagine those same fingers trailing over me, on me.

I compose my fucking face. And I wait for the sight of Zaya to fill my senses. Each time I see her, it makes me feel as if all the time previously I've been looking at nothing at all.

She appears at the top of the stairs like some sort of gothic goddess fantasy. She's tucked one of the framed photographs under her arm, but I have no idea where she got the gown she wears.

Maybe she fucking fashioned it out of pure fucking essence.

My Tempest incarnate.

The gown is made out of some sort of lightweight, sheer silk. Dark blue and barely hanging onto her shoulders, with a wide scoop neckline highlighting her fucking delectable collarbone, the dress gathers under her breasts, then hangs straight down to the floor to pool around her bare feet, trailing behind her down the stairs.

A bruise is slowly darkening where her neck meets her left shoulder. The indentations of teeth marks are clear, but the skin hasn't been punctured. Rought bit her.

I don't imagine licking across that bite mark, or placing my own on the other side of her neck while Zaya moans needily and comes so prettily for me.

The pink-diamond necklace, radiating all its potent energy, hangs over the neckline of the dress, though Zaya usually tucks it away.

She's naked underneath.

She fixes starlit violet eyes on me, offering me a playful quirk of her lips as she scans the barrier of books arrayed across the desk between us.

A literal fucking goddess.

My Tempest always felt poised on a potential edge of pure power, but she's ghosting the footsteps of divinity now.

I'm so, so fucked.

I'm not certain I can even form words. I press my hands

to the desk to stop myself from stumbling up from the chair and throwing myself at her feet.

"Rath," she says, crossing to set the photograph she's carried up the stairs next to the one already on the windowsill.

I can't look away from her, not even to see which photo, which memory contained within it, is worthy of being placed next to her first selection.

When I do finally manage to form words ... well, one word ... it comes out like a fucking benediction. "Zaya."

Then the scent of her hits me.

My cock hardens further, balls tightening so quickly it fucking hurts. I stifle a growl. She's all pungent wild mint softened by her vanilla base, but there's something electric and feral underneath ...

My nostrils flare. I draw deep breaths of that scent in, cataloging it.

Zaya glances at me over her shoulder. Her cheeks flush as she takes in my reaction. "The gryphon," she murmurs.

My eyebrows shoot up in surprise before I can hide that reaction.

Her own eyes widen. Her hands fly up. "No ... not like ... that."

My face flames. I'm not certain I've ever fucking blushed in my fucking life.

Zaya presses her fingers against her lips, quietly giggling. She giggles.

Utterly content, utterly sated.

The universe reorders itself around me. Because in this moment, everything is just ... right. Just as it should be, between us.

I hold out my hand, not entirely certain that I'm in control of my own limbs.

Zaya steps forward to take it, sliding her palm across mine. Energy shimmers in that touch, prickling over my hand and up my arm.

Then with a pretty pivot and a swish of that wet-dream of a gown, Zaya slides into my lap.

As if she remembers.

As if her body remembers.

The wooden desk chair groans beneath us. But she just perches on my thigh and stretches forward, setting her elbows on the desk to survey the books I have open across it.

"What are you researching?" she asks me, as if we haven't practically been at each other's throats for the last few days — all my fault.

I set my right hand on Zaya's hip, compelled to touch her, anchor her on me, but managing to not simply grab her like a fucking beast would, pressing her full over the fucking desk, ass up, pussy bare for my tongue, my cock.

But it's a near thing.

"I'm focused on awry manifestations now," I say, keeping my tone low so my voice doesn't come out desperate and needy.

Zaya's essence dances under my hand on her hip, but it's quiet, settled.

She leans farther forward to run her fingers along the spines of the nearest stack of books, reading the titles, I assume.

I don't imagine running my hand up her back, then trailing my fingers along her arm. I don't imagine capturing her hand in mine, bringing it to my mouth to inhale more of her scent from her wrist. Sucking on her pulse point ...

I close my eyes and send a silent prayer to the universe. A thank you that Zaya is with me. Then I look to see what photo she's brought up the stairs with her. It's the one of us heading out to surf. Zaya is walking with Rought, looking at him and laughing, but she's holding my hand. Our arms stretch between us, and I'm gazing at her like she's my entire fucking world.

"Soul bound," Zaya murmurs, tapping one of the books near the bottom of the stack. "Anything interesting in this one?"

"I've made notes," I say, nodding toward my open notebook even though Zaya can't see me.

But she feels the movement, or was just waiting for the invitation, because she tugs the notebook closer, reading the open page.

"Near the front," I say, feeling lightheaded. "I started with it."

Zaya flips back, pausing in a few places to read. "The necklace holds the power of an intersection point? How is that remotely possible?"

I clear my throat. "Because it hangs around your ... the Conduit's neck. I suspect ..."

She glances back at me over her shoulder. "You suspect?"

I take a breath. "I'm still piecing it together."

She frowns. It's nearly a pout.

I struggle — hopefully only internally — with another urge to press her over the desk and claim that bottom lip for myself. Then get down on my fucking knees where I belong and worship her pussy for as long as she'll let me.

I clear my throat. Again. "I suspect that the powers of the Conduit act like another intersection point."

She blinks. "What? No."

I scrub my free hand over my face. "I'm still researching."

"You think that I'm ..." Her tone is suddenly strained. "That the Conduit is another intersection point?"

I gentle my tone. "I think that nine powerful beings went into ... stasis, one for each intersection point, while one of their ... cohort remained. Perhaps as a linchpin for the protection or barrier spell."

Zaya huffs. "Nine gods, you mean."

I shrug. I've never been someone who believed in gods and goddesses, but I'm almost certain one is perched on my knee. Zaya Gage will not, cannot be denied.

"Rath!" She laughs in disbelief. "You buy into the whole 'they laid down their immortal lives to protect the world from outside influences' doctrine?"

I take a moment to process everything I've read in the last day, and everything that's happened with Zaya — including her returning from the dead. More than once. Then I steadily meet her gaze and say, "I'm getting there."

She exhales softly. And for the first fucking time in our lives together, she drops her gaze. Thoughtful, but not submissive. "I'm ... my aunt believed, but she wanted me to make my own ... assessment."

"I know."

She flicks those violet eyes up to meet mine, gazing at me as if verifying my truth.

I stay still and as open as I can be for as long as she needs to look at me.

"Did you find any more of my aunt's journals?" she asks, turning away just enough to reach the journal I haven't been able to shift, now under a pile of discarded books. She pulls it out.

"There are journals scattered about the shelves," I say, gesturing toward a nearby group of them. They aren't a match to the one in Zaya's hands, and the blank spines don't give anything away about their content. "But I can't read them, can't even open them."

Zaya hums thoughtfully. Still holding the journal, she settles back against my chest. Her gaze is leveled on the armoire across from us. It's closed. With no visible latch or keyhole.

I let myself hold Zaya's hip just a little more firmly.

The armoire radiates an energy that prickles up the back of my neck whenever I'm near it. Or even looking at it, really.

"Maybe the others are in the cabinet," Zaya murmurs. "Or she skipped years ..."

I frown. "Some of Disa's journals are missing?"

Zaya shrugs, pivoting in my lap so she can pull her knees up and tuck her toes under my thigh. I carefully direct her away from my still semihard cock with a gentle pressure on her hip, but she wasn't really heading that way.

"I read the latest entries," Zaya says, thoughtfully smoothing her hand over the front cover of the green leather journal she's holding. "No hints of whatever took her from the property."

I make a noise to let her know I'm listening, but not wanting to interrupt. Zaya was always open and trusting, eager to trade stories and even more eager to seek out information or new experiences. But the reincarnated Zaya — if that's even the proper term for coming back from the dead but still inhabiting the same body — is closed off. Not secretive, but intensely private.

Zaya's gaze shifts to the photographs propped on the windowsill, tapping the journal lightly against her chin. "I wanted to match the dates."

"Between Disa's journals and Mack's photographs?"

"Yeah. It gave me a starting point."

"And ... ?"

"Couldn't find them." She looks at the armoire, then shudders as if abruptly cold. "There's something in there," she whispers. "Something that belongs to me."

I rub my hand up and down her spine without thinking about it.

Zaya turns to look at me, head tilting and hair trailing over one bare shoulder. If she dropped that shoulder just a little more, the gown would simply slide off ... maybe even so far as to expose her breast to my greedy gaze. And if I took a taste then, she couldn't blame me, right?

Zaya's focus drops to my mouth, then back up to peer directly into my fucking aching soul.

I keep my gaze on her face, even as I see her nipples hardening against the lightweight silk of her dress. She only has to shift her leg a bit to the left to feel the ready budge of my cock.

Her gaze flicks to my mouth again, and she lists toward me. Then, blinking, she catches herself, straightening her spine.

I open my mouth to tell her she can kiss me, that I want nothing more than to kiss and cuddle as the morning becomes day, but she looks back down at the journal.

"Actually." She quietly clears her throat. "I found another picture yesterday ... or rather, the day before yesterday ... I'm not keeping perfect track right now."

"Understandable."

She quirks a smile at me.

My heart squelches, then picks up its pace. Its lust. It has to just be all-consuming lust and the staticky bond between us. Because I don't know this Zaya. I don't know this Zaya enough to love her. Again.

She allows the journal to fall open in her hands. "I

found this in the cemetery where Mack was digging when he died. Oh —"

Zaya flinches, and the journal slides off her lap, falling to the floor in a flutter of pages.

"Don't do that without warning!" she practically shouts.

I stiffen, raising my hands. What the …?

"Not you," Zaya snaps, huffing at me. "I'm with Rath in the tower. You don't need my permission." She shakes her head, looking at me. "Why would he need my permission to join us?"

I hear Rought's chuckle from the lower hallway, then his rapid footsteps on the stairs.

"He's … can you communicate telepathically?"

Zaya twists her lips, playing at being peeved about it even though she's practically glowing. "Apparently. I thought it might just be with the gryphon."

Rought, wearing nothing but jeans like he just rolled out of bed and realized he shouldn't wander around the house naked, all but bursts up the stairs onto the upper floor of the tower, grinning madly. "Not just the gryphon!"

Zaya opens her mouth to protest, but Rought lunges around the desk, cups her face, and kisses her robustly.

Robustly enough to press Zaya against my chest. Her sweet ass is now very suddenly nestling my rapidly hardening cock.

I stifle a moan. But I don't quite manage to stop myself from gripping Zaya's hip and grinding up into her. Just a little.

Rought releases her. She's panting lightly.

I manage to loosen my grip on her hip, but she doesn't shift away from my cock.

"We'll have to test that further," Rought says with a grin.

"Which part?" Zaya teases back.

"All of it, from start to finish. Over and over again."

She laughs huskily.

Grinning, Rought steps back and picks up the fallen journal. "What are you two doing up here?"

"Research," Zaya says playfully.

Then she fucking wiggles in my lap.

And I'm definitely no longer just sporting a semi.

Rought chuckles, bending down a second time to retrieve a loose piece of paper that's fallen from the journal and ended up half under the desk. He glances at it. The smile instantly falls from his face. He flips it over to read the other side.

It's a photograph.

Zaya says, "I found that in —"

"Where the fuck did you get —" Rought overlaps her.

They both pause, Rought pale and frowning, Zaya stiff in my lap.

"What is it?" I growl.

Rought passes me the photograph, shaking his head. "What ... that's ..."

I look at the photo. It's Disa with three shifters. For a brief moment, I think one of those shifters is Reck. Which makes no fucking sense because the photo looks as if it was taken in the eighties.

"What the fuck?" I snarl, flipping it over and reading the inscription on the back.

Oso, Ward, Disa, and Ari. Summer 1989.

A visceral emotion more akin to fear than surprise

knifes through me. "Why do you have a photo of our fucking father …"

"And our uncle?" Rought adds.

"What?" Zaya reaches for the photo.

I hold it just out of reach, staring at it so hard, visually documenting every detail, that I'm pretty sure I'd set it on fire if I wielded that power in either of my forms.

"That's the Outcast and the Cataclysm, Zaya," Rought says, his tone way softer than mine. "With Disa. Ari and Oso."

"And who the fuck is the third guy?" I ask, finally ceding the photo to Zaya.

Staring at it, she slides off my lap and takes a few steps away from me.

Even completely distracted, I mourn the newly imposed distance between us. And not just our physical proximity. We didn't need another complication, and that photo —

"Ward," Zaya says thoughtfully. "If he's the only one of the three unaccounted for … then he's the one whose ashes are interred in the Gage family mausoleum. Along with a sacrificial knife with blood somehow preserved on the blade."

"What the fuck?" Rought snarls.

He and Zaya both turn to look at me.

I've already got my phone in hand, punching in my uncle's number.

"Rath," my uncle answers, sounding like I've woken him up. I don't put the phone on speaker. "It's early."

"We're coming over," I snarl. "With Zaya. Who, yes, is still fucking alive."

My uncle sighs heavily.

For just a moment, I feel like a complete asshole. The Outcast dropped just a few weeks ago from a massive heart attack. Also, I've had ample opportunity to inform him of Zaya's return, including at the Outcast lieutenants' meeting yesterday, and I haven't broached the subject. Though I don't doubt that Grinder has been more forthcoming.

But I look down at the photo and up at Zaya, and I'm so fucking incensed that I can barely speak. "You've got secrets, Uncle. Secrets that directly affect us. Did you know that Zaya was fucking alive?"

The Outcast inhales deeply. Then he simply says, "I'll get breakfast sorted," and hangs up.

Riding a wave of utter disbelief, I drop my hand to my side, phone dangling from my fingers.

"That wasn't a no," Rought says, sounding as betrayed as I feel.

"That wasn't a no," I murmur, agreeing.

We both turn to look at Zaya. She blinks as if tuning back into the room, which makes me wonder if she was sensing things on a different level than the rest of us can see or hear.

She grimaces. "I'm going to have to change."

"I like that dress," Rought says, suddenly grinning again. "Does it come in other colors?"

She huffs at him playfully, crossing to the stairs. "I found it in my aunt's closet."

"And why were you digging around in there?" I ask, even though this isn't remotely the conversation we should be having.

Zaya smirks at me, shrugging one shoulder and nearly dislodging the dress precariously hanging from it. I zero in on that point of connection, but alas, the dress holds. "There's a fireplace. And the bed is even bigger. Sturdier."

She gathers the dress in one hand and crosses down the stairs without further elaboration.

Rought shouts a laugh. "Thinking you'll need a bigger bed soon, goddess?"

Zaya doesn't answer.

My brother turns his grin on me, but without Zaya in the vicinity, his amusement fades. "Fuck me. You think he knew?"

"I think outright saying no would have been easier, cleaner." I scrub my hand over my head, then my face. "I know you're busy tracking the dire awry."

"Coda's on that. At least for the extent of this conversation."

"Precious stays here."

He nods.

"I mean it. You need to back me with Zaya."

"It's not going to be an issue. Presh is still asleep."

"Zaya caves to everything and anything our little sister wants."

Rought's grin returns, sloppy and soft around the edges. "Just as it always should have been. Zaya loves that fiercely."

That statement, that proclamation, is like a knife to the gut.

It's also the utter truth. And we almost missed out on all of it.

TEN

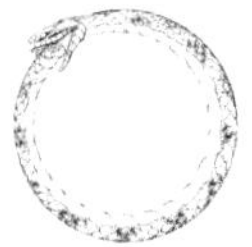

ZAYA

Dʀᴇssᴇᴅ ɪɴ ᴍʏ ᴍᴏʀᴇ ᴀᴘᴘʀᴏᴘʀɪᴀᴛᴇ ᴏᴜᴛꜰɪᴛ ꜰʀᴏᴍ yesterday afternoon — though with new underwear, of course — I hover in the doorway of the guest room across the hall from my own bedroom, checking in on Precious before leaving the property. She's sleeping in the center of the bed under at least two duvets, while DeVille is sprawled bonelessly across the hardwood floor with only a pillow and single blanket, situated between Presh and the door.

I start to ease back, intent on letting the teens sleep.

Presh's head pops up, purple eyes glowing softly in my direction. "Zaya?"

I step into the room, crossing to the young awry before she can scramble out from under all her covers.

"Is it Bellamy?" she asks in a whisper. She chews anxiously on her lower lip, sweeping her gaze across my face as if looking for the truth in my expression.

"No," I say, skirting DeVille to reach the bed and settle on my hip at her side. I give in to the impulse to soothe her, gently running my fingers through her sleep-mussed hair. "You can get some more sleep."

Presh hums quietly in the back of her throat, settling back on her pillow and allowing me just a moment to be with her. Then she reaches up and wraps her fingers lightly around my wrist.

"You'd tell me, right?"

I nod. "You know I would."

Her gaze flicks to the left. Maybe toward her phone charging on the side table, but then she quickly looks away. "I know ... you don't lie to me."

I steel myself, just a little. Because Precious must have questions. She must have a mountain of questions, cobbled together from all the time we've spent with each other but haven't been able to really talk.

But she just shifts her hold to my hand and tangles her fingers through mine. Then, inexplicably, she says, "I don't know my mom."

"No?"

"He ... the Cataclysm ... he said that she left me, but ... I think he might have killed her?" She starts chewing on her lip again, looking up at me through her lashes.

I frown just a little, not quite following the young awry's change of subject. "Do you ... want me to find out? You could give Coda all the information you know about her."

Presh huffs quietly, then hums some more as if taking a moment to think about it. "Maybe. Not now."

"Okay."

"It's just ... I don't have any sisters ... didn't have any sisters either."

Ah. I see where this conversation is going. "Bellamy."

"Right."

"And how do you feel about that?"

"She looks like us … but … it could be another glamour, right?"

I sigh. This isn't the best time for this conversation, but —

"You'd tell me," Presh repeats, firmer now.

"It's not a glamour."

"She's my sister."

"Yes."

She nods, swallowing. "She killed Kris."

"Yes."

"Was Kris … was Kris my mate?"

"I don't think so."

"And you'd know?"

"I didn't look closely, Presh. Not … then."

She drops her gaze, whispering, "But you know … about Andy."

"I know … that you have a multitude of destinies available to you. That you will slip from one path to another, shining bright on this world."

She grimaces. "That's not an answer, Zaya."

I laugh, then sober quickly. "You can't trust Bellamy."

Precious stiffens. "I know that. She killed Kris."

I hold her gaze for a moment. She doesn't look away. "I'm meeting with the Outcast —"

"Oh," she says, already shaking her head. "I'm not going back to the main pack house. He'll never let me leave again."

"Your place is with me now," I say without really thinking about it, as if the universe has channeled through me to voice the claim.

A bright smile swamps Presh's face. "I know."

DeVille groans loudly and deliberately, sitting up on the floor. "If you're making me sleep on the floor, you can at least be fucking quiet."

"Shut up, Andy," Presh grouses, playful and teasing.

DeVille rises, moving to and climbing over the edge of the bed, hair falling all around his face. Then he attempts to burrow into the unoccupied pillows.

Allowing DeVille to distract Presh — which was likely his intent — I stand, heading for the door. Presh half-heartedly kicks at him from under the covers. The young shifter simply pins her in place with his ankle over her lower calf. Presh huffs, but then allows him to settle beside her. Not touching but close enough to almost be snuggling.

"Don't leave the estate, Precious." I pause in the doorway again. "Rath and Rought are coming with me, but Gigi and Coda are here if you need anything."

"Okay."

"That goes for both of you," I say. "You're safe on the estate."

DeVille grumbles in acknowledgment.

I turn away, my mind already shifting to the —

"Zaya?" Precious calls after me softly.

I turn back. She's propped up enough to meet my gaze over DeVille's shoulder.

"Do you ... do you think everyone is redeemable?"

I pause. Redemption isn't something I've given much thought to. Mostly because it's just not relevant to my life. Or it hasn't been.

"I don't know," I finally murmur. "What do you think?"

"I'm still deciding." Precious snuggles back into the bed.

I hover there for a moment longer, oddly ... worried. And waiting for more questions. But DeVille's purr starts up, and Precious sighs contentedly. So I step away, just a little reluctantly.

ROUGHT KEEPS HIS HAND ON MY THIGH FOR MOST of the way to the Outcast MC compound, releasing me only when he needs to shift gears. The roads are damp, but the rain is just the typical early-morning mist. After checking on Precious and DeVille, I found the gryphon shifter in the pristinely restored Ford F-100 idling out front of the house as if I weren't capable of walking all the way to the garage to climb in.

Rath took off on his bike. Coda is still crashed out in the apartment off the workshop, but Gigi is awake enough to keep an eye on DeVille and Presh. Both Cayley and Doc Z returned to work and Outcast MC duties before I made it downstairs.

I'm still not quite certain why I thought wandering around the house in that dress earlier was appropriate — or perching in Rath's lap like he was my fucking throne. But it might be for the same reason I don't feel a staggering sense of relief when we leave the property or, more specifically, the intersection point. Not as I did the evening I picked up Presh, DeVille, and Kris at the warehouse rave ... only two nights ago. Though it feels like at least a week, if not more time, has passed.

I'm carrying the energy of the intersection point more easily, likely because I've reconnected with one of my soul bound. More specifically, I've sealed the bond with the gryphon, and the ties between Rought and me are strengthening. And yes, I'm certain now that those are two different connections.

"Did you ..." My cheeks flush, as if I'm not a fully realized adult. As if Rought's fingers don't only need to shift up about two inches to be touching me in the most intimate of places, that hold meant to be comforting in the now but potentially turning carnal in a mere moment.

Rought flashes a grin at me. "Did I ...?"

"The gryphon ..."

His eyebrows fly up. "The gryphon?"

"No! I mean ... yes, the gryphon and I ... in your body ..." My face is fully flushed now, heated.

Rought's playful leer is not helpful.

Maybe I should try broaching this subject telepathically, though I haven't tried initiating that nonverbal connection yet. It feels even more intimate to invite Rought into my head for this conversation ...

I huff, mostly at myself. "The gryphon holds the soul bond. Though it might be a separate tie. Whatever happened to snip our threads, it didn't affect the gryphon."

Confusion, then utter relief, all but explodes from Rought — and yes, I can apparently pick up intense emotion from him now.

Still looking at me, he veers the truck to the side of the road and throws it into park. A moment later, he's cupping my face and kissing me achingly, tenderly.

"I thought ..." he whispers between kisses. "When I woke up and I could feel you, reach out to you with my mind ... I hoped. I felt that energy shift between us last night ... felt you fill me up ... but I wasn't certain if that was just you, just your essence ..."

"Both of us," I whisper back, wrapping my hands around his raised wrists. Not because I fear him letting me go, but because I crave the skin-to-skin contact. "That energy shift. I think you ... you and the gryphon help me hold the energy of the intersection point easier. Maybe even hold the Conduit power easier."

He presses his forehead against mine, looking me in the eyes and just breathing me in with long, slow, deep inhalations that he holds each time.

"Thank you ..." His voice cracks, hands falling from my face to capture both of mine. "I ... thank you for trusting me."

"I wanted you the first moment I saw you. It felt like you were mine, but I talked myself out of it because I'm not ... because as the Conduit ..."

"You weren't supposed to take on that power for at least a century," Rought says. "We were supposed to grow together before being thrust into all of this."

"But we're here now ...?" I mean it as a statement, but it comes out a question.

Rought doesn't hesitate to answer it. "I'm not going anywhere. And you know Rath is just desperately looking for the right moment to get on his knees for you."

"He's an asshole," I grouse, though without heat.

"We're all assholes," Rought says, suddenly serious. "You're going to need us to be cutthroat assholes, Zaya."

"I'm pretty cutthroat myself."

He hums doubtfully.

"What?! I am!"

"Right ... when is that? When you're rescuing teenagers from berserkers and pouring out the bulk of your blood on a beach in the middle of the unregulated wilds?"

I blink at him. "Are you mad at me? For rescuing Presh?"

"Incensed."

"I should have left her with Chains and Breaker?!"

"My point is, that situation won't happen again because I'll be at your side, or near enough, the next time you mount a rescue operation."

"Sometimes ... the universe moves me." I flick my eyes between his blue-green orbs, looking for understanding in their depths.

"Was that the case with Presh?"

I flush. "Well ... I made that happen."

"Exactly."

I poke him in the chest, then ruin the gesture by smoothing my hand over the same point, luxuriating in simply being able to touch him.

"You lose some of yourself when you die, Zaya," Rought says, voice low. "What is the point of having three soul-bound mates if not to stop that from happening as much as possible?"

I nod, murmuring, "As much as possible ..." just to acknowledge what he's saying to me.

He hesitates for a breath, actually dropping his gaze.

"You ... don't believe me?" I whisper.

"No, it's not that. I know you'll always do what you think is best, but ... I ... we need to have a conversation about Reck."

'Three soul-bound mates,' Rought said while trying to fortify his position. But now he's rethinking that statement.

"My relationships," I say, "or lack thereof, or bond or connections, or whatever you want to call them, are for me to navigate."

"I know," he says. "Always. I just don't think ..."

"I was there," I say, not certain why my back is up about it at all. "I saw Reck with Bellamy in the hotel hallway. I know he's with the Authority. I understand he's not the same kind of asshole as Rath. And you, supposedly."

Rought scrubs a hand over his face, leaning back in his seat to stare out the front window. "I still don't fucking believe it."

"That Bellamy's your half-sister?"

"Fuck me, no."

"She could be Reck's twin." Silence falls between us. The rain picks up. But even as I realize I'm getting cold, Rought settles his hand on my thigh again.

"Ironically, a blood connection will make Bellamy easier to locate," I muse. "Especially if she shares DNA from two sources with Reck. Harlee, Cayley's mage, can probably do it. She'll need to collect the sample directly from Reck. And I'd suggest she doesn't cast alone. Gigi might be coerced to hold a protection circle. Bellamy is powerful ... even I'm not certain what she's capable of. In fact, it might not be a good idea to try to use a blood-based spell against her at all. Something to discuss with the mages ..."

I glance over at Rought.

He's just gazing at me.

"What?"

He shakes his head, then shrugs. "I like you."

"That's good," I say. "Because I'm fairly certain that we're bonded on so high a level that it might really hurt you to get rid of me now."

"I know you're joking ... but ... don't, Zaya. I can't lose you again."

I press my hand over his on my thigh. "Sorry." My own heart aches at even the mere thought of hurting him. "I can't imagine ..."

"Don't," he says roughly, squeezing my thigh. "Don't try. Just stay here with me."

"I will avoid dying as much as possible."

Rought looks at me hard then, nothing playful or charming in the expression. And even though he's seriously calling me out about my lack of self-preservation — which I'm only aware of because it was previously pointed out by Coda — I don't blame him for it. His being hard with me, if only with a single look, if only for this moment, makes me fall for him just a little bit more.

"I like you too," I say, instead of all the other things that want to tumble out of my mouth, out of my mind. The adult me is still holding myself back from the past unveiled in Mack's photos. The adult me is still unsure that the Conduit is a person capable of loving and being loved.

Rought's gaze drops to my lips, and when those eyes flick up to meet mine, they're once again warm and welcoming. "I'm yours."

The words resonate through me, as if he's sent them telepathically as well as voicing them.

He straightens, grinning. "I'll need a full report about what exactly went on with the gryphon ..."

Because, he continues in my head, *I'm pretty certain I couldn't reach you like this when I fell asleep.*

"That's between the gryphon and me," I say, feigning haughtiness. Then I focus on sending my next words along the shimmering bond that now stretches between us. That thread is still thin, but embedded deeply. *But you obviously get to reap the benefits.*

Maybe a ... demonstration?

That could be arranged.

He laughs out loud even as his amusement, his pure joy, filters through to me. It feels as if it curls around my heart, and for a moment, I struggle with the grief that rises in response. Over how alone I've been, and with no chance to even know it.

"Zaya?"

"I need to call Harlee," I say, covering my pity party by reaching into my bag for my phone. I'm still ridiculously pleased at having my unlabeled designer bag back, along with a favorite pair of sunglasses. Maybe being just a little self-centered, a little indulgent, comes naturally to me. "Coda might need some help locating Bellamy. And the sooner she's neutralized, the more time we'll have for … demonstrations."

Rought laughs again, reaching for the phone he's already got propped on the dash and going along with the subject change even as he clearly sees it for what it is. "I got it."

"The mage is on my retainer," I say, just a little stiffly. Because I'm apparently still a loner asshole at my core.

Rought throws me a knowing look. "And who the fuck do you think I work for now?"

His phone vibrates with an incoming call even as he picks it up. He swipes the screen to answer before I can come up with a response to what I'm fairly certain wasn't a question.

"You'd better not be fucking on the side of the fucking road," Rath growls through the phone speakers. "I want these answers."

One of those delicious shivers that apparently only Rath can trigger — even while being a complete asshole over the phone — runs up my spine.

Rought side-eyes me knowingly.

I'm fairly certain the nascent psychic bond between us is way more open on his end.

Holding Rought's gaze intently, I lean toward the phone and drawl, "I'm game if you are."

A choked silence emanates over the speakers.

I tilt my head playfully — for Rought, because Rath can't see me. "You like to watch, don't you, dragon?"

Rath groans over the phone speakers. "Fuuuck …!"

Then he hangs up.

Spinning the wheel and tapping the accelerator to get us back on the road, Rought chuckles, both pleased and amused.

"What?" I say like a total brat. "Am I wrong?"

THE OUTCAST MC COMPOUND SPRAWLS ACROSS A thickly wooded estate set with multiple outbuildings. We navigate a long circular drive that leads to the main house, with a large industrial-looking structure that I presume is a garage and workshop on the far left. Rought stops alongside the front entrance.

Of post-and-beam construction, the massive main house is clad in grayed cedar siding. The plentiful wood-framed windows are in need of a new coat of finish. Multiple gray-wood-railed balconies hang across the front face of the house, as if every room needs its own outdoor space. I have no doubt those railings are scarred with claw marks from years of shifters not bothering with doors and hallways, preferring the two-storey jump.

I can hear the ocean when I exit the truck, leaving my bag but actually remembering to take my phone, but the sound of the surf is faint. Breathing deeply of the misty, woodsy air, and feeling just a little bit lighter without the intersection point roiling under every footstep, I stretch my senses around me. I'm surprised to find that the bottomless well of the intersection point still simmers at the edge of my reach, with no need to stretch farther for it. With the estate twenty minutes up the coast to the north, that power feels much closer than the drive would have suggested.

With my senses so open, I also note that the main pack house isn't filled with as many shifters as I expected, given its sheer size.

"Does this property abut my estate?" I ask Rought as he steps around the truck to join me. I remember at the last moment that it is my estate now, not my aunt's. Though we didn't pass through it, I'm fairly certain that Newport is north of us, between the two estates.

"Outcast territory encircles the Gage estate," Rath says before Rought can answer. The dragon shifter crosses to join us from the garage, where he's presumably parked his motorcycle out of the rain.

Rath is wearing his full cut, including his patched leather jacket, which makes me realize that Rought is still in jeans and a long-sleeved gray henley. Even though we're heading in for an audience with the president of his motorcycle club, who also happens to be the head of his mixed-clan pack.

That mixed-clan designation makes even more sense now that I know it includes a gryphon, a celestial dragon, and a cu-sith. As well as an exceedingly rare kitsune, Cayley, and a pegasus, Doc Z. Plus the marine shifters, Piston and Pepper.

The buttons undone at Rought's neck offer a generous peek at the tattoos literally feathering up his neck. Which makes me think of the gryphon. Again. And more specifically, of our bonding session in the dark of the early morning.

The memory makes me flush like an utter idiot. And lose my train of thought.

Rought chuckles under his breath, ghosting his hand over my back to direct me toward the house and out of the misty rain. He can clearly sense my shift in focus through our new connection. Or rather, our amped-up connection.

"The beaches connect from here to the estate," Rought says. "That's how we came to you when we were too young to drive. It's more direct along the coastline than coming by road. Not that Reck wasn't up to stealing any vehicle he could lay hands on, even at age twelve."

Striding ahead of us, and radiating tension that I know has nothing to do with me — for once — Rath all but pulls the carved wooden door off its reinforced hinges.

I don't recognize the motif etched across the door or along the frame. Mayan- or Aztec-inspired designs, maybe? Both appear practically brand new, likely due to a mage's touch.

"Seems an odd choice. To settle so near the intersection point," I murmur. "Grinder said that the Outcast absorbed a previously established motorcycle club ..."

"About thirty-five years ago," Rought says agreeably. "And we've been actively stretching our borders, more so even in the last five years. That's been Rath's focus since he got back."

'Got back from where' is the first question that pops into my mind. Because despite snuggling in his lap less than an hour ago, I know very little of substance about the middle half-brother who is also supposed to be mine. I go with the more on-point second query. "To ring the estate?"

"Farther north. And south all the way to the California

border now," Rath rumbles from ahead of us. "No one is encroaching on your territory, Zaya."

"You couldn't even if you tried," I say, keeping my tone level as I follow him through the entranceway.

Rath's shoulders stiffen, but he doesn't snip back at me. Instead he shucks off his jacket, hanging it in a paneled closet near the main door.

"You'd never know that my brother's club name is supposed to be ironic," Rought says, only partly teasing.

Rath throws his younger brother a quelling look over his shoulder.

Distracted by the complex display that extends from the front doors throughout the entranceway, I ignore both of them, also letting the line of thought drop. All the moldings, base and crown, every pillar, the entire sweeping stairwell — all of it appears to be hand carved.

Judging only by the exterior, the house seemed almost minimalist in its construction. As if it might have been erected in a hurry, even. The intricate carvings are an odd contrast. Though as I follow Rath through a large living space divided into multiple cozy seating areas, with massive windows open to views of the woods beyond, I see how it all works together.

"The carvings?" I ask Rought.

"The Outcast," he says. "My uncle. It's all his work. He mostly works in totem pole form now. And those are spread throughout the woods and along the property boundary." He eyes me for a moment, then adds, "His version of … warding."

Warding, aka shielding. Or, at minimum, sensor triggers along the boundary of a protected space. There aren't many shifters who can wield essence in that manner, though there are always rumors and suppositions, such as those that follow kitsune. Other than Rought and Rath and possibly Cayley, I've never met a shifter who can wield essence externally.

Of course, such secrets are kept for many different reasons. Not only are essence-wielders vastly outnumbered by those who wield no essence, aka the nulls, but the rarest among us are continually hunted. Either out of fear, or for the power they can be forced to wield for their captors.

I pause to examine the carved post nearest me. Totem poles, Rought said. That's also an odd medium of choice. The square edges of the post between the entranceway and the main living room haven't been rounded. At a glance, the motif doesn't resemble any of the work of the Salish that I've seen, or any of the other Pacific Northwest First Nations known for carving totem poles. Moreover, the Salish are protective about their culture, including their art. Other than the few pieces that have been gifted to Gage ancestors for various favors, I've never seen any of their art outside of a loaned museum collection or in Salish territory.

"Sharing all my secrets already, are you, nephew?" A deep voice draws my attention away from the carved post toward a massive dining area that occupies the entire back corner of the house.

A huge trestle table takes up most of the space, with a long, narrow, and currently food-laden sideboard along the far wall. The pass-through doors to the equally massive industrial-looking kitchen are open on the left. The far end of the table, near the north windows, is casually set for five.

A huge older shifter stands next to the chair at the head of the table. The power he holds is robust but tightly coiled, as if focused inward. Without even looking for his threads, I can already sense that it's his ties to his pack that easily make him one of the most powerful shifters I've ever met.

The Outcast.

Feeling slightly displaced — once again caught between who I was as Zaya and who I now must be as the Conduit — I remove my sunglasses. Then I realize I don't have a bag to tuck them away within. I hold them instead, along with my phone, in one hand.

The Outcast meets my gaze steadily, even after my eyes are revealed.

Ari Guerra — I only know his given name because of the photograph Rath has commandeered — doesn't really look like any of the Guerra siblings, his nieces and nephews. His face is longer, nose more prominent, his skin darker than even Reck, who I'm fairly certain has South American heritage from both sides of his bloodline. The Outcast's straight black hair is long enough to tuck behind his ears and threaded through with thick strands of gray. His eyes are a light blue. He's dressed in a thin sweater that's slightly ragged at the cuffs and hem. Torn blue jeans. Barefoot.

As I approach under the Outcast's gaze — fixed but not unwelcoming — I see that light-gray starbursts radiate from around his pupils. Each eye a different pattern. I don't believe that those markings are connected to or evidence of his beast, though. Because I can't sense any shift in his essence, not as I do when the gryphon peers out of Rought's eyes.

The jagged edges surrounding his pupils almost look like healed-over, decades-old scar tissue.

From what?

Not a physical injury. A shifter of the Outcast's stature, given enough years to heal, would be able to grow back even lost limbs and damaged eyes.

He's almost as big as Rath, easily six foot seven inches. Though the cane he's leaning on and the careful way he occupies the space diminishes his presence. The cane appears to have been roughly carved out of bone, though I don't know what sort of beast has a femur that long.

A furtive look exchanged between Rath and Rought, who have placed themselves on either side of me, indicates that something is different about the Outcast's presence. Or something about his presence concerns them, at least. Perhaps he's recovering from an illness or sickness? Hence the cane.

I don't take a closer look.

A shifter of the Outcast's power would sense any shift in my essence, his connection to the rest of his pack weaving palpable threads through the room. Plus we're allies, our territories sharing the same country. Or more specifically, the Outcast territory surrounding the small sovereign domain I've inherited.

Having stood steadily silent under my regard, the Outcast raises his left hand, tapping the first three fingers over his heart. Thankfully he doesn't bow his head as if in prayer. "Weaver, you bless this house, this land, with your presence."

"I am but the spool, not the weaver," I say, keeping my voice as even as I can when confronted by an annoying bit of religious doctrine.

I'm suddenly hyperaware that this shifter knew my aunt — likely intimately given their proximity in the photo Rath has tucked away somewhere. Which means the Outcast actually knows something about the power I now hold as the Conduit. His reverent gesture tells me he *believes*.

The elder shifter huffs, clearly amused by my denial.

Thankfully, he directs his attention to his two nephews,

first Rath, then lingering on Rought. "I see," he murmurs. "You're no longer one of mine. I thought I felt a shift."

Rought steps forward and offers his uncle a folded bundle of black fabric. I didn't notice him carrying it.

It's his cut. The leather vest that displays his club patch and declares his allegiance to the Outcast — the motorcycle club and the shifter at its core.

The Outcast takes Rought's offered cut with a nod, transferring it to the hand still holding the cane. He then wraps his free hand around the back of his nephew's neck, pulling him closer to rest his forehead on Rought's.

A gentle energy shifts between them, and they stand like that for long enough that I realize I'm holding my breath.

"I understand more than you know," the Outcast says quietly.

"That's why we're here. Now." Rought steps back to my side the moment his uncle releases him.

"Is it?" The Outcast raises a questioning eyebrow at both his nephews.

"You should eat," Rath says gruffly.

The Outcast chuckles, but he obligingly steps back to prop the cane against the chair and settle at the head of the table. He tucks Rought's discarded cut at his side.

Trailing Rath, Rought steers me around the table toward the sideboard, which appears to hold enough food for a small army, most of it in warming dishes. Granted, the three shifters actually are a substantially sized army, not even including what I bring to the mix.

I pick up a plate. Rought takes it from me, quickly filling one edge with the exact pieces of sliced fruit I would have gotten for myself.

"Our bond negates your bond to the Outcast?" I ask in

a low murmur, even though there's no chance that any of the sharp ears in the room don't hear me.

"Yes," Rought says easily. Then he scoops perfectly fluffy scrambled eggs onto a quarter of my plate.

"As it should," the Outcast says from the table.

Rath pivots with a plate literally piled with protein — more of the scrambled eggs, two types of sausage, bacon, and ham — and places it in front of his uncle. The serving of food to his pack leader is casual but filled with meaning.

"Where's your brother?" the Outcast asks, meaning Reck.

"Not invited." Rath begins steadily building an identical plate of food for himself.

"And why is that?" the Outcast asks, picking at his eggs. The only nonprotein item on his plate appears to be a single roasted tomato.

Rought fills the remainder of the space on my plate with crispy hash browns. Then he winks at me when he catches me watching.

It's possible I'm drooling, just a little. And not just over the mound of potatoes. If I could fall for my gryphon shifter all over again, I probably would in this moment.

"And one of those tomatoes?" I ask in a whisper.

"I've got you," Rought says, already spearing a tomato with a serving fork.

I reach for the now-full plate, but with a tiny shake of his head, Rought pivots to deposit it before the seat to the Outcast's right. Then he pulls out the chair for me.

I sit, wanting to playfully protest but also aware that I'm the Conduit in this room, not the lovesick schoolgirl I dissolve into when I'm around Rought. Not that I was ever like that as a …

Well, I guess I don't know how I was around any of my

soul-bound mates when I was young. Nor have I had the privilege of attending an actual school.

Rath settles with his plate directly across the table.

"Please eat," the Outcast says to me.

I obligingly take a bite of the hash browns, following it with another, far more generous bite. They are perfectly crispy and salty on the outside, fluffy and starchy on the inside. With maybe a touch of paprika?

The Outcast grins at me, nibbling on a piece of bacon. He's barely touched any of his other food, even though Rath is already a quarter of the way through his just-as-full plate.

Rought sets a freshly pressed apple juice next to my plate, then lowers himself into the chair next to me. He, at least, has some potatoes mixed in with his mound of protein.

The Outcast looks pointedly at the empty setting to Rath's left, requesting a response to his inadequately answered question without asking it again.

"He's Authority," Rath states evenly, still shoveling food in his mouth as quickly as he's chewing and swallowing.

"He's one of your bond group."

Rath's fork pauses in midair for a moment as his gaze flicks to me.

The Outcast follows his gaze.

I take a sip of my apple juice. "Not my call."

"It is always your ... call, weaver." The Outcast frowns, glancing at Rought and Rath again.

"That's not why we're here," Rath says.

"Yes. I do note that you're still wearing your cut. Your bond, as nascent as it is between Zaya and Rought, is incomplete."

So the Outcast can scent soul ties, or maybe even all essence-imbued bonds. It's another intriguing glimpse of the power he holds, though that sensitivity might be due to the bond — through both blood and pack — that he holds with his nephews.

"This is about you, Uncle." Rath still sounds perfectly calm, even deferential. "Not us."

"Tell me, then."

Rath nods thoughtfully, but then crams another hunk of ham in his mouth, chewing. The dynamic has shifted between him and his uncle. Loyalty coming into play, maybe? Now that Rath is in the room with the Outcast, he's hesitating, even though he seemed geared up for a confrontation from the moment he saw the photo in the tower office.

"You knew my Aunt Disa," I say, stepping in where I totally don't belong to get the answers Rath and Rought appear to need. Because this really isn't my set of secrets to unravel. It's not relevant to the *now* I'm navigating.

The *now* I'm navigating rather poorly, given my handling of Bellamy — even if I'm only going to admit that to myself. I'll keep that in mind as all the drama of my aunt's life and death keeps sucking me in.

The Outcast leans back in his chair, pushing his still-full plate of food a few inches away from him. "I did."

I reach my hand across the table. My arm doesn't even span halfway. Rath tugs the photograph free of some inner pocket in his cut, then passes it to me, easily reaching across.

I place it face up on the table, then slide it over to the Outcast.

He leans over to look at it rather than touching it.

A shifter who commands a motorcycle club the size of the Outcast, as well as a portion of an entire country, for over thirty years, is smart enough to not touch something passed to him by a person of my power.

He exhales sharply, sounding almost pained. Then he laughs quietly, head tilted as he almost reverently touches the edge of the photo.

"So perfect," he murmurs, as if not aware he's spoken out loud.

And I know. I *know*.

"You were one of my aunt's chosen."

"No." He sighs, settling his palm over the photo as if blocking it from his sight is the only way to force himself to look away. With his arm extended, he settles back in his chair and fixes his gaze on me. "I was her soul-bound mate."

"What?!" Rath blurts.

The Outcast ignores his nephew, his eyes glued to me. "What is wrong with your bonds?"

"My aunt didn't have soul-bound mates," I say calmly, ignoring his question. Though my heart is making a solid attempt to lodge itself in my throat.

"Three of us," he says, matching my even tone. Though his gaze is so intense that I'm tempted to look away.

I don't. But it's unusual for me to be intimidated at all.

"As you have three," the Outcast adds.

"I don't have three." Because I need the conversation to move much, much quicker, I offer a truth of my own. "My bonds have been stripped from me."

The Outcast frowns deeply. "That isn't possible, even if you rejected —"

"I would never," I insist, because I know that much, at least. I know it.

The Outcast flicks his gaze — questioning and clearly angry — to Rath, then Rought. "What have you done? Is this why Reck isn't here?"

"This is about you," Rath says roughly. "About your fucking secrets and how they might have impacted us. You knew Disa. You knew Zaya wasn't dead. You let us believe —"

"I don't get involved with the Conduit's business. I protect as much as she'll let me, but I no longer have the right —"

"We're your blood!" Rath shoves his chair back, shooting to his feet. Then, finding himself with all of our attention on him, he paces, clearly trying to level out.

"Sit," the Outcast says after a strained moment. The command is mild but pointed.

Rath stiffens, clearly thinking about ignoring — or at least trying to ignore — the essence-enforced demand. Then he throws himself into the chair, which creaks warningly under his weight. His gaze on his plate, he attempts to finish what remains of his breakfast in a few fierce bites. Clearly stifling himself.

I didn't really understand, not until watching Rath struggle in this moment, what it must have been like to be on the other side of all this. Abandoned and forgotten by his soul-bound mate. By me. And then to find out that our elders, those most trusted to guide and protect us, had knowledge of it. Or even more nefariously, that they had a hand in keeping us apart.

"Just so I have this clear," Rought drawls, deliberately deepening his Southern accent. "You were soul bound to Disa Gage, the Conduit. But you still took my mother as your chosen, bite-bonded mate."

The levels of tension in the room expand sharply and abruptly, almost suffocatingly so.

I forgot about Rought's mother. And his twin half-sisters, the children of the Outcast and his mother.

"Soul-bound mates can't fucking cheat on each other," Rath says darkly. "Can't have children outside of the bond."

"Rejected mates can," the Outcast says, suddenly weary. He rubs his hand across his face. "Oso certainly proved that. Over and over again."

Rought and Rath share a grim glance.

"Oso?" I murmur, not making the connection to the name on the back of the photo that the other three make immediately.

"The Cataclysm," Rought says roughly. "Our evil fucking sperm donor. That's what my uncle is using as his justification for fucking my mother."

The Outcast sighs heavily.

"The Cataclysm," I repeat inanely.

Fuck. They mentioned the Cataclysm in the tower, didn't they? Still, my stomach drops and my mind empties even though I suddenly, rather desperately, need all of this to connect or click together. I need the entire picture, the entire tapestry, so I can move on. I already need to move on from all of this.

I don't like the weave unfolding before me. Not the ragged-edged design, and not the loose threads still waiting to be woven. Or snipped.

All of it out of my control.

Because this is my fate, my past and present, seemingly melding together with my aunt's past. I cannot direct my own fate. I can only nudge the trajectory of others'. I'm caught within destiny's grasp.

Or I was before I became the Conduit.

Now ... now my own beliefs, my own truths, are being upended, unraveled.

The Cataclysm was my aunt's soul-bound mate. The

father of Presh and Rought and Rath and Reck and even Bellamy was my aunt's soul-bound mate. And now his children are mine — or they were supposed to be mine. The half-brothers at least, though my connection to Presh feels fated as well.

"Yes," the Outcast finally says. "The three of us are half-brothers, like Rought, Rath, and Reck. Soul bound to the Conduit, drawn to her after she claimed the intersection point. Claimed it and needed to defend it." His eyes cut to me, as if his mention of defending the intersection point has a deeper relevance.

I'm still struggling with the revelations far closer to the surface. "You ... but that would make you ..." With too many fragments of the past whirling in my head, I struggle to pull together a coherent thought. "Really old ..."

The Outcast barks out a laugh.

The tension in the room breaks with a practically audible snap. We all slump back in our chairs, unable to do anything, ask anything else — and there are so many more fucking questions — until we absorb what's already been revealed.

"Please tell me," I finally ask in a whisper, my throat still clogged, my chest tight. "I understand it might be difficult, but —"

"It's not," the Outcast says gently. "Though I take it your aunt passed almost four weeks ago?"

"Yes. How did you ..."

I glance at the cane and think about the diminished feeling hovering about the Outcast despite his robust ties to his pack.

I think about discovering my aunt's chosen. All dead. I even vaguely remember Rath grilling me about why I assumed Ingrid had a heart attack.

"Have you found Devlin?" The Outcast glances at Rath and Rought, both still rooted in their chairs, food forgotten.

"No," I say. "But it appears that all of my aunt's chosen died with her. As best we can assess the timeline."

He hums, a quiet knowing mixed with a hint of grief. "I only survived due to the pack ties."

Something about that hum, about the shift in his energy, or maybe even the shift in our dynamic, puts me on edge. "Your bond wasn't as severed as you thought."

"Perhaps the universe intervened," he says coolly.

"In which event?" I ask mockingly, not quite understanding my own mounting ire. But it cuts through all the overwhelming disconcertion, so I cling to it. "My aunt's death or saving you from following her into the After?"

The Outcast's fingers curl into a fist. His hand is still resting over the photograph on the table. His previous reverence was a ploy, maybe. To make me feel welcome? Or a hollow attempt to renew our association — the motorcycle club and the Conduit, living in such close proximity.

But I am not my aunt. I'm not the Outcast's rejected mate.

Beside me, Rought shifts in his chair, firmly planting his feet and leaving space between him and the table.

Rath narrows his eyes at his uncle, shoulders angling toward him.

I don't drop the Outcast's gaze. I refuse to cede any ground, any energy to this male with all his fucking secrets. All his lies to his nephews, by omission or otherwise.

Or at least I won't cede any more ground than I already have.

The Outcast huffs out a breath that's not quite a laugh. Then he relaxes, just a little. "I forget," he murmurs as if speaking to himself, his gaze once again on the photo partially hidden under his now-splayed fingers. "What it is like to sit across the table from …"

He catches himself before completing the thought.

I don't let it go, though.

"I'm not my aunt," I say. All the mysteries that aren't my purview, all the places I should be focusing my attention, and I can't let this go. There's some connection in all of this, something to do with my aunt's untimely demise and my still … disjointed … acceptance of the Conduit powers.

"You've got your mother's charisma and the general shape of her face. But otherwise, you are so very much of your father's bloodline," the Outcast says.

Every word is a challenge, pressing me into, containing me within, the role he's granting me and allowing nothing more. Especially the deliberate mention of my father's bloodline. The suggestion that he knew, that he knows, either of my parents well enough to see them in me.

I lean slightly forward. "I'm not some child in pigtails playing on the beach anymore. I don't even remember that girl. I'm the fucking Conduit. You will treat me accordingly."

"Or what?" he asks almost gently, but with a mocking twist to his lips. "Do you think my nephews will allow you to strike at me?"

"What the fuck is happening here?" Rath slams his hand on the table before I can escalate the situation. The dishes and glasses all jump a half inch, sloshing my apple juice everywhere. "We need answers, not pissing contests."

"I am not beholden to you," the Outcast says, barely glancing at his nephew. "I owe you no answers. My past is not for your purview. For you to question, to tear apart."

Rought jumps up from the table. "You're bonded to my fucking mother! Does she know you were soul bound to Disa?"

"And you fucking lied to us about Zaya," Rath says, quietly malevolent. "You knew, you had to fucking know. Even with the three of us in the fucking hospital, you always have eyes on the estate. You let us believe she was dead."

Those repeated accusations fall around the Outcast, now stone faced. His hand on the table, over the photo, clenches again.

I let the silence linger, the sound of Rought's and Rath's breathing heavy within it, as I click together a few more of the clues. My sharpened ire is making it easier to focus.

"On top of bonding with anyone who's not your crux, or having biological children outside that bond group, it should also be nearly impossible for soul-bound mates to murder each other," I say. "That little complication must have been in the book you just read, right, Rath?"

Rath shakes his head, not in denial, but trying to focus on my words rather than giving in to his obvious need to lunge across the table and throttle his uncle.

The Outcast's gaze — hard and rimmed with all the immense power at his command — flicks to me and holds there.

"It wasn't my aunt," I say, already knowing that truth, at least. "You said she rejected you. If she'd been the one to murder your brother Ward, whose ashes she secretly interred in the family mausoleum, then why not kill you and Oso as well? That would have severed her bond to you much more efficiently."

Tension etches across the Outcast's face.

I'm not sure that Rought or Rath are breathing anymore.

We're all poised on the edge of these secrets, ready to slash and rend.

"Did you kill me as well?" I ask, even though I'm not at all certain I want that answer. "Did you take the dire-wrought sacrificial knife my aunt interred with Ward's ashes and that picture ..." I nod toward the photo still pressed under the Outcast's fisted hand. "Did you steal my child-hood and my soul-bound mates from me?"

Rought stifles a moan, abruptly settling back in the chair next to me. His hand falls gently on my thigh, only half hidden under the table.

"No, Tempest," Rath whispers mournfully. "Whatever else our uncle has done, he didn't take you from us."

"Is that what happened that night?" The Outcast's voice rasps with barely contained emotion. "He used the knife?"

"No," Rath says definitively — but with no elaboration.

But I know now, just from voicing those simple questions ...

I know what my mates are trying to ... not keep from me, but spare me from. Until I'm ready to know the truth of my first death. The death that cost me all of them.

I focus on the current secret I'm trying to untangle. I'm tired of getting constantly sidetracked by outside influences. "Oso killed Ward, and Disa banished both of you for it."

"There was no definitive proof," the Outcast insists. Sounding like someone who just can't believe that his brother killed his other soul-bonded brother.

"You think," I say almost gently, "that the Conduit didn't know who killed her own soul-bound mate? You think she didn't feel a section of her soul rip asunder? And if Oso would murder his own brother ... for what? Jealousy? Or did he think that would consolidate the power shared between you three?"

"That's not how it works ..." Rath murmurs.

"I cannot speak to my brother's mind," the Outcast says, getting testy again. I doubt anyone ever challenges him, at least not in public. "I can only —"

"You think living without your three universe-gifted mates is easy?" I really don't want to hear his justifications. "You think she didn't spend every day feeling disjointed? As if every time she died, parts of her weren't put back in place properly? That she didn't constantly feel as if she was walking the earth on a slightly different level than everyone else, destined to see all, but never to truly connect with anything, anyone?"

I'm shaking now, tears rolling down my cheeks.

And I know. I know I'm not talking about my aunt anymore. The parallels between us are too much to ignore.

The Outcast takes a shuddering breath. "Disa took Ingrid as her chosen within a month. Mack within six months. She even took Grinder for a spin a few years later."

I laugh, so harshly that it physically hurts. "And that makes her the villain in your story? That she needed the support? She couldn't trust either of you, could she? Who else would have had the power to harm the soul-bound mate of the fucking Conduit except you or your brother? And that dire-wrought knife? You think those are just an easy purchase from any corner store? Ward's murder was premeditated. You were likely next. And when Oso realized that the deaths of his soul-bound brothers didn't come with a power boost? What then? Murder my aunt? Try to take her power, claim the intersection point?"

"I don't know," the Outcast says, anger and grief edging his words. "She banished me. But I stayed as close as I could. I built the Outcast MC to fortify her borders."

"And that's just sad," I say, spite now pouring out from my sundered soul. "Pathetic, really. The Conduit doesn't need protection, she needs —"

"I won't have some child question decisions made before she was even fucking born!"

The Outcast slams his fist down on the table, standing in the same motion. Energy, his power, explodes through the room, shoving dishes, cutlery, chairs, and Rought and Rath all away. The two of them tumble back in a mess of limbs amid flying shards of wood and porcelain.

The table partially shatters under the blow, falling to pieces at the Outcast's feet. The photo gets lost in the destruction.

The Outcast stares at me where I still sit, disbelief swiftly overtaking his anger.

Not a single iota of his power tantrum has touched me.

I stand, taking a step toward him, hearing Rought shifting behind me. Wood clatters to the floor as he moves, his chair seemingly torn apart, or perhaps crushed under his weight. Rath has taken out one of the carved support posts in the living room before crushing the nearest set of couches.

Hopefully, the second floor isn't about to drop on top of us. That might actually hurt.

"Not only am I not a child," I say quietly to the Outcast, icy calm now, "but that childhood was all but stripped from me. And I can't help but think that you bear partial blame for those missing years. Whether due to your past actions or negligence or some direct intervention thirteen years ago … you carry the responsibility for the fact that my own bonds have been ripped from me."

I'm close enough to touch him now. I raise my hand, hovering it over his chest.

He flinches even as he tries to cover that reaction, his fear of me. I doubt that the Outcast has been truly afraid in decades. At least not for himself. "I didn't know."

"You did," I say. "Because even if the boys all thought I was dead and reported that to you, your territory surrounds my aunt's. Like Rath said, someone, one of your scouts, would have seen me leave the property. There is no way, so fresh from being dead, that my aunt could have arranged to teleport me. She didn't even know that I would survive that night. Even now, as the Conduit, the complications are too risky to even attempt to move me in such a way."

Something flickers at the edge of my mind …

A sense of wind pressing me back, and rock underfoot. Then a dark, stormy night.

And screaming.

So much screaming — shouts of disbelief, and pain. Then terror. The power of the intersection point aching through my bones, as if rejecting me …

Or … unable to connect with me.

I shove it all away.

The actual memory of the only time I have been teleported follows. In the aftermath of my mother's death, in the arms of my absentee father. Not that Disa gave him much of a choice about the absentee part. I might have only been nine, but that particular memory is crystal clear.

I shove that thought away as well.

"I didn't know for certain," the Outcast insists, shifting his feet to stop from swaying. "Not until recently."

For a moment, I can't remember what we're discussing in the aftermath of the elder shifter's power play.

"How recently?" Rought asks from behind me.

Right. My death.

The Outcast's gaze flicks between both his nephews, Rath having moved to boxed him in from the other side.

"Cayley," I say, more pieces of the puzzle click, click, clicking together. "Cayley is bound to you. And she saw me in Tokyo. Even with me securing the invitation from the Phrontistery and the scholarships after rescuing her sister, Kiki would have needed permission, your permission, to leave your territory. Cayley would have been forced to give you something to explain all of that, even if she refused the Authority when they interrogated her."

"What?" Rath exclaims. "What interrogation with the —"

"Eighteen months," Rought says hollowly. "You've known for certain that Zaya was alive for at least eighteen months."

The Outcast raises his hands, placating his nephews — but not surrendering. "Telling you what I only suspected wouldn't have fixed your severed bonds. I knew they had to have been muted or compromised somehow, either by Zaya's death or ..."

"Or ...?" I ask.

"Some other intervention," he adds, covering the pause though I know that wasn't what he was about to say. "The bonds had to be compromised. Otherwise the boys wouldn't have believed you were dead, Zaya. Not even with Ingrid's and Mack's confirmation. They would have felt you." He locks his gaze to Rought's over my shoulder. "Especially you, Angel."

"Don't call me that," Rought rasps.

Rath slowly starts to unbutton his cut. "Have you got what you need, Zaya?"

I'm not certain. I don't know that I needed any of this information, nor that I'm done asking questions. But I nod anyway.

"Give us a quick moment, goddess," Rought says, ghosting his fingers down my spine.

So instead of fucking with the Outcast's threads like I so desperately want to, I lower the hand I'm still holding only inches from his chest.

Because their uncle is right, though for the wrong reasons.

I won't hurt him. His punishment is for his blood, those few he should hold allegiance to, to extract. It's not as if he had an intact universe-gifted soul bond to supersede his blood bonds.

Rought presses a kiss to my temple, both of us still staring at his uncle.

The Outcast finally drops his gaze, though his shoulders remain squared, his stance firm. I notice that he lost his cane during his temper tantrum.

Leaving the remainder of my answers behind, assuming the Outcast can provide them, I cross around him, stepping carefully through the debris now littering the room.

Rath yanks off his cut, crumpling it in one hand. He leans into me as I pass. I pause just long enough for him to brush a kiss against my cheek. Essence shivers across my skin. The kiss is utterly chaste, but full of promise.

I traverse the living room in reverse, noting again that a house that should be teeming with shifters is oddly empty. Not even Rought's mother and sisters are here.

Did the Outcast send them all away after Rath's call, to protect them from me? As a simple reflex? Perhaps he expected retribution. But for what, exactly? For keeping me from my mates?

I glance back over my shoulder. Rought and Rath have crowded around their uncle, but all three of them are watching as I leave. Just before I cross out of their line of sight, Rath throws his discarded cut at the Outcast's feet.

I turn my attention forward — where it always should be — and exit through the front door, my heart weighted with even more questions than I had when I entered.

ELEVEN

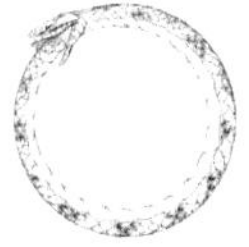

Slowly crossing toward the woods only a few meters from the north side of the house, I breathe in deeply in an attempt to settle my mind. I'm more than a bit staggered by the secrets my aunt was keeping. Though I also understand that Disa was always clear that her role, her duty — as dictated by the universe — was to live in the present. As she raised me. As I'm now supposed to be.

If I allow myself to be truly maudlin for a moment, though, I'm not certain anyone raised me in the traditional sense after my mother died. Of course, other than the intermittent visceral flashes I've been experiencing in the last few days, I am apparently missing large portions of thirteen years of my life.

More secrets kept from me by my aunt.

Someone always fed me, someone tutored me, someone was always around — a rotation of aunts and uncles, mixed with a few cousins, following some schedule that kept them near enough. But never close enough to form actual familial bonds. By my aunt's edict? Because I was the Conduit's vessel?

Maybe Disa always planned to explain it to me ... that's what her note implied, yes?

I'm sorry for everything you are about to discover
and that I wasn't the one to tell you.

Or maybe that note was penned out of regret for everything my aunt was leaving for me to hold. Did she think I wouldn't be haunted by her death? Or the past she'd hidden from me? Maybe she thought she'd trained me better than that. Maybe she thought I would simply step into my role and wait for the universe to move me where it willed.

"I'm never going to know," I whisper to myself, as if I need to chastise myself out loud for it to truly sink in. I'm beyond the tree line, weaving through evergreens now. "I'm never going to know, so what's the point in rolling the questions around in my mind?"

The ground between the huge conifers is bare, packed down in places, a combination of the still-chilly late-winter weather and the dozens of shifters who must run through these woods on a daily basis. I don't have a great sense of the history of the area, but I presume it would have been clear-cut well over a century ago, when the settlers attempted to strip this land of its resources and seize it from the First Nations. Back when the territories were first united, only to be torn apart into separate countries with the vast stretches of the wilds in between.

Even if they weren't second growth, it seems unlikely that the trees would be this large without help, presumably from multiple mages with earth affinities. Though this thick growth could simply be a side effect of the Outcast building a strong, unified pack filled with rare and powerful shifters.

I let those niggling thoughts fall away, allowing myself to just breathe. The air is mossy and damp. Comforting. If I were anyone but me, anyone but the Conduit, I might have assumed I was breathing in essence.

I am me, though.

I'm immune to more than just malicious spells.

I walk apart.

Except ... I recall the essence shifting between Rought and me as I rode him on the couch. And an echo of the grip the gryphon had on my hips as he pinned me to the bed only a couple of hours ago.

I could reach for the tether that binds Rought and the gryphon to me now. As tenuous as it still feels, I know I could find it, touch it. Maybe even strengthen it by reaching through it, brushing my mind, my consciousness, against my soul-bound mate.

I'm not so alone anymore.

I'm also not so childish as to seek out that connection in a minor moment of confused melancholy. Rought's conversation with his uncle is far more important than me suddenly feeling like I wouldn't mind a cuddle.

I find the first carved totem another dozen steps into the trees.

This carving is rougher hewn ... as if made by claws, articulate but deadly. The Outcast's claws — or rather, the claws of whatever beast he transforms into. Unlike the smoother, more considered carvings in the house, the wood here has been left to weather. The grayed totem stands about a foot taller than me. I have no idea what the markings represent, or even whether it's a language or pictographs. Perhaps only the Outcast can read them. Perhaps he's a member or a descendant of a lost tribe.

I don't touch the totem. I don't wish to trigger or dispel the boundary ward.

The power of the Outcast — both the shifter and the club he created — isn't under my purview. I'm not some ... autocrat. Or savior. I neither make rules nor enforce them. I don't even bring balance or protection. Not on a global scale, at least.

Not unless or until the universe deems it necessary.

As I wander farther, juggling thoughts of all my aunt's secrets and what I was taught was my fundamental role, the sound of the surf picks up. Wisps of low-lying fog tell me I'm nearing the coastline. I pause among the trees instead of continuing. Breathing, settling. I can't remember the last time I set foot in nature like this ... the last time I voluntarily hiked or biked or swam in the ocean.

It takes a moment, as if I have to truly settle my mind to catch it without actively reaching for it, but I can feel my connection to Rought. Or rather, I can feel where he is. That connection is quiet, though not as tenuous as I previously deemed it. Still, I hesitate to reach for it, even tentatively, because I don't want to accidentally overpower it. Which is more of a feeling than a rational thought.

I have a soul-bound mate. Someone — or something, perhaps the trauma from my first death — tried to tear Rought and me apart. But the gryphon ... Rought's beast hadn't manifested yet. And the gryphon held the bond.

Even the idea is overwhelming. I'm sure Rath will scour the library looking for supporting documentation. But ... maybe ... the dragon and the cu-sith hold the other two bonds?

My aunt had three soul-bound mates as well. I don't understand the intricacies involved in her choosing to sever those bonds, but she never told me about any of it.

She never told me that maybe I didn't have to carry everything on my own.

I ignore the condemnation I feel rising underneath my own thoughts — the childish anger threatening to overtake the purely rational conclusion.

Disa thought she had more time. Another century at least before the vessel would wear thin, before the Conduit power would pass to me.

I start making my way back to the house. Despite my tumultuous thoughts, the tiny knot anchoring me to Rought is a warm glow in my chest.

Maybe Disa was right about the past not mattering.

We all have to live in the present, after all.

I tug my phone free from my pocket, honestly surprised that I've got the device on me. I'm also carrying my sunglasses, which is just short of a miracle. Maybe I'm not as easily distracted as I thought.

I'm swiping Coda's passcode sequence on the phone screen before I consciously make the decision to do so.

The pack house comes into view through the thinning trees.

A large SUV — clearly Authority issue, though its hulking exterior isn't marked with their insignia — speeds up the drive, abruptly skidding to a stop as if the driver has spotted me through the tinted windows.

"We're on it," Gigi growls over the speakers of my phone.

"On what?" A chill slithers down my spine as I keep my eye on the SUV.

The phone suddenly feels weighted in my hand, as if anchored by a strand of fate. The fate that placed it in my pocket, that saw me reach for it to dial Coda without conscious intent.

I pause, waiting. No other essence stirs around me, but I'm suddenly certain I'm hesitating in the moment before a *knowing*. As if the universe is also waiting, waiting to see which way the threads are about to shift.

Or what they're about to snag.

A long, weighty pause settles between me and the combat mage on the phone. There are very few things that would concern Gigi enough to take that testy tone with me. With anyone, really.

The passenger-side window of the SUV rolls down as the vehicle backs up, letting me see within it.

Reck.

The last time the universe paused around me was right before the cu-sith strolled through the shifter and berserker battle on the streets of Newport. Right before I made a choice — a personal choice — to send Precious off without me and to save those dozens of shifters from the death emanating from Reck's beast.

I'm not at the edge of a minor twist of fate.

I'm on the precipice of a full-blown *knowing*.

"Get in," Reck calls to me, blunt and biting.

"You're 'on what,' Gigi?" I raise the phone closer to my mouth to repeat the question.

"Precious slipped away while I was showering," Gigi says over the speakers. "With the boy."

"You're tracking her phone?" Freed from the momentary pause in the universe, I cross steadily toward Reck. Not rushing, but not avoiding what's coming. I'll move quickly if Presh needs me, but jumping to conclusions while the universe realigns around me — if that is what's going on right now — is never a good idea.

"I've got it," Coda says from somewhere in the background. "Give me my fucking phone, Gigi."

"You. Focus!" Gigi snaps at the awry tech. Her voice sounds closer to the phone speakers as she addresses me. "Sorry, Zaya. It took me a moment to wake the asshole supreme once I realized the kids weren't on the property."

"Zaya!" Reck glances from me to the front entrance of the house. "Move your fucking ass."

"Text messages, not as wiped as the baby awry probably thought ..." Coda mutters in the background. "She's been texting an unknown number ... this routing code, though ..."

"Authority?" I ask, walking right up to the open window of the SUV to meet Reck's dark-eyed gaze. Then I deliberately look into the back seats. Empty.

"Who are you talking to?" Reck asks darkly.

I'm not certain he has another tone. At least not when addressing me.

"Who's that?" Gigi asks over the phone speakers.

"I'm not sure," I say. Then I say to Reck, "Are you my long-lost soul-bound mate? Or are you an Authority agent right now?"

He grimaces.

I'm not sure which option displeases him the most. But it's likely the soul-bound thing.

"Carlos Guerra," Gigi says, speaking to Coda somewhere in the background. "Sergeant of the Major Crimes Unit, Cascadian Division. Club name Reck. For obvious fucking reasons."

"I have a fucking eidetic memory, you know," Coda grouses.

I can hear the awry tech's fingers flying over their keyboards now.

"Were the text messages to Presh from you?" I ask Reck.

Deliberately, dismissively, he shifts his attention to the front doors of the house. "Get in, Zaya."

The strength with which he's gripping the wheel and the tense way he's holding himself gives him away, though. He's angry, likely perpetually, but he's not indifferent.

He's pretty to look at in profile. But it's clear that Reck doesn't know me — past me or present me — very well. I don't respond to demands from anyone but the universe. And the universe hasn't moved me yet.

"I don't have him." Coda's voice shifts closer to the speakers. "I don't have his phone, Zaya. I should easily be able to jump from you to him." There's a brief pause, then a frustrated snarl. "Fucker. He's running one of those Authority black boxes."

Reck, still not looking at me, smirks like a total asshole.

I tilt my head, considering him. "I can see the resemblance now. I couldn't before. Just a sense of the familiar. Of course, I had just died the day before I found the picture. Dying tends to make everything a little hazy around the edges for a few days."

Reck turns his head just enough to narrow his eyes on me, assessing but also threatening. "Resemblance to who?"

"Your father. Though it's an easy guess that Bellamy is your twin."

Anger, maybe even pure hatred, etches across his face. "It's not an easy guess!"

"What's that?" Coda asks. "More info, Zaya. I've been asleep for a few hours, and Gigi won't give me another energy drink."

"You've had three in the last fifteen minutes," Gigi snaps from the background.

"Oso Guerra," I say, not quite certain why I feel the need to needle Reck. Because I honestly don't think he looks like his father, and Coda already knows everything we know about Bellamy. "The Cataclysm."

"You have a picture of the Cataclysm and you haven't sent it to me?" Coda snaps. "What the fuck, Zaya!?"

"Rath has it," I say, hovering my hand over the window frame of the SUV, reaching for all the essence spells layered over it, embedded into the steel and paint. Those protections are likely also restricting Coda's reach. Or ...

"Maybe the SUV is the black box," I say.

"Don't," Reck snaps, as if he knows what I can do with a simple touch. "We might need that. Get in!"

"I'll have the black box disabled in a few minutes," Coda says. The tech sounds focused, present.

Reck jerks in his seat, as if he's just stopped himself from making a grab for my phone.

I raise a questioning eyebrow.

He grinds his teeth. Then he says, "We might need that protection as well."

"Coda protects me in the digital realm," I say mildly, using their name for the first time since the call began.

Surprise flits across Reck's face — followed by unfiltered avarice. Yeah, I didn't think he'd miss that little tidbit. Then he grimaces, presumably at my knowing look. And because I've just openly declared the awry tech to be under my protection. The Authority has been hunting Coda for years.

"I've got the last logged location for Precious," Coda says. "Sending you a route. No eyes on her yet." No cameras or satellite, the tech means. "And I think they're still on the move."

My phone screen flashes, then a map appears. A marker blinks southeast of our current location.

"How long was your fucking shower, Gigi?" I ask,

unable to hide my ire. "The kids are practically on the Idaho border!" Okay, that's a massive exaggeration, but they are in the middle of fucking nowhere at least an hour away, maybe more. And seemingly heading toward the border because there's nothing else out there.

"I didn't know I was babysitting a fucking flight risk," Gigi snarks back.

I don't answer her. Coda mutters something that I don't catch. I stare down at the map, looking at it with intent. I don't recognize the location. The *knowing* still doesn't kick in.

I turn my phone toward Reck.

He looks at the screen, then nods stiffly.

"I'm ... I'm sorry," Gigi says over the speakers. "Zaya. Fuck. I'm ... you never ask for favors. I'm ... sorry ..."

I don't respond to that either. I have no fucking idea how Presh and DeVille got off the property without the combat mage noticing. But I also know that determined teenagers can pretty much do whatever they want if they don't care about the risks.

Coda mutters something in the background again. It could be "Enough ..." But it might also be "Gear up."

"I'm sorry," Gigi whispers again.

I hear what I assume is the door to Coda's trailer opening, then closing.

"I'm here," Coda says over the phone speakers, firm and focused. "Who has the kids, and why are they using Authority tech?"

"What?" Reck snaps.

"Don't tell me you didn't know, Sergeant," Coda purrs maliciously. "Your fellow agents are deep in the Cataclysm's pockets."

"That's a new twist to me as well," I say mildly, though

I'm thinking about the bit of vid that Coda found of Reck's agents meeting with Devlin. Are Wilson and Shaw in the employ of one of my aunt's rejected soul-bound mates?

Reck's expression blanks, all his intent hidden behind that false, almost-too-pretty facade. "We're wasting time," he snaps at me, then he glances over at the house again. "Get. In. The. Vehicle."

"The camera Rought installed," I say promptingly, keeping my gaze pinned to Reck, watching for any shift in his expression, any shift in his essence. "At the top of the drive?"

"First thing I checked," Coda snaps. "Before sending Gigi out on foot with a tracking spell. A spell, by the fucking way, that doesn't fucking work on this fucking estate." Coda inhales deeply, calming their tone. "I have continual feed running from that and the three other cameras Rought installed for me. The tech doesn't have a problem with the energy boiling out of the fucking earth there, not since you ... gave me access. But I've already scoured it for clues."

Reck has given up all pretense of dismissing me or ending the conversation. I can see him analyzing everything Coda's saying, forming questions. I smirk at him, and not playfully. His energy, even through the protections coating the SUV, seriously bothers me. I actually had less trouble with the cu-sith. There's something pure, true, in the grim reaper's malicious power.

Reck twists his lips, as if stopping himself from baring his teeth at me.

So the feeling is definitely mutual.

Severed bonds or not, the contrast between my reaction to Reck and his brothers, Rought and Rath, is stark.

"The kids aren't stupid enough to have exited the property via the driveway," Coda mutters over the phone. "So they had to be on foot."

"They didn't get this far away on foot," I say mildly.

I would have to reach through the protections coating the vehicle to truly look at Reck, truly see him. And I hesitate, not only because of his earlier caution but also for personal reasons. And yes, I'm aware that the Conduit shouldn't have personal reasons for not doing something. But looking at someone's threads is invasive, even with consent. Reck is too powerful to not know the touch of my essence. To not remember the touch of my essence.

And my essence as a teenager wouldn't even have been a whisper of the power I now hold. That I'm still struggling to hold.

"Stop looking at me like that," Reck snaps. "I wouldn't hurt Presh. And ... I won't hurt you."

"You can't hurt me," I say automatically, stiffly.

"Can't I?" he says coldly. "Your soul-bound mates might be the only beings capable of —" He cuts himself off, grimacing. And dropping his gaze.

"Maybe that's why ..." My eyesight suddenly goes hazy at the edges. My fingers twitch, subconsciously curling into a two-finger hold. As if by mulling through all the revelations from the last twenty-four hours, I'm suddenly and involuntarily drafting the threads of the past through my fingers, trying to untangle them. Or maybe trying to properly ply them together into one unified whole? Ready to be rewoven into the fabric of the universe —

"What are you doing?" Reck asks sharply.

I refocus on him. "What?"

He shakes his head, grinding his teeth. " 'Maybe that's

why …' what?" He asks the question as if it's been pulled from him against his will.

"Why my aunt rejected her soul-bound mates after Oso murdered Ward."

Reck blinks. All of his pretense and masks fall away. Just for a moment.

I don't make him wait for clarification. "The three half-brothers, Oso, Ward, and Ari, were soul bound to my aunt. After Oso killed Ward, my aunt severed her other bonds. But maybe that wasn't a punishment. Maybe that was self-preservation."

"What the fuck …" Reck wraps his left hand across his forehead and rubs both of his temples. Then he exhales harshly. "That doesn't change the present."

"No, it doesn't."

"We need to go now," he says, reverting to his Authority persona even though none of what he's doing, nothing he has been doing with or without his agents, is sanctioned. Especially any interaction with me, the Conduit. "Just you and me. Bellamy is threatening DeVille, and then Presh, if anyone else comes with us."

I reach for the handle of the passenger door without further hesitation.

The universe tugs at me — hard and away from the vehicle, away from Reck.

Muta twists on my extended arm, taking his bush-master form in an instant. Seriously heavy and completely pissed — over being abruptly awoken, I presume — he twines up my arm, over my shoulder, and around my neck.

"I don't have the black box disabled yet," Coda says over the speakers. "Should I loop in Rought?"

"Not yet," Reck says, answering for me. His gaze is riveted to Muta.

The death god trapped in the form of a huge snake rears partially up off my shoulder, hissing when this display of dominance results in his head getting covered in my hair. He looks ridiculous, like he's wearing a wig.

I see Reck's lip twitch as he suppresses a smile.

Unfortunately, those annoyingly full lips thin as the Authority Reck personality takes over again. "Bellamy was clear about the sequence of events that need to happen now. Give us a fifteen-minute head start."

"Bellamy's schedule ..." I say. "And why would Presh voluntarily leave the property? What is Bellamy holding over her?"

"Nothing," Reck snaps.

"Nothing," Coda says over the phone, oddly agreeable. "Not according to the text messages."

"Just her soft fucking heart," Reck mutters. "And the promise of a sister."

"And an inference that Bellamy needs help," Coda says dryly. "To escape the Cataclysm's clutches."

"Same thing," Reck huffs.

"Redemption ..." I murmur. My stomach anxiously churns as I recall the tail end of my conversation with Presh.

"What?" Reck snaps.

"Isn't Bellamy already being aided by your agents?" I say, more to rub it in than to confirm it.

"Yes," Reck huffs, pissed about actually confirming it. "It wasn't clear before that they ..." His nostrils flare as he takes a breath, then corrects himself. "I didn't think they'd come for Presh."

He's not lying. I don't think he's lied to me once. Yet. He knows ... he knows that much about me, at least. And he knew my aunt as well. The Conduit is hard to lie to, to hide anything from. Not if the universe needs us to know the truth.

"Maybe Bellamy needs help getting away from both the Cataclysm and the Authority," I say, as if I'm actually thinking it all through. I'm not, really. I'll react in the moment as I always do. I'm just giving the universe a chance to weigh in for a second time.

"This exposes them," Coda says over the phone speakers, fingers flying over multiple keyboards in the background. "Don't worry, Sergeant …" The awry tech sneers Reck's title. "I'm putting a tidy little info pack together for you to deliver to your Authority superiors. Not that the Conduit will be held accountable for whatever actions she's about to take."

Reck's gaze flicks across my face, as if truly seeing me as the Conduit, not as the girl he knew, for the first time. But his expression once again hardens as it settles on Muta. The bushmaster has managed to untangle himself from my hair.

"I'm not going to hurt you," he repeats.

"You don't believe that," I say mildly. Guessing rather than truly knowing.

"Don't read me," he snaps. "If I say it, it's the truth. Get in the fucking SUV, or Bellamy is going to use DeVille's life force to fuel a teleportation spell and take Presh back to the Cataclysm."

I get in the SUV.

The universe tries to force me back out, so strongly that my movements are jerky and uncoordinated.

"Stop fucking around," Reck snarls.

I laugh joylessly, already knowing where all of this is leading. It's probably not a great idea to die only days after my last death, which was only three weeks after the previous death. What would happen to the Conduit power if the vessel can't be revived? Would it fall to another? Even if I'm the only currently living vessel? Could anyone not bred or destined for that power actually hold it?

I don't think so.

So what, then? If all the essence that fuels the earth, that protects us, flows through the Conduit and that power doesn't have its vessel — me — does it all just slowly wither and die?

Reck hits the accelerator, practically fishtailing down the drive.

My shoulder slams into the door, the sharp pain pulling me back into the present. Where I belong.

I buckle my seatbelt.

Muta settles in my lap.

My phone goes dead.

The universe tugs at me, again and again.

I'm not supposed to be with Reck. Maybe I'm not supposed to go after Presh at all, just as I wasn't really supposed to rescue her at the diner. Or to snip Chains's threads to save her.

I'm fucking with someone's destiny right now. Or I'm about to.

Two days ago, I would have said that as the Conduit, I had no destiny, no fated path. But in this moment, I have a feeling I might be about to reweave a section of my own tapestry.

And it's going to hurt.

It always does.

"Was it you, then?" I finally ask, resting my head back against the seat and watching the road speed by.

Fifteen minutes ago, we left the ocean and any sign of thriving civilization behind us, entering into another stretch of the wilds. But unlike the unclaimed or unaffiliated coastal regions of Oregon, here on the edge of the barrens, only the remnants of a once-verdant landscape remain. The ruins of farmhouses and barns. The occasional rusted coil of barbed wire on a broken section of fencing. Even the flora and fauna have been slow to reclaim this land. It's still overcast, but we've even left the rain behind.

Muta in my lap is fixated on Reck. My phone is still seemingly dead in my hand. Coda must be seriously pissed at me for willingly sitting inside a literal black box. We've been driving in silence for almost an hour, taking the highway due east.

"Was it me what?" Reck snaps, as if he loathes talking to me, loathes being in the same space as me.

"Was it you who killed me?" I ask evenly. "You who severed all our soul bonds?"

Reck takes a breath — then another, even more ragged. His hands tighten on the steering wheel until the molded leather and steel groan under the pressure he's exerting.

"No," he rasps. "It wasn't me. Not ... by my hand, at least."

He carries some sort of guilt over my first death. And Rought seems to think Reck's done something that makes him dangerous to me, for me.

I give him space to elaborate. He doesn't. Though the tension threading through his hands and up through his shoulders eases a little as more minutes, then another quarter hour, pass in silence.

The landscape continues to change around us as we

close in on the barrens and the essence-scorched plateaus that run all the way to the base of the Rocky Mountains just over the border into Idaho.

Reck has been driving at double any reasonable speed limit the whole way. Not that I've seen any posted signs or monitoring devices. And even though the road is nearly dead straight and not that badly maintained, the vehicle doesn't run smoothly at this velocity.

The multitiered breakdown of the political landscape of North America over a century ago destroyed much of the verdant farmlands, the vineyards and orchards that once defined this area. Closer to the mountains and rivers, nature is slowly reclaiming the territory. These so-called wilds are vastly different than the overgrown sections of the coast that the Outcast MC is claiming and rehabilitating. Rather than slowly crumbling from neglect as it is along the coastline, any hint of civilization has been scrubbed from these lands.

Random ranger-overseen outposts pop up all along the highway, all the way through the rest of Oregon and into Idaho. I'm fairly certain those outposts are more for emergency situations rather than being continually occupied. Again, the overall governance of the wilds of Cascadia is ... spotty.

If I were to roll my window down, I might catch the scent of dire-mage-wrought essence still etched deeply into the earth. Or of the weapons the nulls deployed to stop those mages from claiming this previously resource-rich land.

A trio of my Gage ancestors stepped in to quell the conflict in this area, then helped define and fortify the newly drawn borders between Canada to the northeast, the Navajo Nation to the east, and California to the south.

Not that the name 'Gage' appears in any null-written history books. Within those pages, only the deployment of a weapon of mass destruction is mentioned. With nothing of note about the miraculous recovery from that nuclear fallout.

"It's ironic," I say, catching sight of essence scorch marks still marring the barren rock out my window. "For a dire awry to choose this as her meeting spot."

"The border between Cascadia and California isn't as fortified as the border between Cascadia and the Navajo Nation." Reck flicks his thumb to indicate the GPS map on the dashboard. We're still at least an hour away from the location pin that has updated three times on Reck's map, always moving farther east. As if someone is silently sending through new coordinates. "Even so, Bellamy can retreat in two directions from here, then cross into Canada or the US."

"The United States is practically walled off."

"It's the border between the US and the Federation, and between the Federation and Mexico, that's fortified to that extent. Everyone who shares a border with Cascadia and California has been easing crossings for the last decade or so, especially trade."

I hum thoughtfully, not all that interested in the conversation. Though the fact that Reck is speaking to me with actual civility is a nice change. International borders never impacted me much as Zaya Gage, and they certainly don't impact the Conduit from moving where the universe wills her.

And yes, I'm still ignoring that the universe actively doesn't want me in this vehicle, or with Reck, or perhaps both.

My phone screen flickers, then blacks out again. Either

Coda is still working on breaking through Reck's Authority-issued black box, or the awry tech is just letting me know they have eyes on me.

Another fifteen minutes pass in silence.

So many lost years, lost memories, and shared moments stretch between me and the shifter at my side. Yet neither of us has anything to say to the other.

"You don't remember," Reck finally says as if picking up my thoughts, not even glancing my way. It's a confirmation, not a question. "You don't remember us. You don't remember that night. You don't remember dying."

"I have vague memories of waking," I say, keeping my gaze out the side window.

It hurts, I realize. Somewhere buried deep inside me, it hurts that he obviously doesn't give a shit about me. Mack's photos and my conversations with Rought and Rath truly had me believing differently.

Reck takes another breath as if to speak, still not looking at me. But he doesn't voice whatever follow-up question he had.

"There are no threads between us," I say.

"I don't know what that means," he snaps.

"Had you manifested your beast?" I ask, slightly detached. Not numb, but focused, waiting for whatever the universe is trying to shield me from. "That night. When I died. Had you manifested?"

"It wouldn't have made a difference against him," Reck says, not wholly believing it. The half-lie filters through to me easily.

"So yes."

"What does it matter?"

"Rought hadn't transformed into the gryphon yet," I say, still weaving together that section of my past, of my missing bonds. "And Rath transformed in the aftermath, correct? The dragon manifested to help heal him."

"More like save his life," Reck mutters grimly. "Why would it matter now, Zaya?"

I think about that question for a moment. I think about the maliciousness that Reck and his beast practically breathe. I think about being drawn to Rought, and even to Rath, despite the absence of anchored bonds.

"You're supposed to be mine," I say finally. He doesn't feel like mine at all.

"I was never fucking yours," Reck snarls. "And I won't have you now."

"Our destinies were once entwined," I say, ignoring the sharp ache radiating through my chest.

He scoffs. "Believe whatever you want."

"Disa thought she'd rejected her soul-bound mates," I say, surprised at the evenness of my tone.

"So?" he snaps.

"So her death nearly took the Outcast with her, just like all her chosen died."

Reck finally fixes his gaze on me. I instantly wish he were looking at the road instead, and not only because he's still driving way too fast.

His gaze is filled with utter loathing. No matter his repeated declaration to not hurt me, Reck Guerra hates me. Utterly and unequivocally.

I try to shrug it off. "Soul bonds might not be so easily severed. If the Conduit herself couldn't snip them."

"The threads you mentioned," he says.

"Yes."

"You said there aren't any between us."

"There aren't."

"I'm not interested in your fucking games, Zaya. What the fuck is your point?"

"You're driving me to my death right now," I say casually.

He huffs nastily. "I already told you, I'm not going to hurt you."

The half-truth brushes against me. I flip my hand, as if I can capture that snarled false declaration in my palm.

Reck flinches, inadvertently jerking the steering wheel just enough that the SUV swerves across the road. He curses, slowing to get us back in the proper lane. Not that we've seen many other vehicles. Crossing through the barrens isn't for the casual traveler and certainly isn't a preferred trade route.

"Stop fucking with me," he says.

"Stop lying to me," I say mildly.

He stiffens. "Bellamy can't take you."

"And your agents?"

He huffs dismissively.

I let the silence stretch between us for a moment. "Who killed me?" I finally ask. "Who crossed through the boundaries of the intersection point unimpeded? Was my aunt there? Rought said he — you all were banished from the estate. Was that in the lingering aftermath? Or as a result of my death?"

Reck's grip tightens on the steering wheel again. His lips are pressed against his teeth so hard that they're white. His jaw is etched in tension.

"Is my murderer still alive?" I ask. "After facing off with my aunt? How is that possible?"

"It shouldn't have been," Reck mutters. "It never should have fucking happened in the first place. You should have been safe from him!"

I know now, even without Reck actually voicing the name. It's clearer even than I gleaned from the conversation in the Outcast's dining room. Who could stand against my aunt? Or who could at least flee from her, leaving me dead at her feet?

"I tried to banish Rath," I say, sounding thoughtful even if my head is mostly empty.

"What?"

"From the estate. He grabbed me —"

"What!?"

I wave off his concern, not bothering to analyze it. "But even after I claimed the intersection point, he walks the land without permission."

"I'm not fucking following what you're saying, Zaya."

I finally look at him, indulging in doing so for a moment. He's beautiful, even in profile.

He's supposed to be mine.

But he's not. He's not mine.

"My aunt is dead," I say. "At least a century before her time."

"I know."

"She had tea with someone the afternoon she went missing. Though I'm guessing on the timeline a bit. Someone lured her from the property with some issue ... some emergency. Was it you?"

"It wasn't."

He's not lying.

"What is your fucking point?" Reck snaps. "I didn't kill Disa."

"You wouldn't have been capable of it."

"Right. But?"

"Someone obviously did."

"Well, it wasn't me, it wasn't my agents, and it wasn't Bellamy," he says. "So you're perfectly safe."

"No," I say, finally looking away from him. "My aunt was perfectly safe with you. You were supposed to be mine."

"I'm not fucking yours!" He shakes his head, trying to settle himself.

I let it go. I don't have any proof of anything yet, and I hate mucking around in supposition. I hate guessing.

Reck glances at me, then away. He shifts his hands on the wheel, then plays with the climate controls on the console.

The silence that fills the vehicle now is sharp, filling with a slow creep of bitter malevolence.

A text message appears on the console. *Ten minutes, asshole.*

The pinned location on the map shifts. Again. As if Bellamy has sent an update. But we're near now.

"I'm on my fucking way, you fucking bitch," Reck says.

His words appear on the console a moment later. He must have pressed some button on the steering wheel to connect to his phone, which is connected to the SUV. Or routed through the SUV to get around the black box?

"Smooth," I say. "Clear. Precise. Not at all incendiary."

"She claims to be my fucking sister, and she tried to fuck me!"

"No," I say. "She pretended to be me, and you tried to fuck her."

"Same thing. It's fucking sick."

"Either way?" I ask, just a little mockingly.

He spares me an irate glance.

I still don't feel drawn to him, not even remotely. I understand he's objectively gorgeous. Dark and deadly.

That his beast must lend him immense strength. Even extra powers, perhaps. I assume his senior position in the Authority might even beguile some people. But not me.

"What?" he snaps, chafing under my regard.

I shrug. "There aren't any threads between us."

"Stop saying that!"

"Why?"

A middle finger emoticon appears on the console.

Reck scoffs, flicking his fingers toward the message. "See? Just a fucking child playing at being a villain."

"I suppose it takes one to know one," I say.

"Now who's the child?" he mocks.

"Still you."

"We're not having this conversation."

"What conversation? The one we're currently having?"

He inhales. That press of malevolence all but boils around him. Then he exhales and reins it all in.

Impressive.

"Nothing matters more than Presh," he says calmly.

"I agree. Presh ranks incredibly high in the things that matter."

"This isn't banter." He loosens his hands on the steering wheel, relaxing into his seat. All deliberate adjustments. "I don't fucking love you. I never fucking loved you. I would fucking sacrifice you in a moment if it meant saving any members of my family."

Those measured words — rephrased but voiced for the second time — ache through me.

They're also clearly a lie.

I'm not certain which parts are false, but am presuming it's the mention of not loving me in the past.

I'm also not certain why Reck needs to make his position so clear. "I heard you the first time," I say quietly. "And I know."

"You know?" he mocks. "The great and terrible Conduit knows all."

"I know." I look at him steadily. "That you're about to sacrifice me."

"I said I wouldn't hurt you. I'm tired of fucking repeating it."

"That's not the same thing, though," I say. "Not in your mind."

"Don't pretend to know me."

"The great and terrible Conduit knows all."

"Fuck you," he sneers.

The road twists ahead of us, cutting toward the foot of the mountains. I look out the side window, to where the clouds have dissipated over the arid plains. A congregation of vultures circle in the near distance, wings splayed and coasting on the wind. The universe tugs at me, almost half-heartedly.

As if it knows the decision has already been made.

"So that's what you did," I say, running my thumb across the blank screen of my phone. I should text Rought, even if Coda has already reached out. That's ... proper, right? To reach out to my ... lover before —

"What?"

"You didn't kill me," I say. "But you did sacrifice me to save Rought and Reck."

"Zaya ..." His voice cracks. The utterance of my name is packed with barely concealed pain.

"I understand," I say before he can cover his reaction. Or explain it. "I would never expect to matter to anyone, and certainly not more than your brothers. Previously soul bonded or not."

The SUV navigates a final turn. The mountains fill the horizon dead ahead of us now, snow still covering their craggy peaks. But a flattened vista spreads out to the right.

In a deliberately cleared area just off the road, a single squat concrete outpost is set to the side of a paved lot. The crumbling pavement is overgrown with dead weeds at the edges. The steel front door of the outpost is barred, with a fluorescent-yellow emergency phone hanging to the right. No windows. A satellite dish is secured to the roof. Presumably, an emergency kit and rations, as well as temporary shelter, can be found within as long as the phone works, the satellite connects, or a ranger is on-site.

For the sake of whoever might otherwise be here, I hope the outpost is remotely monitored, with no rangers around. Because Bellamy stands next to an older sedan in the lot. Her athame is in one hand, a cigarette in the other.

No sign of the Authority agents or their vehicle.

I have no doubt they're here, though.

Presh and Deville are pressed together in the back seat of Bellamy's vehicle.

Reck veers off the road, almost rolling the SUV. Then he brings us to an abrupt stop a few meters away from Bellamy.

I lay my hand on the door handle. The universe gives me one final tug. Then that energy slips away, leaving me to my choices. Muta curls around my arm but doesn't revert to his bracelet form.

"Zaya," Reck says again, gaze riveted to Bellamy but his attention on me.

Ignoring him, I step out of the SUV.

TWELVE

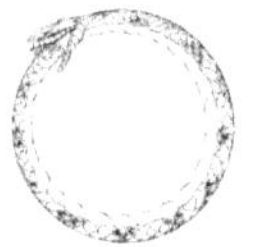

Bellamy takes a long drag from the cigarette as I approach. In the back seat of the sedan, Presh jerks forward, mouthing words. She's not whispering, though. An iridescent red-tinted essence collar rings the base of her neck.

"A collar?" I sneer at Bellamy. "Really? Because Precious is such a threat."

"I couldn't stand the chatter." Bellamy flicks the cig away. It lands on the pavement a few feet from her, bouncing, the tip still glowing.

"And yet you started the conversation." I stop a few strides away, aware of Reck a step behind me and to my left — closer to Bellamy's car.

"Monitoring your ward's communications? How invasive of you, Zaya." Bellamy picks at something on her lip, then lightly spits. "Fuck, when I nicked it from the kid, I was hoping it was weed of some sort. But they're just old-ass, mass-produced shit." She sighs affectedly, leaning back against the car.

"Bellamy ..." Reck snarls.

Her dark-purple-edged, whited-out eyes flick to him, ire abruptly infusing her expression. "I'm not interested in your words either, brother."

"Don't fucking call me that."

"Why?" she mocks. "Because all of our other siblings are good enough to rescue but me?"

Reck hesitates.

"He knows, you fucking moron," Bellamy scoffs dismissively. "He knows that every time you get the chance, you abscond with another of his bastards, tucking them away in some hidden part of the world. Presumably for your own nefarious purposes."

"Fuck you. You don't —"

"You still haven't figured out that he doesn't give a fuck about the boys."

That stymies Reck's instinctual protest. For a moment, at least.

"Because the awry gene is dominant only in his female offspring?" I ask, focused and calm. I have no idea yet what the universe was tugging me away from, because I get no hint that I can't handle whatever Bellamy is about to throw at me.

"He thinks so," she says, feigning detachment.

It's interesting to me that no matter how powerful these two are, no matter how arrogant, neither of them uses their father's name when speaking about him. They actively avoid doing so. And I already have a hint of the why — just not the how.

Bellamy told me as much when she mentioned having seen my necklace before. It just took me a while to weave that together with all the other hints, including her connection to the Authority agents, and those agents meeting with Devlin ...

And Presh fleeing when she saw a cage being brought into her father's compound. When she saw Bellamy, from afar, for the first time. Before that, he had kept Bellamy apart from the rest of her siblings, including her twin.

A twin now standing at my side, yet not with me at all.

The Cataclysm was involved in my aunt's death. Her rejected soul-bound mate. Someone so powerful and so vicious that his children — who likely also rank among the most powerful figures in the world — are utterly terrified of him.

Reck finally finds his voice. "None of this is fucking relevant right now. Let Presh go."

"I'm not holding her per se."

"I'm not interested in your sick mind fucks, Bellamy," Reck snarls. "I don't care what shit he put you through. You think he hasn't tortured us all? Taken everything we love? Tainted anything we treasured? You never should have laid hands on Precious."

Bellamy steps away from the car, squaring off with her pissy brother.

"The power play between you two can wait," I say. Then I turn my attention to Precious and DeVille, who has his arm wrapped protectively around Presh's shoulders. "Get out of the car. And Precious? That collar can't hold you."

Precious's eyes snap to mine. The purple infused through the deep blue of her irises isn't even remotely subtle now.

Bellamy chuckles darkly. "You haven't trained her particularly well."

"I've had three days. Two of which have now been spent being annoyed by you."

Bellamy opens her mouth, already snarling.

I lean a little closer, cutting her off. "Also, there's been no awry weak enough to test her strength against. Luckily, she now has you to fulfill that role. I'm sure she'll soon learn your worth in her life."

"I thought we were sidelining the power plays," Reck drawls. His attention is firmly fixed on his younger sister in the car.

"Go ahead," I say to Presh, nodding encouragement.

Bellamy pivots just enough to have eyes on Presh, keeping her body angled toward us.

Precious glances at her long-lost sister, then at me. I lift my free hand — Muta is still weighing down the other arm like the asshole he is — and wrap my fingers around my throat.

Presh nods, swallows, and then wraps one hand around her neck, covering the red-tinted, essence-fueled collar. Her dark-purple eyes flick to Bellamy, and she glowers at her sister.

Bellamy laughs, sharp and too bright.

The collar writhes under Precious's touch, then visibly tightens. Presumably that's Bellamy's control, though I can't feel whatever power the dire awry is playing with because it's literally nothing to me.

Precious soundlessly gasps for air, eyes widening in fear.

Reck jolts forward.

I raise my hand to him. "No."

He actually listens to me.

"Precious," I say mildly, "this is nothing to you, it's completely beneath you. You are better, more pure, than your sister could ever hope to be."

Bellamy narrows her eyes on me, clearly insulted.

Cheeks pinking, Precious takes a shuddering breath. At

her side, still holding her as much as she'll allow, DeVille looks like he isn't breathing either.

Then, still soundlessly, Precious laughs.

I can practically feel the amusement, the honest joy, roiling off her.

The collar dissipates under her hand.

Bellamy huffs.

"Be glad it wasn't me you tried that with," I say, my tone still perfectly level. "I would have snapped it right back at you, just as Precious could have done, and you would have been on your knees, begging for your last breath."

Reck's gaze snaps to me. I can feel the heat of his regard. I ignore him.

"You knew that Precious is under my protection," I say. "No court, no law, no authority can take her from me now. Nor will anyone even attempt to prosecute me for how I choose to enforce my guardianship."

"She came to me," Bellamy says, sounding just a little shaken. "She chose to sneak away to see me. You can't kill me because she's a stupid kid."

"Hey!" Precious cries from the back seat of the sedan.

"I'm not speaking to you, Bellamy," I say. "Or at least not solely to you. Am I?"

I allow my gaze to slide past the dire awry, looking behind the sedan and slightly to the right. In a seemingly empty area of the paved lot surrounding the outpost, a simmer of essence catches in the sunlight, hovering about an inch off the dusty pavement. A concealment ward. "Your mage is powerful."

"The Authority attracts powerful people," Reck says mildly. Not remotely shocked by the hidden presence of his agents. The two of them, at a minimum. "Get out of the car, Presh."

Precious glances between us all. Bellamy is all but ignoring her supposedly kidnapped victims now. The younger awry reaches for the handle of the door.

"Other side," Reck says. He wants to keep the car between Presh and DeVille and the Authority agents behind their ward, currently listening to our conversation.

DeVille opens the door on his side, climbing out first, then reaching into the back seat for Presh. His eyes are bright with essence. Too bright.

"Reck," I murmur.

"I see it."

DeVille is on the edge of transforming into his beast. First-time transformations are chaotic under the best of circumstances — and with Presh at the center of everything going on here, that's disconcerting. As an awry, Presh might be naturally essence proof. But if he's lost to his beast, DeVille could accidentally maul her before I could take a single step to intervene.

"Reck," I say again quietly, trying to sound calm.

"Can you just trust me for once in your fucking life?" he snarls, just as quietly.

Bellamy snorts derisively. "Trust you? Why should she? I don't even know you, and I already know the levels you would —"

"I'm already fucking sick of your fucking voice," Reck snarls viciously.

DeVille's head snaps up, reacting to Reck's aggression. He's cradling Presh's hand in his own, guiding her out of the car and coaxing her to keep her head down. Too close.

He's way too close to Presh with his essence that bright in his eyes.

I can feel Reck's hesitation. His gaze flicks to Bellamy,

to the still-empty space behind the dire awry, then back to DeVille and Presh.

"You came here to protect Precious," I say.

Bellamy snorts again. Her arms are crossed, athame still in hand and now resting along her bicep. In the sunlight, her eyes are almost white. That's disconcerting, even to me.

Muta finally coils up to rest over my shoulders, leaving my right arm tingling from his weight. The death god trapped in the body of a bushmaster flicks his tongue out, tasting the essence shimmering in the air. His gaze is focused over Bellamy's shoulder.

The death god's intent aligns with my own.

Finally making a decision, Reck crosses around the front edge of Bellamy's vehicle. Moving to protect Presh.

Bellamy eyes him with loathing, muttering, "Like little sister can't handle her own fucking mate."

I'm not surprised that Bellamy has so easily picked up on the ties between Presh and DeVille — because those bonds have strengthened from the events of the last couple of days. From Bellamy manipulating and killing Kris. But I ask instead, "Doesn't bright light bother you?" My own eyes lightly ache even behind my dark-tinted sunglasses. Unfortunately, any of the mage-crafted glasses I've tried instantly fizzled under my touch.

Bellamy blinks, slightly thrown by the question.

"Your eyes?" I say. "The headache must be constant."

"What do you care?" she snaps, arms falling to her sides.

I shrug. "Just stalling."

She huffs. "Glasses are a liability in a fight."

I glance at her, raising a mocking eyebrow. "No one should ever be able to get close enough to you for that to matter, awry." I hit 'awry' hard.

"You don't know what it's like to be me," she says.

Reck gets Presh situated between himself and DeVille, shielding them both as much as possible with his body. Then he herds them back toward his SUV — and all those layers of protection he didn't want me to fuck with earlier.

So the asshole shifter isn't without some reasoning skills.

"Last time I rescued Presh," I say thoughtfully, "I made it all worse."

"Why tell me?" Bellamy asks, fingers flexing on her sacrificial dagger.

"Just reminding myself."

She opens her mouth. But the Authority agents not-so-patiently waiting finally deem Reck far enough away — and exposed on all sides — to attack.

The concealment ward melts down into a ring hovering four feet high in a swirling circular flow of essence. Its circumference is just large enough to surround agents Wilson and Shaw, plus a hulking SUV identical to Reck's. Blond hair still smoothed back into a tight bun, skin still sun-kissed, Wilson twirls her wand over her head with a controlled rotation of her wrist. Ruddy-skinned and red-haired, Shaw flashes his beast's elongated canines, though he maintains his bulky human form. Both of them still wear their Authority-issued suits.

"Now!" Shaw snarls, his beast too present in his voice. He's not completely in control.

Her expression carefully blank, unfeeling, Wilson slashes forward with the wand as if cutting through the essence ringing them. The ring splits once, then twice more as she repeats the gesture.

She flicks the wand three times. Three long lashes of power launch forward — one toward Bellamy, one toward me, and a final lash toward the retreating trio.

Shaw instantly lunges forward, racing behind Wilson's casting as if they've practiced this maneuver hundreds of times.

Bellamy spins, spattering me with warm liquid and barely getting a shield up between herself and Wilson's admittedly impressive casting. Turning a concealment ward into tripled containment wards is seriously masterful wielding. It also takes a lot of power, draining the caster.

The repurposed warding slams into Bellamy's shield, driving her back against the car.

The second essence rope comes up against me, against everything I am … and simply encircles me, unable to grab hold. I reach for it instinctively. And just as I threatened Bellamy earlier, I grab its tail and whip it back at its caster with a flick of my wrist.

The third strand targets Reck as he shields the kids while they run for the SUV. DeVille stupidly wrenches away from the older shifter's loose hold and throws himself in front of Presh. The essence hits him directly in the chest, throwing him back into Reck and Presh, taking both of them off their feet.

Reck curls around Presh, protecting her from the pavement.

Wilson screams in frustration, presumably at being hit with her own casting.

Shaw, who was running for Reck or maybe Presh, hesitates — just long enough for me to tear free the containment spell still trying to erode the hasty shield Bellamy constructed, then fling it toward the shifter.

Partially dispelled, the repurposed spell is only strong enough to wrap around Shaw's legs, slowing him down rather than stopping him in his tracks. He face-plants into the pavement.

I throw a look Bellamy's way, finally taking a moment to wipe the spatter of blood off my face. The warm liquid that hit me a moment ago. "Stop fucking cutting yourself," I snap.

She blinks for a moment, then snarls back, "I do what I have to."

Already moving forward to intercept the Authority mage, I simply shake my head at the dire awry. Wilson is pulling power into her wand, readying to channel another strike. And she's not going to bother with something as gentle as a containment spell this time.

Behind me, Reck is on his feet and crossing toward Shaw as he tears through the last of the containment spell wrapped around his ankles. Shaw's hands are clawed, face bloodied from his fall but already healing.

Presh is trying to get the spell off DeVille, but he's thrashing and snarling against its hold so viciously that she can't get near him.

"In the SUV, Presh!" Reck snaps.

Wilson points her wand at me.

Shaw, having also decided I'm the biggest threat — and he's not wrong — takes a running leap at me.

An all-encompassing roar rips from DeVille. He transforms with a crack of bones and a twisting of flesh. The containment spell attempting to hold him is ripped asunder as the young shifter involuntarily takes the form of his beast. Claws score the pavement. Ridiculously long fangs — four of them, two upper and two lower — bite at the air as DeVille, as his beast, writhes in utter agony.

Reck pivots back, raising his hand and screaming, "Stop!"

He means it as a caution to Precious, who's still reaching for DeVille. But essence fueled by his fear, his terror, flares from him. It explodes outward, actually buffeting me.

Everyone just stops. Except for Reck and me.

Shaw, in the middle of his lunge toward me, pauses, balanced on one foot. Wilson holds, her essence gathered all around the tip of her wand, ready to unleash it toward me. Bellamy, blood dripping down both forearms now, is in the middle of pushing away from the sedan to seemingly step between me and the mage.

And DeVille is frozen in his beast form, crouched on all fours, neck arched back, massive maw yawning wide in pain. His fur is a lighter gray around his face, chest, and belly, but dark gray, spotted and striped in black, along his massive body.

He's a fucking smilodon — more commonly known as a prehistoric sabertooth tiger.

His hair color in human form makes much more sense now.

Reck takes a shuddering breath. His disconcerted dark-eyed gaze flicks to me, as if I have any answers for him regarding his own power.

I shrug.

He fucking glowers at me, totally pissy again in an instant.

Precious breaks Reck's hold first, hands flying to her face as she takes in DeVille.

"Get in!" Reck shouts.

She jerks, then stumbles back toward the SUV.

Energy snaps out from Bellamy toward Wilson. Dark-tainted essence writhes around the still-frozen mage, collecting along her extended wand. The wand snaps in her hand, and the spell coiled ready within it implodes — taking Wilson's hand with it. Her mouth drops open in a soundless scream as she clutches her severed limb to her chest and drops to her knees.

"Huh ..." Bellamy says, tilting her head thoughtfully.

Shaw completes his lunge, landing within reach of me. His hand extends toward my neck, claws primed to rip out my throat.

Rogue agent or not, Shaw killing me clearly wasn't his original directive. Unfortunately, pushing people past their original intent is a fairly common side effect of me just being me.

Muta strikes first, fangs dripping with venom as he latches onto Shaw's wrist. The canine shifter screams. The death god twists in midair, flipping off my shoulder to twine around Shaw's forearm, then biting him again and again.

Shaw stumbles back a few steps.

DeVille — or rather, DeVille's beast — crashes into Shaw from the side. I catch sight of a stunned Reck over the beast's massive shoulder. Then DeVille is crushing Shaw's head in his massive maw, fangs buried deep into his skull.

Muta falls to the pavement, coiling in on himself and hissing pissily. He's clearly displeased that DeVille has claimed his kill, never mind that it would have taken fifteen minutes before his venom imploded Shaw's heart.

"That's going to be hard to heal," Bellamy mutters. She steps back like she's uncharacteristically afraid some of Shaw's blood is going to get on her.

Sabertooth DeVille starts all-out mauling Shaw, who is very clearly dead. Then he's batting the agent's limp body from one side to the other, like a cat with a mouse.

Reck, seemingly recovered, strides toward Wilson. "Stop that," he says to the sabertooth as he passes.

The sabertooth snarls at him pissily, but listens. He

abandons Shaw's bloody body, settling down to lick that blood off his paws. His eyes are a blazing yellow, no hint of DeVille in their depths.

I'm not sure he's going to fit in the SUV for the drive home.

Still on her knees, Wilson has recovered a shard of her wand and is in the process of using that shard to channel enough essence to cauterize her wrist. She looks up at Reck as he approaches, terror finally breaking through her deadened indifference.

"We were just following orders," she says pleadingly. "We've been tracking Bellamy —"

"Lie," Reck says.

"It's the Authority mandate —"

"Lie."

"Reck —"

"That's not a name you get to use," he croons with deadly intent. He crouches, almost lovingly cupping Wilson's cheek.

"We're loyal," she insists. "Loyal to you. And even though she's awry, we would never have hurt your sister —"

In a blur of motion, Reck snaps Wilson's neck.

She falls to the ground at his feet.

Presh stifles a scream, drawing the sabertooth's attention. He rises onto all fours and slowly pads toward his soul-bound mate. Not even a hint of violent intent in the movement.

Reck gazes down at Wilson. "More lies," he murmurs thoughtfully.

"Well, that's one way to tender your resignation," Bellamy says mockingly.

It's also an effective way to stop me from asking questions and getting any answers from either Authority agent now.

Still crouched, Reck fixes his malevolent gaze on his newly revealed sister. "I still have you to turn in."

Bellamy slips behind me, laying her athame across the front of my neck. "I don't think so."

"Seriously!?" Presh cries, grabbing fistfuls of the longer fur around the sabertooth's neck as if she might be able to slow the beast down if he decides to charge again. "You said you needed help!"

"What I need," Bellamy says, "is leverage. And insurance."

I smile involuntarily, ignoring the blade lightly pressed against my skin. I can't decide if Presh is just extremely gullible, or whether she's so pure hearted that she actually does believe that everyone deserves grace and forgiveness. Redemption.

So much so that she's willing to speak for Bellamy even after she murdered her friend Kris.

That morality, that goodness, is a completely different sort of strength. And perhaps an indication of the power Presh will eventually wield.

Reck shakes his head, straightens, and crosses toward Presh and the sabertooth. He notably stays on the far side of Muta, though, not getting between me and the coiled bushmaster. Muta, not remotely concerned about me, continues to sulk. Or it's possible he likes the sun-warmed pavement.

"Take care of that, would you, Zaya?" Reck says over his shoulder. "I've got to get DeVille back. I'm not interested in having my interior shredded."

Bellamy tightens her hold on me as Reck moves, as if she thinks he's just feigning disinterest.

He isn't.

The athame slides harmlessly against my skin.

"Seriously?" Bellamy mutters, echoing Precious from a moment before. "He really doesn't give a shit about you. So … that was a hate fuck? When he thought I was you?" She pauses, curling her lip. "Not that the asshole was capable of getting hard enough to actually penetrate."

"As much as I enjoy having conversations with a knife to my throat," I say, curling my fingers around Bellamy's wrist, "let's not."

She shudders under my touch. To be perfectly honest, I'm not a fan of the press of her discordant energy either. It raises all the hair on my arms and prickles at the back of my neck.

"You promised!" Presh cries, pulling my attention to her.

The young awry hangs out of the back passenger side of the SUV, glaring in our direction. The sabertooth tiger attempts to climb into the vehicle with her, over her, but she shoves his face away. There is no way he'll ever fit in the back seat.

Reck appears to be moments away from slaughtering everyone, starting with the ridiculously long-fanged tiger.

"You promised, Bellamy!" Presh shouts, pressing her hands against the base of the sabertooth's neck, trying to straight-arm him away from her. "You said you needed help!"

"I lied, you utter fucking moron," Bellamy shouts back, sounding more like a pissed-off elder sister than a deadly dire awry.

"You didn't!"

"I did!"

"Zaya!" Reck snaps, getting his arm around sabertooth

DeVille's neck and yanking him back. The tiger is double his size, but Reck moves him, then holds him away from Presh, seemingly easily. "I will fucking leave you behind!"

"Are all my siblings this fucking stupid?" Bellamy asks. "The gryphon has a bit of that Greek god thing going on, but that doesn't mean he knows where to stick his —"

Still holding her wrist, I easily twist out of Bellamy's hold, pivoting to look at her. Her arm is now extended between us. She blinks, disconcerted. I pluck the dagger from her hand.

Sickly layers of misdeeds and residual from multiple sacrifices coat the blade. Bellamy has cut more than just herself with this dagger, and each time, she's fortified it with more and more dire-wrought essence.

All of that crumbles under my touch. Until the athame is nothing more than a decorative knickknack.

The dire awry's disconcertion flicks to the dagger in my hand, shifting from disbelief to sharp anger. "You have no fucking right!"

"I do, actually."

"Given to you by what fucking —"

"The universe, I suppose."

She tries to twist her wrist free from my hold. Then, when that doesn't happen, she yanks down hard, over and over. Dark-tainted essence, born of frustration and a mounting fear, infuses the sticky blood still covering her forearms. Those barely healed cuts well with fresh blood. Potent blood.

But whatever spells she's trying to manifest fizzle under my touch before she can even direct them to a purpose.

She tries again and again. Blood flows from the gashes she previously made in her arms. Then when all that fails to impact me, previously healed scars on those arms begin to burst open. Blood drips down from the arm still extended between us, pours down along the arm she's raised toward me in an attempt to quell my simple touch.

Her eyes blaze, all but whited out now. Her lips turn blue against the pallor of her tanned skin.

She's draining her life force.

Bellamy is formidable. She'd be even more powerful if she learned to pull power to her from natural, unlimited sources.

Against anyone but me.

"I won't ..." She gasps as if the words have been wrenched out of her depleted lungs. "I won't be his any longer."

I tilt my head, blinking as threads of destiny spark around us, as if called forth by Bellamy's declaration. Presh, DeVille, and even Reck blaze in the corner of my eye. Layers of complex, multicolored threads of fate — of life force, as some call it — twine around each of them, binding them together, linking them with me, then streaming outward in all directions. So many vibrant paths extend from Precious specifically that —

"Look at me while you're killing me," Bellamy snarls, slumping against my easy hold on her wrist.

"That, you're doing yourself," I say mildly, though I do turn my attention back to her.

She laughs, already sounding near dead. "Can't even grant me an easy death ..."

The crack of bones and a muffled scream from the direction of the SUV let me know that Reck has coaxed DeVille back into his human form.

I take a moment to look at Bellamy's threads. I've never met a dire awry before, and I still don't remotely understand why she needs to reach for power in her blood or in the life force of others in order to cast.

A thick rope of fate — quickly darkening to black under my gaze — is wrapped around her neck as if strangling her. A blackened tangle of threads is centered over her heart ... all the edges seemingly ... cauterized. I have to angle my head, peering out from the corners of my eyes to catch a glimmer of the cobweb-gray threads that stretch toward Presh. I assume they extend to Reck as well. The sibling bonds.

A single thread stretches from Bellamy directly to me. I cup my free hand around it.

"What are you doing?" Bellamy shudders under my hold. Involuntarily reacting to the touch of my power, rather than trying to get away from me. "What are you doing?" she repeats. Her voice is thin, but ... awed?

"Presh!" Reck shouts. "Fuck!"

Rapid footfalls herald Precious's approach, and then she's at my side with all her glorious destiny blazing around her.

"Zaya, please," she pleads.

I close my hand around the thread that ties Bellamy to me. Are we linked in this moment simply because I'm holding her upright as she dies? Or are we linked because —

"Zaya!" Presh reaches for me. No, for us. She hovers her hand over where I'm still holding Bellamy's arm aloft.

"Don't touch her, Precious," Bellamy snarls, protective and fierce even with her dying breath. And that's a choice in and of itself, isn't it?

What a tangle of lies Bellamy has woven. An uneven and patchy tapestry. What did the dire awry do when she was called to the compound and found that a cage had been set up for her little sister ...

Did Bellamy even know she had siblings before that?

Did she help Precious escape?

The younger awry seemed to slip away from Federation territory so easily, even if she mixed up the train stops. Did Bellamy have a hand in that, only to then be tasked with getting Precious back?

She's desperate now. And not because she's dying.

Dying might honestly be a relief for her, though Bellamy's too fierce to admit that, even to herself.

The tangle of cauterized threads over her heart expands … almost as if it's taking a breath. Then a half-dozen of the ends waver, lifting, reaching …

"You've been killing yourself one thread of fate at a time." My voice is remote, weighted with power. "Every time you sacrifice another for energy, you kill a little more of yourself."

Precious shudders. The hand hovering over mine shakes. "Please, Zaya …" she whispers.

Bellamy sobs, just once. In grief and fear.

But not for herself.

"Please," the dire awry quietly begs. "Don't hurt her … don't hurt … sister …"

Precious lays her hand over mine, angling her head to catch my attention. She reaches up and pulls off my sunglasses, tucking them away in the pocket of her lilac hoodie. When she meets my gaze, her eyes reflect the purple nebulas blazing from my own eyes. "Zaya. If Bellamy goes back to him, he'll force her to make more of those berserkers. To make up for the ones we all killed."

I look back at Bellamy. She's pale, wavering on her feet. Blood no longer drips from her arms. That tangle of blackened threads over her heart rustles again, reaching out for …

Precious?

"What do you see?" I ask the young awry.

"You," she whispers reverently. She squeezes my hand lightly. "You are so beautiful."

I laugh, completely involuntarily. Only Precious could gaze at all the power I carry — both great and terrible, as Reck mockingly called it — and call me beautiful. "What do you see of your sister?"

She swallows, then turns her gaze to Bellamy. "She's dying."

"Yes."

Bellamy chuckles weakly, swaying forward and back. "I concur."

Precious tightens her hold on me. I grip Bellamy, keeping her on her feet. The young awry raises her other arm. Her hand shakes as she points to Bellamy's neck and then at her heart. "There and there ..."

"Yes," I say. "What do you want to do about it?"

"Fuck me," Bellamy groans. "This is not a good time for a mentoring session."

Precious glances back at me, eyes wide but not afraid. Determined. "Can we ... remove the ... bad essence?"

I step closer to Bellamy, lowering our arms between us as I do. Then I reach up and tug the noose of essence free from around her neck.

A strangled scream makes it through Bellamy's clenched teeth. Her neck is bruised in a mottle of dark colors edged in yellow.

I look down at the rope in my hand. "Still dying."

"Is that ..." Presh bites her lip. "Is that ..."

"Bellamy's last strand of destiny," I say, ignoring the thread that still links me to the dire awry because I'm not yet certain what to make of it. "It shouldn't be black."

"Um, okay." Presh huffs. She narrows her eyes on the thread lying limply across my hand, then steps closer to gaze at the tangle of threads clustered over Bellamy's heart.

Once more, a half-dozen or so of those threads shiver, their blackened tips reaching for Presh.

Energy shifts behind us a moment before Reck lays his hand on Precious's shoulder. The red and deep orange of his life force coils around the both of us.

"I'm fine," Presh snaps testily at her older brother. "Zaya is here."

"Zaya," Reck spits, "can't be trusted when she's otherwise occupied."

I'm not certain what he means. And with the final weave of Bellamy's fate displayed before me, I don't remotely care.

Ah, right.

That's what he means.

Still ... this is all interesting ...

"What do you see there, Presh?" I ask, nodding toward the knotted ball of threads over Bellamy's heart.

"A ... wound?" She hesitates, hovering her fingers just a few inches away. "Multiple wounds."

I hum, still intrigued. "And what do you feel like doing?"

"Time to stop fucking around," Reck growls.

"Right now?" Presh asks, ignoring her brother. "With those ... cuts?"

"Yes." I glance down at the inert dark-red rope of fate in my hand. "We can walk away, and Bellamy will likely die —"

"No!" Presh presses her hand over the mess of threads clustered around Bellamy's heart. "No!"

The young awry's energy wells. The cauterized threads

try to knot around her fingers. Bellamy stifles another scream.

"I'm sorry," Presh sobs, though her tone is determined, focused. "I'm so sorry."

"What the fuck is going on?" Reck asks, clearly unable to see what Presh and I can see.

Presh draws more energy, more essence, from herself. Instinctively, I think.

"Gentle," I say. "Careful. Don't pull too much."

The snipped ends of the blackened threads burrow into the back of Presh's hand. She flinches but doesn't pull away.

"Think about smoothing over that wound you see," I say. "Maybe like you're applying an ointment. Or maybe it's more like sewing the edges together. Or ..." I don't know anything about healing, really. And certainly not on the level that Presh seems driven to do. These aren't wounds in Bellamy's flesh, but ...

"It needs to be debrided," I say — but I'm not the one speaking now. The universe has decided to chime in, through me. "The damaged life force needs to be removed to allow —"

"I see," Presh whispers. And with another push of her power, the tangle of threads dissolves into nothing under her palm.

The thick rope of life force in my hand jerks as if suddenly infused with more energy. I let it go. It slowly retracts, sluggishly twisting around Bellamy, but not cinching around her neck.

Bellamy gasps, stumbling and clutching her chest.

I also let her go.

She collapses against her sedan, shuddering and

sobbing. The wounds on her arms have healed over. Even the older scars are barely visible.

I turn to Presh, cradling her face in my hands and gazing down at her. She blinks up at me reverently. Unafraid.

"Soul healer," I murmur, understanding just a little more about the intricate destiny that surrounds Precious. "How blessed the world is to have you."

Her eyes fill with tears, but it's joy that radiates through her. "Soul healer," she whispers.

"So utterly precious." I smile, then press a kiss to her forehead.

Essence flows from me to her — a blessing, a benediction. A promise of protection and love.

"What the fuck?" DeVille groans from somewhere behind Reck. "Why am I on the fucking ground?"

"That's where you fell, Andy!" Hands on her hips, Presh whirls around to chastise him. "And you're way too heavy to pick up!"

I meet Reck's gaze. His expression is open and awed. He looks moments away from falling to his knees before me.

I don't like that look at all.

Not from my once-soul-bound mate. Not from the Authority agent he chose to be. Because visions of a cage to tuck me safely within always follow that sort of look. Tuck me away to worship. To possess.

I narrow my eyes at him.

He flinches, then curls his lip into a snarl.

That's better.

"It's not like I can choose where I fall," DeVille grumbles, brushing himself off as he gets to his feet. He's wearing sweatpants that I assume Reck generously got on him after he passed out from transforming. "Every fucking bone in my body hurts."

Presh launches herself toward him, practically skipping. Beaming.

With a bare moment of hesitation, he sweeps her up in his arms, twirling her around on unsteady feet.

Presh throws her arms around his neck. "You should see your tiger!"

"A tiger?" DeVille shouts. "What the fuck? But my mother is a —"

"A sabertooth tiger!" Presh squeals. "He's so sweet."

DeVille blinks at her.

She slaps at his chest. "Put me down, you oaf."

DeVille, now completely confused, lowers Precious to her feet, then runs his hand through his hair, looking to us for confirmation.

I nod helpfully. "Big, scary."

"Total ass," Reck mutters.

DeVille's gaze drops to Shaw's mutilated corpse. His brown skin visibly pales as he raises a shaky arm to point at the body. "Did ... that ..."

"Don't worry," I say blithely. "Muta had already killed him. You just made that death come a little quicker. And probably less painfully."

"Less ... painful ..."

DeVille bends over at the waist and throws up. Hunks of bloody flesh spatter the ground and his bare feet. "Oh, fuck. No!" He throws up again. Presh rubs his back, keeping her feet well away from the spew zone. "What the fuck is ... that ..."

"That would be bits of Shaw," I say.

"Really, Zaya?" Reck snarls.

Before I can respond, Bellamy takes that moment to keel over.

Presh abandons DeVille, racing toward her sister. Reck intercepts her, grabbing her around the waist and yanking her off her feet.

"Enough of this shit," he snarls. "We're completely exposed out here. It's past time to fucking leave."

Bellamy starts convulsing, seizing.

I cross to her, somehow already rolling her onto her side before I've even decided to move. She stops trembling under my hands. I touch her chin, angling it and wondering if I should find something to put between her teeth.

Presh flails in Reck's hold, landing a well-placed kick to his groin, no doubt inadvertently. He grunts, pained, and drops her to her feet. She stumbles.

Muta suddenly appears next to Bellamy's head, flicking his forked tongue in her direction.

"Oh, now you step up," I grouse to the death god.

He ignores me. Of course.

Presh scrambles away from a still-cursing Reck, coming down on her knees next to her newfound sister.

Bellamy cranes her head back to look me in the eye. The light lavender of her iris has expanded and deepened slightly in tint, leaving only a thin ring of dark purple on the edge. As if Presh's healing has also cleansed her essence.

Those eyes are wide and unseeing, though.

"He's coming," Bellamy whispers. "That was always the plan. To lure you away …"

"Me?" Presh asks.

Bellamy's eyes flick from her sister back to me, slowly focusing. "The Conduit. He almost had you, but you slipped away. Sneaky goddess."

"Zaya?" Presh asks again, confused now.

"No," I say. "Not me. The Conduit."

Because I know now. I *know* why the universe kept tugging me away from Reck. Because nothing has happened here that I couldn't handle, even without guidance. Nothing has happened. Yet.

"You are the fucking Conduit," Reck snarls, stepping closer.

"I'm only the vessel." And I'm suddenly hollow within. Again.

I convinced myself, somehow, over the last few days ...

I convinced myself I was more. That I was a person who could make actual choices, build friendships, maybe even have and reconnect to soul-bound mates.

"I'm sorry. I'm ... I didn't have any other choice," Bellamy whispers. "Run if you can. He's not strong enough to take you from the estate. Not yet anyway."

"I never get to run," I say.

ACKNOWLEDGMENTS

With thanks to:

<u>My story & line editor</u>
Scott Fitzgerald Gray

<u>My proofreader</u>
Pauline Nolet

<u>My beta readers</u>
Anteia Consorto, Theresa Daigle, and Gael Fleming.

<u>For their encouragement, feedback, & general advice</u>
FaRo Society (esp. the Discord crew)
Hailey Edwards
Carrie Ann Ryan

<u>For their art</u>
Jay Aheer (Simply Defined Art)
Eternal Geekery
Barbara D Soares (drsoaresrex.com)

ABOUT THE AUTHOR

Meghan Ciana Doidge is an award-winning writer based out of Vancouver, British Columbia, Canada. She has a penchant for bloody love stories, superheroes, and the supernatural. She also has a thing for chocolate, potatoes, and cashmere.

For recipes, giveaways, news, and glimpses of upcoming stories, please connect with Meghan via:
www.madebymeghan.ca
info@madebymeghan.ca

facebook.com/MeghanCianaDoidge

instagram.com/meghancianadoidge

tiktok.com/@meghancianadoidge

ALSO BY MEGHAN CIANA DOIDGE

<u>Novels</u>

After the Virus

Spirit Binder

Time Walker

Cupcakes, Trinkets, and Other Deadly Magic (Dowser 1)

Trinkets, Treasures, and Other Bloody Magic (Dowser 2)

Treasures, Demons, and Other Black Magic (Dowser 3)

I See Me (Oracle 1)

Shadows, Maps, and Other Ancient Magic (Dowser 4)

Maps, Artifacts, and Other Arcane Magic (Dowser 5)

I See You (Oracle 2)

Artifacts, Dragons, and Other Lethal Magic (Dowser 6)

I See Us (Oracle 3)

Catching Echoes (Reconstructionist 1)

Tangled Echoes (Reconstructionist 2)

Unleashing Echoes (Reconstructionist 3)

Champagne, Misfits, and Other Shady Magic (Dowser 7)

Misfits, Gemstones, and Other Shattered Magic (Dowser 8)

Gemstones, Elves, and Other Insidious Magic (Dowser 9)

Demons and DNA (Amplifier 1)

Bonds and Broken Dreams (Amplifier 2)

Mystics and Mental Blocks (Amplifier 3)

Idols and Enemies (Amplifier 4)

Instincts and Impostors (Amplifier 5)

Endings and Empathy (Amplifier 6)

Misplaced Souls (Misfits 1)

Awakening Infinity (Archivist 0)

Invoking Infinity (Archivist 1)

Compelling Infinity (Archivist 2)

Awry (Conduit 1)

Grand Romantic Delusions and the Madness of Mirth

(Part 1 & 2)

Snag (Conduit 2)

Novellas/Shorts

Love Lies Bleeding

The Graveyard Kiss (Reconstructionist 0.5)

Dawn Bytes (Reconstructionist 1.5)

An Uncut Key (Reconstructionist 2.5)

Graveyards, Visions, and Other Things that Byte (Dowser 8.5)

The Amplifier Protocol (Amplifier 0)

Close to Home (Amplifier 0.5)

The Music Box (Amplifier 4.5)

Moments of the Adept Universe 1

Recon Mission: Bee (Amplifier 5.5)

Soulmates, Doorways, and Other Unruly Magic (Dowser 9.5)

www.ingramcontent.com/pod-product-compliance
Lightning Source LLC
Chambersburg PA
CBHW070616300726
48975CB00006B/1828